IMPIOUS

A wicked murder mystery from Yorkshire

RAY CLARK

THE
BOOK
FOLKS

Published by The Book Folks

London, 2022

© Ray Clark

ISBN 978-1-80462-006-9

www.thebookfolks.com

"Wickedness is a myth invented by good people to account for the curious attractiveness of others."

Oscar Wilde

Chapter One

By the pricking of my thumbs
Something wicked this way comes.
– William Shakespeare, *Macbeth*, Act IV, Scene 1

Friday

Katie Tunscroft couldn't believe her luck when she'd taken the call on Wednesday. The shop had lain empty for months. Katie had worked for the estate agent for nearly a year, without one inquiry for that particular property during that period. And suddenly, out of the blue, a very positive lead. Initially, the building had been in the wrong part of town for attracting custom, but recent investment had changed all that.

She had no idea who he was; neither did the rest of the staff, nor the manager, Alf Crossley, and he'd been there since the Jurassic period: he knew everyone and everything. The client said his name was Hubbard. He didn't live in Yorkshire, but he'd passed through Morley recently, and both the shop and the location were perfect for what he wanted. She'd asked what that was. He'd politely declined to answer.

Katie suddenly stopped thinking about the shop and more about her weekend. The one she had planned with her friend, Portia – a spa in Harrogate: top-class hotel, room service, massages, facials, swimming, the lot.

Katie had agreed to drive. It was more of a demand really. She absolutely loved her Chillout Purple Fiat 500. She'd wanted one of those since the first time she had laid eyes on it. Her father had agreed to stand as guarantor and Katie had wanted all the extras that the dealership could offer: spoilers, mudguards, wind deflectors.

Her father had claimed it was a waste of time and money. The salesman said it enhanced the resale value of the car. The only thing it enhanced was the salesman's wages, her father had said. Nevertheless, the salesman had talked Katie into it without too much effort; her father had tried to talk her out of it with plenty of effort. She had disagreed, lost her patience. And on it went. But she still had the car.

Walking down Queen Street at nine-fifteen in the morning, Katie was in a world of her own. She had a coffee in one hand, with her phone in the other checking her messages. A number of people passed, bidding her a good morning. She waved and smiled but she had no idea whom she'd greeted.

Katie wondered if she could call her client again and make absolutely sure he was coming.

Portia interrupted that thought by FaceTiming her.

"Where are you?"

"On my way to work."

"Oh, your mysterious client," said Portia. "At least your job is interesting, and you get out and meet people."

Katie smiled. Portia had a job at one of the salad warehouses on the outskirts of town. She worked weird shifts, as did everyone there. Most of them never complained but then again, most of them were foreign; happy to take whatever was on offer and, according to Portia, they all worked really hard and rarely spoke out of turn.

"So, do you know anything else about him?" Portia asked.

"What do you mean, anything else?" replied Katie. "I don't actually know *anything* about him."

"What time are you meeting him?"

"About ten o'clock. But I'm only five minutes away from the shop. I'm outside the Town Hall now."

"What do you think he's like?"

"How should I know? I've never met him."

"But you've spoken to him," persisted Portia. "You must have some idea. What does he sound like?"

"Old," replied Katie. "He has one of those smooth voices that you associate with older people."

"Older? More experience, then."

"With what?"

"You know what," replied Portia. "Has it been that long since you've seen any action?"

"Portia, for God's sake, I don't want to discuss my love life in the middle of the street."

Katie was approaching Brunswick Street. "Look, I'm nearly there, Portia, I'll to have to go."

"Okay, but how about some lunch?"

"Yes. I'll give you a call."

Katie ended the session and put the phone into her pocket. She wrapped both hands around her coffee. It was mid-November and the weather was turning. The first week had been lovely, dry and sunny. The second had been awful: freezing cold winds and heavy rain. Now there was a ground frost that refused to move, and generally lower temperatures.

She turned into Brunswick Street, passing a number of recently opened businesses: Oscars, Edge Hair Clinic, The Seven Hills Bar, and a place called Vixen. Fifty yards in front of her she spotted the shop. It was situated on the corner of a wide alley. It was simply the most uninviting premises she had ever seen: grey double-door front, two storeys with darkened windows and grey painted concrete ledges. The windows were so grimy they allowed no view of the inside. Behind the shop, about twenty yards further down Brunswick Street, was a passageway, allowing access into a backyard.

Alf Crossley had told her the building had started out life as a blacksmith's shop but she hadn't found any evidence of that. It had also been a bakery, a florist and a greengrocer.

Her phone suddenly rang. Katie answered a call from Brenda, in the office: would she pick up some milk on her way back in?

Katie agreed, ended the call, and then fished through her pockets for the keys. As she pulled them out, they snagged on the fabric and hurtled towards the side of the road, heading for a drain cover.

"Oh my God, no," shouted Katie. If she lost them she'd be in trouble. Luckily she didn't. Katie bent down, scooped up the keys and rammed them into the lock before anything else went wrong.

She opened the door and stepped inside, into a small vestibule, large enough for only two people. A number of letters and circulars littered the floor, most appeared to have been there for months. She kicked them into a corner with her right shoe. The building smelled damp and musty but that was only to be expected. She had no idea when anyone was last in but the windows must have been shut tight since they left.

Katie noticed a hook on the wall to her right, where she immediately placed the keys. She dropped her handbag on a window ledge, along with a folder, and then prized the plastic top from the cup. Steam rose up. She took a few sips, savouring the vanilla flavour. It was expensive but worth every penny.

She checked the time again. Approaching nine-thirty. She took another sip of coffee, bit the bullet and opened the door leading into the main shop.

As she entered, she could see her breath from the hot coffee she had sipped. Ahead of her, the room was a large open space, with an almost empty floor save a few old cardboard boxes, and some more envelopes. Shelves had been mounted on two of the walls. The windows were dark and impenetrable, and the place was littered with cobwebs. She hated spiders. They were harmless enough but everywhere they went they did so at the same speed as Usain Bolt. You had no idea where they were going to end up – she doubted they did.

She stared ahead of her, one hand on the coffee, the other on her phone. She noticed another door in the wall opposite, leading into a smaller room. She was imagining all sorts of things now; ghosts, serial killers, aliens. That would teach her to watch *Paranormal Caught On Camera*. Katie had no idea why she watched it anyway; she could never sleep afterwards. But it was so addictive. It frightened her half to death and the last thing she ever wanted was to meet up with something from the afterlife, but it was so bloody fascinating, the things people had filmed.

Katie took another sip of coffee, and then decided to check out the smaller room.

She approached the door, her footsteps resonating around the building, but thankfully that was the only sound.

"For God's sake, Katie," she said to herself, "man up."

She laughed at that: a woman manning up.

Katie opened the door, still smiling to herself. But the smile didn't last. She instantly recoiled, screamed, dropped her coffee and fell backwards all in one movement.

Every nerve end in her body was on red alert. Her legs felt hollow, her stomach turned and the only thing she had the strength to do was gaze on at the sight before her.

"Oh, Jesus."

Chapter Two

Phil Patterson stared out of the shop window, taking in what was going down on Queen Street. People were out in their droves, pushing prams, dragging shopping trolleys, holding conversations, greeting each other.

Business was good. Customers were loyal. He was the only butcher in the street, surrounded by a number of cafes and takeaways: The Spice Lounge, Nigellas, Chicken Cottage, Lime Tree Bistro. Most – if not all – used him when buying their fresh meat.

He wasn't one of these fancy deli butchers that sold every modern dish you could think of. He was a straight down the middle, old-fashioned butcher offering fresh meats, pies, pasties and hot sandwiches; everything laid out in steel trays and on steel counter tops. His shop stood opposite a number of hair and beauty salons and estate agents. He picked up all the trade.

The clock on the wall told him that it was nearly ten. They'd already had one busy spell with workers dropping in early for breakfasts, buying pies for dinner. Emily, his right-hand woman was making tea in the back room. Another hour would probably see the start of the dinnertime rush.

"Penny for them," said Emily.

He turned, taking the mug from her. "Probably not even worth that much."

Emily smiled, sipping her own tea. She was a strawberry blonde, carried a little too much weight, a little past her best but she was a diamond. She'd worked in the shop ever since it had opened, years ago.

"Can't be all that bad."

Patterson sighed. "Probably isn't, but I sometimes wonder what life is all about. Why are we here? Where are we going? Is there more to just working all hours?"

"Oh, dear, that is a bit deep. I thought you loved this shop."

"I do," said Patterson, "but I've butchered all my life and to be honest I've never really been anywhere, never done anything else *with* my life."

"Is that what you were up to this morning?" asked Emily. "When you asked me to cover for you?"

Patterson tapped his nose and pursed his lips.

"All in good time, Emily."

"You'd miss this place if you ever did anything else."

A fracas outside the shop diverted their attention. Two car horns blared. A pair of angry drivers faced each other, mouthing obscenities, though Patterson doubted that either one knew what the other was saying.

Emily turned away. "A bit of the old male testosterone rearing its ugly head again."

"Looks like it," said Patterson.

"Anyway, as I were saying, you'd never do anything else. You love the customers, not to mention the money." Emily's expression suddenly darkened. "Apart from this one, maybe."

As Patterson turned, Emily slipped off into the back room.

"Oh fuck, not him again."

The man had probably spent ten minutes studying everything in the window, and would no doubt spend another ten inside, questioning Patterson on everything else.

The rough old dog had the appearance of a totter, a rag-and-bone man, dressed in a shabby old overcoat that had seen far better days. In fact, you wouldn't even *give* it to a rag-and-bone man. His face was tanned, lined, weather-beaten, as if he'd spent his life working outside. His hair was grey and down to shoulder length, and Patterson noticed that he had odd-coloured eyes: one brown and one green.

He had grey frayed trousers tucked into a pair of Wellington boots, gloves with no finger ends, and a flat cap. Despite his appearance he was quite tall, broad-shouldered, well-built, and didn't appear to have missed many meals. His voice was smooth, his manner eccentric, but despite being reasonably polite he still annoyed the shit out of Patterson.

Emily had gone into the back room so there was no one else to serve him.

The man crept into the shop and studied what was on offer behind the only glass counter Patterson had, as well as the steel trays on the top containing a variety of different cuts of meat.

"Morning," said Patterson, in an effort to be friendly.

"Is it?" replied the totter.

"Was when I last checked," muttered Patterson under his breath, placing his cup under the counter.

"Pardon," said the totter.

"Checked," said Patterson. "It's time I checked the ovens."

"Not when you have a customer," came the reply. "And you should speak up, young man. That's the trouble with your generation, you mutter too much. Wouldn't have happened in my day, you'd have had it knocked out of you."

Patterson found that idea quite appealing, knocking the fuck out of someone – especially him.

"Where's this from?" asked the totter, pointing to the rump steaks.

"Well, if I didn't know any better," replied Patterson, "I'd say it was a cow, though which one I wouldn't like to guess. But I could find out for you."

The man spun round. "You know what I'm talking about."

"Be a first," muttered Patterson.

"Pardon," he shouted, reaching up and poking his ear.

If the old bastard had a hearing aid it would make Patterson's day. He remembered in his younger years teasing an old man with a hearing aid. Whilst having a difficult conversation, Patterson spoke lower and lower until the old guy turned it up full. Then Patterson shouted. The old man nearly had a heart attack.

"Thirst. A right thirst, this morning," shouted Patterson, reaching for his cup and holding his drink aloft.

The totter flinched and stepped backwards, nearly colliding with the teenager behind him, who was no doubt after a hot sandwich. Though why, Patterson couldn't imagine, he was dressed in a school uniform so that's where he should be.

"Watch out, Granddad."

"Pardon," said the totter, swinging round. "I'll give you granddad."

"In your dreams."

"Shouldn't you be at school, young man?"

"Surprised you remember what school is," came the caustic reply. "Anyway, I would be if you wasn't in here asking all sorts of awkward questions."

The totter turned to Patterson. "Never had all this cheek in my day, need a good horsewhipping, some of them."

Luckily for the teenager, Emily had reappeared and knew exactly what the schoolboy wanted. She quickly launched a bacon sandwich in his direction. He put the money on the counter before disappearing with an evil-eyed expression, giving the old totter a wide berth.

"Cheeky young bugger," shouted the totter, glancing at Patterson. "I blame the parents."

"Yes," replied Patterson, eager to change the subject and be rid of his least favourite customer. "You wanted to know what qualifications the cow had. I believe it came with a Mensa certificate and did once appear on Mastermind, where its specialist subject was offal, and judging by what I heard, that's exactly what the cow was."

The totter tutted and glanced at Patterson as if something had recently died and he'd found it.

"Are you trying to make me look stupid?"

"You don't need my help with that," replied Patterson.

"No," said the totter. "It must be yourself you're trying to make look stupid, then, and *you* don't need *my* help." A long silence ensued before the totter said, "I never know when to take you seriously. You want to grow up."

Patterson would have loved to tell him to fuck right off and harass another butcher, wondering if that would be serious enough.

"Take no notice of him, love," said Emily to the man. "As I mentioned the last time you were in, all our meat is top quality, locally sourced and humanely slaughtered."

"Yes, my dear, I remember. You mentioned Proctors Farm if I'm not mistaken?"

"Yes, love," replied Emily. "Been dealing with them for years. We wouldn't have it any other way."

"I was merely checking because the last lot of meat was excellent."

He leaned forward, his demeanour having changed now he wasn't putting up with Patterson.

"Lovely to hear it, now what can I get you, love?"

"*What can I get you, love,*" mimicked Patterson, slipping into the back room, keeping himself out of sight, and his mouth closed.

The totter narrowed his eyes. "I had no desire to upset his lordship, but I care for animals and I need to know they are treated with respect."

"I shouldn't worry about him, love, he's seen his arse this morning, that's all."

"Rather him than me," laughed the totter.

Emily laughed at the remark as well. "Couldn't have put it better myself."

Patterson could still hear the conversation in the back room and wished to Christ Emily would hurry up and serve the man. He slowly washed his cup and by the time he finally came out, the totter had gone.

"You want to watch what you're saying, Patterson," said Emily. "He just spent fifty quid with us. Bought a nice piece of fillet and a few other things."

"He just winds me up with all those questions."

"Don't let it get to you; he pays your wages, remember. And I'll tell you something else, not all of the meat is for him. He has a couple of horses stabled up with Joe Proctor."

"Fucking hell," said Patterson. "He doesn't feed the fillet to the horses, does he?"

"No, you daft beggar. He buys some of the meat for himself, and the rest for his dogs. All top quality, mind. All I were saying was, he knows Proctor; so he knows what he's getting from us."

Patterson suspected he might be a rough diamond, better for knowing. But there was still something he didn't like about him.

"Have you any idea who he is?"

"None at all, other than what I've just told you. Don't know where he lives, or in fact anything else about him."

"Do you know anyone who does?"

"No," said Emily. "I just appreciate the amount of money he spends in here. Without people like him we wouldn't have a living."

"I don't have your patience, Emily. I wish I had."

"You haven't had much of anything lately. You certainly haven't been yourself. Maybe a change of career *is* what you need."

Chapter Three

Detective Sergeant Sean Reilly pulled the pool car to a halt on Brunswick Street outside the shop. Both men jumped out and approached the building. A young PC stood guard over the scene, one that Detective Inspector Stewart Gardener hadn't seen before. He had short black hair; much thicker on the top than it was down the sides, which appeared shaved. His uniform and boots were clean and Gardener suspected he was on the ball, as he also noticed scene tape around the perimeter of the shop, and a box of scene suits in front of the door.

Gardener glanced at his watch. It was only ten-thirty in the morning. A lot appeared to have happened in a short time since the job first came in: girl finds a body, calls 999, informs the police; the control room dispatcher sends a local uniform officer to check it out. He confirms it is a body, puts a cordon in place and asks for CID.

The young girl standing to their right was perhaps the same age as the PC. She had straight black hair down to her shoulders, blue eyes, thin nose and thick red lips. She was dressed in a pale blue two-piece trouser suit with a white blouse and a blue silk scarf around her neck, topped off with a knee-length Mackintosh, which he doubted was doing much to keep her warm with today's temperature.

Gardener thought she was very attractive but given what she might have seen inside the shop her complexion appeared to have been bleached. She was talking to someone on the phone but as he drew nearer, she cut the call.

"I'm sorry," she said.

"What for?" Gardener asked, smiling, hoping it might put her at ease.

"That was my friend on the phone. We'd arranged to meet for dinner. I've cancelled. After what I've just witnessed, I don't feel like eating now... or ever."

Reilly slipped around the corner of the shop and scurried further down Brunswick Street. He stood by the entrance to a passage, which led to the rear of the building.

When he returned, he said, "I thought I might have a wee look to see where it leads, see if there was anything obvious that might help, but your man has his scene tape over that bit as well."

Gardener glanced at the PC, flashed his warrant card and introduced both himself and Reilly.

"PC Richmond," replied the PC. He nodded at the girl, "This is Katie Tunscroft. She found it."

"It?" repeated Reilly.

"When you see it, you might feel the same way," said Richmond.

"How bad is *it*?" asked Gardener.

"Bloody awful," said Katie. "Scared the shit out of me." She put her hand to her mouth. "Sorry, didn't mean to say that."

"I've heard worse," said Gardener.

"He's said worse," added Reilly, staring at his partner.

Katie smiled. "I can imagine, judging by what you must have seen." She continued. "I didn't even know if it was real at first, it never moved. It was so bloody creepy."

"It's definitely real," said Richmond.

Gardener glanced at Richmond. "Can you tell me anything about the scene? What do we have?"

"A corpse," replied Richmond. "Can't tell you whether it's male or female or how the hell it ended up like it has."

"Is it that bad," asked Reilly, "that you can't tell what sex?"

"Can't tell anything about it," said Katie. "I mean, who does that sort of thing? Who plants a body in an empty shop?"

"You'll see what we mean when you take a look," said Richmond.

"It is dead?" asked Gardener. "You have checked?"

"I have, it wasn't easy," said Richmond, "but I'm sure it's dead."

"It wasn't easy," repeated Reilly. "I think we need to see what we're dealing with, boss."

Gardener noticed the population of Morley beginning to assemble outside the shop so he turned and asked Katie Tunscroft to quickly summarize her version of events.

"You didn't touch anything?"

"Too right I didn't. I was out of there pretty sharpish. But I might have contaminated the scene," she said, as if she knew what she was talking about, or watched a lot of TV.

"How so?" Gardener asked.

"I had a cup of coffee with me, didn't I? Dropped the bloody thing."

"I think we can understand that given what you've told us," said Gardener. "And you didn't see anyone lurking around before you entered the shop?"

"No."

Gardener asked Katie if she would like to sit in the patrol car where it would be a little warmer. Once he and his partner had assessed the scene, they would come back and ask her some more questions.

She nodded, moving towards the car. Richmond produced a scene log, which both officers signed before suiting and booting and entering the building.

On doing so, Gardener noticed a pile of envelopes over to one side, and a set of keys hanging on a hook. He pushed open the door into the shop. The room was large and led into a smaller room behind. Considering the shop was empty there wasn't much mess.

The smaller room was where it was all happening. Gardener walked further in so he could gain a better view.

Centre stage was their corpse, wedged into a chair with no seat, facing the back wall, and a back door leading to what Gardener suspected would be outside. To the left of the body, he noticed an open cupboard, which as far as he could see was empty. The corpse was wrapped very tightly into a blue polythene shroud, which was the only way he could describe it.

Gardener glanced at where the hands should be but they were also covered, as were the feet. He edged into the smaller room, squeezed up toward the cupboard in an effort to face the corpse, but that was of no help to him because the whole head was also encased within the shroud.

No part of the body whatsoever was on show. As Gardener was wearing gloves, he reached out for the wrist of the corpse to check for a pulse, despite thinking he would be wasting his time. He couldn't feel anything.

"What in God's name has happened here?" asked Reilly, kneeling and glancing underneath the seat.

Gardener peered around the room. It was empty. The only inhabitant was the corpse in the chair – nothing else: no waste cardboard, no envelopes or flyers, no cutlery or crockery. It had obviously been used as a kitchen at some point because at the far end, under a window was a sink with one mixer tap. He walked over and glanced into it. The sink was empty.

"I've no idea," said Gardener.

He stared at the door leading to the outside. The long rectangular window within was broken, the lock ripped away from the frame, and the wood around it splintered.

"Forced entry," said Reilly.

"We might strike lucky with prints," said Gardener, "but it's not likely. Whoever is responsible for this will have covered their tracks."

"Be a bigger area for the SOCOs and the PolSA team to concentrate on," said Reilly, staring outside. He then pointed to the floor. "There's nothing under the chair to catch any body waste."

"Probably no need," said Gardener, "the way it's been wrapped up."

"Makes you wonder where this poor bastard's been, and for how long. He must have been killed somewhere else and then brought here."

"I'll go with that, Sean."

Gardener studied the body more closely, trying desperately to make out any features. Another confirmation of death was no rise and fall of the chest, and no breathing sounds.

"Do you think it's male or female?"

"Hard to tell, too tightly wrapped," said Reilly.

Gardener touched the blue polythene, caressing it between his gloved fingers.

"It's quite thick, industrial grade. Could prove interesting if we can find out what it is, where it was produced and who sells it. Whatever has happened to the body is pretty much contained within this wrapping."

Reilly also felt around the body itself. "Everything appears to be here: hands, feet, head. It all appears to be together. I can't feel any excess fluid built up around the feet, so God only knows what we're going to meet when Fitz gets inside there."

"I can't smell anything associated with an aged corpse," said Gardener. "I know the inside of this place is musty but that's about all I can smell. I wonder how long it's been here."

"Surprisingly enough, that back door has been forced and there are no wee predators in here, so my guess is not that long."

Gardener turned and searched the small room once more, hoping to find something that might offer a clue. He sighed. There was absolutely nothing to suggest how the body had met its grisly end.

Reilly pulled the back door further open, glancing outside. He pointed to the ground. Most of it from the passageway was concrete but there also appeared to be a soft layer of mud and grass, some of it overgrown. The yard was a scrap man's delight, with a number of pallets, broken and rusted gates and an old washing machine. But in the middle of all that, Gardener noticed two very slim tracks, perhaps from the wheel of a cart.

"That might be helpful. It also confirms to me that he or she was almost certainly killed somewhere else and brought here."

"Let's hope somebody's seen something for the witness statements," said Reilly.

"You'd like to think they had," said Gardener.

The SIO returned to the corpse, once again feeling his way around it. As his partner had suggested, everything appeared to be in place, the body seemed to be in one piece. He wanted desperately to slit open the polythene, see what was really going on underneath, but it was more than his life was worth.

"I really don't think there is a lot more we can do, Sean. We need everyone here: the team, Fitz, the SOCOs, PolSA. It's a full-on murder investigation as far as I'm concerned. We'd better call them in and leave them to it."

Chapter Four

Back outside the shop, Gardener slipped over to the pool car and retrieved a quilted jacket. He wasn't sure whether or not it was his imagination, but it felt colder now than when they had entered the building. Before leaving the premises, he'd placed a call requesting the teams to attend, including the Home Office pathologist. Like most crime scenes, he figured it was going to be a nightmare.

Reilly had gone scouting around the area. It wasn't long before he was back.

"Can't spot any CCTV."

"Pity," said Gardener, glancing around at the shops and the houses.

On the opposite side of the road was a bar called The Bottle and Tap. The small side street in which they were standing was called Brunswick Alley. It had one long building on the corner, which Gardener thought might be a number of flats.

"There're plenty of houses but God knows what any of them would have seen," said Reilly, glancing up and down.

"It's going to be awkward, Sean, we don't even know *when* the body was dumped."

"Probably the middle of the night, knowing our luck."

Gardener agreed and strolled forward to the end of Brunswick Alley. The first thing he saw was a skip, with nothing of any interest in it, but it couldn't be ruled out. The rest of the area was a small yard for the back of the buildings, in which to dump rubbish or park your car.

He glanced at his watch, hoping it wouldn't be too long before everyone turned up. He and Reilly discussed talking to Katie Tunscroft but dismissed that idea; there was no point starting with her and having to break off for the team.

Gardener asked Richmond to extend the scene tape from the front of the shop, all the way across to the building on the opposite corner of Brunswick Alley. Whilst he did that, Gardener and Reilly strolled up Brunswick Street, past the shop, ducked under the tape and continued to the rear of the building.

Gardener noticed a pair of gates in reasonable condition, which suggested they were regularly used, a wooden fence, three different coloured wheelie bins – which would have to be searched – and some small piles of rubbish.

"Boss," said Reilly, pointing to the ground. "They look to me like the same track marks we saw at the back of the shop."

Gardener bent down and studied them, taking a couple of photos on his mobile. He knew the SOCOs would also do that but it didn't hurt to have a backup.

Another ten minutes of mooching around was interrupted by the arrival of his team in three different cars. Gardener quickly assembled them outside the front of the shop and explained the presence of the unidentified corpse within.

"Male or female?" asked DC Colin Sharp.

"We don't know," Detective Inspector Gardener replied.

"You don't know?" questioned PC Julie Longstaff.

"Christ, boss," said DC Dave Rawson, by far the bravest of the bunch. "I know you're knocking on a bit, but–"

"I wouldn't complete that sentence, if I was you," said Reilly, "not unless you want to be back walking the beat."

Gardener laughed and went on to explain what his partner was talking about.

"Jesus," said DC Frank Thornton, "this must be a first. Can't say we've ever had one wrapped in a bin liner before."

"It's hardly a bin liner, Frank," said Gardener. "This stuff looks military grade."

"Oh, God," said DC Bob Anderson, blowing into his hands. "The last thing we want is another military nut to deal with."

Detective Sergeant Sarah Gates agreed, stamping her feet on the ground. "God only knows what Fitz will find when he gets inside."

"Did I hear my name taken in vain," said the pathologist, creeping up behind them.

"God forbid," said Reilly. "Given your time of life I'm surprised you heard anything at all."

Dr George Fitzgerald, the Home Office Pathologist, otherwise known as Fitz, smiled but deigned not to reply.

Gardener asked the team if they could split up and work through all the basic police procedure, which would mainly include house-to-house, and calling in on as many businesses as they could to ask if anyone had seen anything dodgy in the last couple of days, or anything they considered out of the ordinary.

Two white Transit vans pulled up on the road near the back of the shop, at the entrance to the small alley leading behind. Teams of officers jumped out and began unloading equipment, which included the paper suits and shoes they would need.

Once his own team had split up, Gardener took Fitz through what he had found, before leaving him to his own devices on the inside. There would be nothing further that he or Reilly could achieve by going back in. They would simply waste valuable interviewing time with Katie Tunscroft.

Gardener turned his attention to the rear of the shop, where he noticed Steve Fenton, Head of SOCO walking toward him. Gardener took him through what he'd found but clarified one important point.

"As soon as you enter the shop, Steve, I'd like someone on the body immediately. I need fingerprinting and DNA testing, and then I'd like it down the mortuary as soon as possible because I want a meeting with Fitz before close of play today, so I have something to discuss in the incident room."

Fenton nodded and retreated to address his own team.

Chapter Five

Andy Blanchard strolled toward Trident Fitness, opposite the ASDA store on Howley Park Road in Morley. TF was a one-storey building resembling an old tyre-fitting shop. At the rear of the main building stood a number of other outlets that had perhaps been workshops, or tyre-fitting bays. The building sported a large car park at the front but Andy wasn't driving.

He hunched his shoulders slightly, pulling his rucksack closer. It was colder than he had imagined, and he was only dressed in a T-shirt, jeans and trainers.

As he reached the door, he opened it and allowed two other bodybuilders to leave before he entered. They nodded their appreciation. He didn't know them but had seen them around the place a few times. He often felt that everyone using the building was here for the same purpose, and as such there were no superior egos. Everyone was willing to help someone else.

He slipped through the main hall and into the changing rooms. He felt like really giving his system something to think about today.

One hour later, Andy was back in the changing room, sweating like a bull. He pulled his chilled drink from a fridge in the corner, sat on a nearby bench, and took a long swig. The ice-cold liquid as it made its way down his throat into his stomach was refreshing.

When finished, he placed the bottle on the bench. "I needed that," he said to himself.

"Not surprised," said Niles Beckett.

Startled, Andy smiled. "Sorry, mate, didn't know you were there."

Niles took a seat next to him. He was a weightlifter in a different league to Andy. He was twenty-three with coffee-coloured skin and muscles on his muscles. He trained seriously because he wanted to represent England at the Olympics.

"No worries, Andy. Are you okay?" he asked. "You were really going for it in there, man. Me and a few of the lads were impressed but worried at the same time, know what I mean?"

Andy drank some more of his water. "I'm okay."

"You sure? You seem pretty down, man, as if you had something to prove."

"Doubt I could prove owt to you lads," said Andy. "You're way out of my league. I'm just an ugly old brute trying to keep himself in trim... and probably failing."

"Come on, man, don't run yourself down," said Niles, sipping more of *his* water. "I reckon you could keep up with the best of them in your day."

"I've only ever really done it for fun," said Andy. "I take it a bit more seriously now. I'm not in the building game so I need to do something to control the weight."

"Yeah, some of the lads reckoned you were handy with the tools. You own a bit of property as well, don't you?"

"I have a few places," replied Andy.

"If I leave you my number maybe you could let me know if you have anything," said Niles. "Me and Corrine are looking to move in together."

"Well done, son. What sort of a place are you after?"

"Nothing special to start with, just something to get us out of the parents' place, know what I mean? A two-up-two-down in a quiet place will do us."

"Leave it with me," replied Andy, taking in more water, now feeling a little cooler and a tad better.

"Not your tenants, is it, man. They not giving you any grief?"

Andy laughed. "No." He put his bottle down and stared at Niles. "I'll tell you what, I reckon I have some of the best tenants I've ever had at the moment. I know they want stuff doing to the house now and again, but they provide me with a good living. I don't charge too much, and I look after them. And why wouldn't I, they're my bread and butter? I want them to stay."

"Nice to hear it," said Niles. "I've seen these programs about nightmare tenants and slum landlords, but you don't strike me as one of them. So if it's not them that's bothering you it must be something else."

"I don't want to bore you with my problems."

"Don't be daft, man. We're all friends in here."

Niles was right, and Andy knew it. Andy felt himself relaxing in Niles' company, and suddenly he found himself opening up a little.

"If you must know, it's my dad."

"Oh," said Niles, with a more concerned expression. "Is he not well?"

"I couldn't tell you."

"I'm not with you."

"I haven't seen him for years. He went out to work one day and never returned. I were eighteen."

"Never?"

"No, never came back. Nearly forty years ago today. And I'll tell you something, it's never sat right with me."

Andy sat back a little. "I know I'm boring you now, but it's all I can really think about when the day comes round."

"You're not boring me, man. Me and the other guys all have respect for you. Christ, if that happened to my old man, I think I'd be the same as you. It's not right, is it? You mean, he went out of the door, and that was it? Full stop, you never laid eyes on him again?"

"That about sums it up."

"How did you feel?"

No one had ever asked Andy that question, and as such, he had to think about the answer. Finally, he said, "Lost."

"I think I'd be a bit more than lost. Were you close?"

Another good question, thought Andy.

"I reckon we were. He'd always been there for me, see. If I had a problem, *we* had a problem, until it was sorted."

"That close. You were lucky." Niles' expression was one of sudden surprise as his eyes widened and his hand went to his mouth. "Sorry, I didn't mean it to come out like that. I don't mean you were lucky to lose him, lucky to have him. Some guys never have that. Did you tell the police? Stupid question, I know."

"Oh aye. There were a big investigation. They looked into all sorts of stuff; even checked *us* out: me and my mam, see if everything was on the level."

"Did they find anything? I don't mean with you and your old lady."

"Well they never found *him*," said Andy, "so I suppose, no, they didn't."

"They never found nothing? Not even a trace, where he went?"

"No, nothing. It's like he walked out of the house, out of his life, out of *our* lives, and just ceased to exist."

"Fuck, man," said Niles. "That's heavy stuff. How did they leave it?"

Andy finished his drink. "I'm not real sure. They just said they'd keep everything on file and visit it on a regular basis to see if anything turned up."

"And has it?"

"No."

"Be one of them cold case things," said Niles, drinking more water. "I've watched some of that CSI stuff, that's what they call it – cold case."

Andy laughed. "You sound like you know your stuff. Maybe *you* should have been looking for him."

"Have you never heard anything since?"

"No," said Andy, pulling his towel from his rucksack, ready for a shower. "Not a thing."

"Hasn't there even been a sighting of any kind?"

Andy sat back, deep in thought. "I don't think there has, well none that I've ever heard about, and I'm sure I would."

"God, that's some heavy shit," said Niles. "I can't imagine what you went through. What does your mother think about it? She must have known him better than anyone?"

"She never understood it. For years, she never accepted it. Used to lay a place for him at the table every mealtime. She kept his clothes washed and pressed. She moved out of their bedroom but she kept it immaculate, in case he ever returned. I think she must have accepted it eventually. She used to talk about nothing else. She's getting on a bit now, but she never really mentions it anymore."

"Bet she still thinks about it, though," said Niles. "What do you believe in your own mind?"

Another question that took Andy back, one he had to think about. "Honestly?"

"Absolutely."

"I think he's still out there. I honestly believe he's still alive and that one day he'll come back into our lives with some kind of explanation."

"Have to be pretty fucking mind blowing, if you ask me."

Andy laughed. "Yeah, that's one way of putting it. Be worth hearing, though, wouldn't it? I sometimes wonder if that's why I've never had a serious relationship with anyone; never had kids. He'd never meet them, would he? Never hold them."

"Maybe not, Andy, but I bet if you asked your mum, she would have wanted grandchildren. She would have wanted to hold them."

That one sentence silenced them, made Andy feel very selfish. He'd never actually considered that one.

Eventually, Niles said, "What's the last thing you remember?"

Andy stared at Niles. "That's an easy one. He were a right keen chess player. He spent hours teaching me the game. To this day, I savour them memories, of the games we played. He believed that chess made you a better person, because it allowed you to look at life differently, allowed you to solve problems more readily. I think he was right. Trouble was, it didn't help me to work out what had happened to him, or to find him."

Andy grew silent again, and then said. "We started a game of chess in the parlour of my old mum's house on that very morning. Before he left for work, he made his move and he put me in check. He said, there you are, something for you to think about."

After some time, Niles said, "Have you ever made your move?"

Andy glanced in his direction. Lifting the towel and slinging it over his shoulder, he rose from the bench.

"No, it's still in the same position as we left it. I really do believe one day he'll walk back in and we'll resume the game. He'll want to see where I move next."

"You've had a lot to cope with but you've done well for yourself, brother," said Niles, to Andy's back.

Andy raised his right arm as a gesture. "I'll let you know about that house."

Chapter Six

Gardener and Reilly were at the front of the shop, gazing in at the activity. Within the last few minutes the empty building had come alive, resembling something of a Tom Cruise film set. Staring up and down Brunswick Street, Gardener saw the locals had gathered to try to catch a glimpse of what was going on. He also noticed that Katie Tunscroft was now *outside* the police vehicle, puffing on a cigarette.

"We need to speak to her, Sean, while everything's still fresh in her mind."

Reilly grabbed a pad and pen from his inside pocket.

As Gardener approached, she immediately dropped the cigarette and stepped on it. "Sorry."

"No need to apologise."

"There will be if my boyfriend finds out," replied Katie. "I gave these things up six months ago. Vowed I'd never smoke another."

"That was before you entered the shop," said Reilly, defending her.

"I've gone through three in the last half hour. God that was awful in there. Frightened me to death. I mean, who does that? Is it someone's idea of a sick joke, or what?"

"You'd be surprised what some people do for a laugh," said Reilly.

"I can't imagine anyone finding *that* funny. *Is* it real?"

"We assume so," said Gardener.

"You mean you haven't checked?" asked Katie.

"We're not allowed."

"I thought you were in charge."

"Looks can be deceiving," said Reilly.

"Oh, God," said Katie, shivering. "I can't even begin to imagine some of the things you have to deal with. I couldn't do it. I couldn't do your job, having to put up with stuff like that all day long, every day."

"It's not every day," said Reilly, as if that excused it.

"Or all day long," said Gardener. "Would you like to go somewhere warmer, Miss Tunscroft? Have a coffee, maybe?"

"No, I don't think I could. I think I'd just like to answer your questions and go home. I couldn't stomach anything to eat or drink."

Gardener nodded, starting with her basic details. He ascertained that she lived with her parents on Scotchman Lane in Morley, and she was single.

"Which estate agent do you work for?"

"Crossley's on Queen Street."

"Is it part of a chain?"

"No, it's independent."

"And is it someone called Crossley who owns it?"

"Yes, Alf Crossley."

"What's he like to work for?"

"He's really good, quite laid back. Been in the game for years."

"Seems rather odd that this shop has lain empty for a year, and when a client wants to view the place, someone breaks in and leaves a body."

"I know, can't see him being too happy."

"Has the client shown up?"

Katie checked her phone before replying, "No."

"Have you heard from him?" Reilly asked.

"No."

"Have you tried to call *him*?" Gardener asked.

"To be honest, no," replied Katie. "I've been too busy trying to get my head around it."

Gardener nodded. "Can you tell us anything about your client?"

"I know his name is Hubbard?"

"Does he have a first name?" asked Reilly.

"If he did, he never told me."

"Can we have his contact number?" Gardener asked.

Katie gave it to them and Reilly called the station, told them what he knew and asked for a call back if they managed to speak to him.

"Did you get any more details from him?" asked Gardener. "Address, for example?"

"To be honest, I didn't," replied Katie. "But we have all that sort of stuff back in the office. Alf will certainly have it."

"How was today set up?"

"Initially, it was a phone call, and then he emailed me confirmation."

"Sounds like he was keen," said Reilly.

"He seemed confident."

"Perhaps he's local, knows the place," said Gardener. "Did you only ever speak on the phone?"

"Yes, never met him."

"Did he ever call from a landline?"

"Not that I can recall. I only ever had the mobile number. But that's not unusual nowadays, is it? Everyone has a mobile but not many have a landline."

"True," said Gardener.

"Did you ever call him out of hours?" asked Reilly.

"Yes, a few times. He nearly always answered. If he didn't, I'd leave a message and he'd call back as soon as he could."

"So you never suspected anything untoward from any of the phone conversations that you had?" questioned Gardener.

"No, nothing. He seemed…" Katie paused. "Well, he seemed really nice."

"Did he sound local?" Reilly asked.

"Not really. I never detected an accent. The only thing I can really remember of the phone calls is that he had a voice like James Mason."

"James Mason?" questioned Gardener. "The actor, James Mason? I'd have thought you'd be too young to remember him."

"I am," laughed Katie. "I only know that because my dad loves Mason's films. He used to make me watch them all the time."

Gardener found that funny, because his own dad was very similar. He loved all the old black and white kitchen sink dramas. If Gardener had a pound for every one he had been made to watch he'd be quite rich now.

"Do you know if he ever spoke to any other members of staff?"

Katie screwed her eyes together. "I'm not really sure, you'd have to ask them. There might have been an occasion once when he called me and I wasn't around, so someone took a message, but I honestly can't remember who."

"Do any of the others know him?" asked Reilly. "Or have they heard of him before?"

"Not as far as I can remember. If anyone has, it would be Alf. He's older than Morley itself, had the shop since God were a lad, knows everyone."

"Did Mr Hubbard ever give any indication of what he was going to do with this shop?" Gardener asked.

"Not that I can recall," said Katie. "Up until now this side of the town hasn't drawn much custom. Getting better now, though, because more places are opening up around here. That's new." She pointed to The Bottle & Tap. "So maybe he'd hit on something that would work and decided here would be right."

"Who actually owns the shop?" Reilly asked.

Katie's expression was blank. "Do you know, I really don't know. Alf will have records."

Reilly laughed. "Bet you don't call him Alf in the shop."

Katie rolled her eyes. "God forbid. Very traditional is our Alf."

Gardener found it strange that she didn't know who owned the shop, especially if she had been working the case and in line for closing the deal. Maybe she was suffering the effects of shock.

"I take it you guys will be going to see Alf Crossley."

"As soon as we've finished with you, Miss Tunscroft."

Gardener didn't expect that to be much longer, as he didn't feel there was anything more she could tell them, or much more that he could ask her, for now.

At that point, Reilly's phone chimed. He stepped back and took the call, which ended quite briefly.

"Turns out it's a burner, and it's out of service," he said to Gardener.

"What is?" asked Katie.

"The phone you've been calling, Miss Tunscroft. Looks like it's a pay-as-you-go burner phone and now it's disappeared."

She put her hand to her mouth. "Oh my God. Does that mean I've actually been talking to the killer all along?"

"It's a distinct possibility," said Gardener.

Katie's expression darkened. "This is just awful. He's been playing me with no intention of ever renting the shop?"

"Doesn't sound like it, Katie, love," said Reilly. "Sounds like he wanted you to find the body."

Katie's knees buckled but she remained upright.

"How sick is that?" she shouted. "He's been using me? What kind of a game is that he's playing? Oh my God." She put her hand to her mouth yet again.

"What's wrong?" asked Gardener.

"I've just thought of something: what if he knows me, and he's watching me? What if I'm next?"

"It's not very likely, Miss Tunscroft."

"Seems to us that he just wanted what's in that shop found," said Reilly.

"Why?"

"Who knows?" said Reilly. "There's no rhyme or reason with most of these people."

"How did he get in?" asked Katie. "Do you think he has a set of keys?"

"He might," said Gardener. "At the moment it looks like he's forced the back door. But, as you've just mentioned, all of that may have been staged because he does have keys."

"How the bloody hell would he have the keys?" Katie asked, more to herself.

"Has there been *any* interest in the place?" asked Reilly.

"No, it's been on the market a year or so. Not one phone call."

"So, to your knowledge," said Gardener, "no one has ever been to see it, and no one has ever asked for the keys?"

Katie shook her head. "No."

"The mystery deepens," said Reilly.

"Okay, Miss Tunscroft," said Gardener. "I think that's all for now. Would you like a lift home?"

"No," she replied. "It's not far and I think I need to clear my head. The walk might help."

"If you're sure," said Gardener. "We'll send someone round later to take a formal statement."

Katie nodded.

Before departing Gardener asked if he could have her phone, which he dropped straight into a Faraday bag.

"What about my boss?" Katie asked. "He's going to wonder where I am and what's going on."

"We'll tell him," said Gardener. "He's our next port of call."

Chapter Seven

"I don't often get a visit from the police. It must be something serious."

Alf Crossley pretty much resembled everyone's favourite grandfather. He was overweight with a round face and a bulbous nose and grey hair and round, wire-rimmed spectacles. He wore a grey pin-striped suit with grey loafers. He was now sitting behind his desk in an aged leather seat, which was probably his favourite judging by the condition. The office was clean and smelled fresh, and was sparsely furnished with a desk, two filing cabinets, two wooden cabinets, a wastepaper bin and a green check-pattern carpet.

"I'm afraid it is, Mr Crossley," said Gardener, favouring the warmth of Crossley's office to the streets outside. He went on to explain what Katie Tunscroft had found earlier in the day.

"A body? A *dead* body in the shop?" said Crossley, blinking several times and raising his arms in the air. "Oh my dear Lord. How is Katie? Is she still there? Did she find it?"

"We took the liberty of sending her home after we'd spoken to her. And we said we'd send an officer round later in the day to take a formal statement."

"Is she okay?"

"A little shaken," said Gardener, "but it's understandable."

Crossley sat forward and cupped his hands under his chin. "I must call her later and see how she is. How awful. Do you know who it is?"

"No," said Gardener, preferring to leave it at that, and ask questions of his own. "How long has Crossley's been here?"

"A long time, Mr Gardener. My father, God rest his soul, started the business in the Seventies. I took over in the Eighties. So, as you can see, we're well established, especially considering we're not part of a chain."

"Have you ever been approached by a chain, for a buyout?" asked Reilly.

Gardener understood why he'd asked. If Crossley had been made an offer, and then declined, it may have caused animosity, which might be a reason for someone to dump a body in one of their premises.

"No, Mr Reilly. There's enough business to go round."

"How long has Katie been with you?" Gardener asked.

"About a year, fifteen months, maybe."

"What are your impressions of her?"

"She's very good. Always pleasant to customers, has a good understanding of the job. She's certainly helpful, and willing to go the extra mile. Not something you usually find in someone so young these days."

"She lives with her parents," said Reilly. "Have you met them?"

Crossley seemed perplexed by the question. "Yes, they're nice people as well. Why do you ask?"

"Just trying to build up a picture of Katie and her home life."

Crossley nodded.

"No problems that I know of, Mr Reilly," Crossley said. "She is courting. They've been together for some time now and there is talk of settling down and buying a house. You don't suspect her of any wrongdoing, do you?"

"We have to treat everyone as a suspect at the start of an investigation, Mr Crossley," Reilly said.

"Me included?"

Gardener ignored the question.

"Any customer problems?"

Crossley laughed heartily. "All the time, Mr Reilly. I imagine you've never been an estate agent and I don't mean that demurely, but every day is a problem. Dealing with all this, as you can imagine, brings us our fair share of disgruntled customers who don't understand why things just don't happen when they want them to. It can be a nightmare."

At that point the door opened and another member of staff entered, carrying a tray with three cups of tea and a saucer of biscuits. Gardener saw his partner's eyes light up.

Eager to move the matter on, Gardener opened the line of questioning that they were really there to pursue.

"So, who owns the shop in Brunswick Street?"

Crossley took a sip of tea before answering. "I'm not really sure, Mr Gardener, I'll have to check the records."

That was clearly someone else's job because Crossley picked up the phone and relayed the order.

"How long has it been on your books?" asked Reilly, carefully selecting the biscuits he required.

"A year, maybe… I'll certainly be able to tell you when Nadine brings the records in, but my best guess would be a year."

"Have you ever met the owner in person?" asked Gardener.

"Can't say I have," replied Crossley. "I believe everything was either conducted by telephone or emails."

"And how have your services been paid for?"

"At the moment they haven't. There hasn't been anything to pay. On this particular contract we're working on commission. Once we arrange to either sell it for the owner, or let it, then we'll take our cut."

The door opened and Nadine walked in with a thick manila folder, passing it over to Crossley. He took it and thanked her, and she left. Crossley delved into the file, studying it before revealing his information.

"It was purchased a year ago, but the owner decided to let it almost immediately."

"Is that usual?" asked Reilly.

"It's not *un*usual, Mr Reilly. Maybe the buyer changed his mind and decided he would get more money renting it."

"And who was the buyer?"

Crossley went back to the file. "It says here the registered owner is a company called WEB Enterprises."

"Where are they based?"

"According to this, Hemel Hempstead."

"Do you have a number?"

Crossley nodded, and passed it to Reilly, who removed his phone from an inside jacket pocket.

"Does the owner of WEB Enterprises have a name and address?" asked Gardener.

Crossley checked the file.

Reilly placed his phone on the desk. "Out of service."

"No surprise there," said Gardener, with a sinking feeling.

"Hubbard is the name," said Crossley.

"Hubbard?" repeated Gardener.

"Yes," said Crossley, "a Mrs Wendy Hubbard."

"How interesting," said Gardener.

"What do you mean?" Crossley asked.

"Katie Tunscroft's client, who was coming to view the shop was called Hubbard."

"It could be a coincidence," said Crossley.

"We don't believe in them," said Reilly.

"Does WEB Enterprises have a different mobile to the one Miss Tunscroft gave you this morning, Sean?"

"Yes."

Reilly then dialled the station and gave them the number and the necessary details on file and asked them to check out what they could.

"I don't like the sound of all this," said Crossley. "So the owner of the shop makes an appointment to view his own premises, doesn't show up and then you find a body in it?"

"It would seem so, Mr Crossley," said Gardener. "If it's all the same to you, we'd like to take Katie's computer with us. We already have her phone, and we'd also like access to those records you have."

"Consider it done, Mr Gardener. I'm not stupid enough to throw client confidentiality at you. If this goes public it could be very bad for business."

Aware there was nothing else he could do for the time being, Gardener was very eager to seize everything he could as fast as possible and return it all to the station so his team could make a start.

"Are all your staff here today, Mr Crossley?"

"Yes, we're only a small outfit so we only have four full-time staff, including Katie."

"Okay. I'll send round two of my officers to take statements from the rest of the staff for our records."

Crossley nodded.

"Do you have a high staff turnover?" Reilly asked Crossley.

"Not at all, Mr Reilly. All my current staff have been here for years, ten or more, apart from Katie."

"Everyone happy?"

"I'd like to think so," said Crossley. "In fact, I sincerely hope so. I've always told them all, if ever they have a problem, come and see me. There's nothing we can't sort out over a cup of tea."

Gardener nodded, preparing to leave. A number of questions ran through his head. Who was being targeted here; the estate agent, the police, Katie, someone else not yet in the equation? What part did Hubbard play in it all, if that was really his name?

Chapter Eight

Back outside the shop on Brunswick Street, Gardener noticed it was still a hive of activity, particularly for the SOCOs. Members of his own team were conducting interviews on the street with anyone who would listen despite the temperature.

Steve Fenton suddenly appeared and advised them that he and his team had performed every test known to man on the material covering the body, and he would have the results as soon as possible. He informed Gardener that the body had now been transported to the mortuary.

Gardener glanced up and down the street. The crowd had thinned out and all that remained around the crime scene tape were the press with their cameras, not to mention a television news crew.

"What's going on here, Sean? We have an empty shop, a body wrapped up better than NASA suit up their astronauts, two people called Hubbard at the centre of the mystery, both with burner phones that are now out of service, and the company that appear to be running things are in Hemel Hempstead?"

"Well summarized, boss. Might be true as we know it, but by the time we've finished wading through it, I doubt if the Hubbards will exist."

"That certainly won't help us. I'd like to know what's happening with the Hubbards, if we can ever get hold of them."

"I doubt we will, but if we do, will we find that one has killed the other?"

"Possibly. Do you think they're local?"

"I can't imagine Hemel Hempstead having anything to do with it," said Reilly, "that's just a cover. I think you're on the right track, whoever did this is local."

"I agree," said Gardener, "they know the area."

"Well enough to blend in, I should imagine," added Reilly. "They've done all this without really being noticed."

"That's the only way they could have got themselves in and out," said Gardener. "It looks as though it's been well planned. Possibly under surveillance for weeks and they've picked out the shop deliberately."

"I don't think the forced entry at the back is genuine. Perhaps they had keys, but they've made it look like that."

"That doesn't look good for the estate agent," said Gardener. "It's hard to think that anyone at Crossley's had anything to do with this, but stranger things have happened."

"I certainly didn't get that impression from young Katie Tunscroft, or Crossley for that matter."

"Those cart tracks might offer a clue of sorts."

"Only if witnesses had their eyes open," said Reilly. "What's with all the wrapping?"

"They obviously don't want us to see what's going on immediately."

"Maybe so, but they're not stupid. Everybody and his brother watches CSI and detective dramas these days, they know we *will* see what's on the inside before long, so why bother with all that shit?"

"It's a game, Sean. Whoever they are, they're playing a game with us, and we've met enough of that sort in our time."

Gardener turned and glanced down the road where Brunswick Street met Queen Street. More press had gathered. They would want interviews but it was pointless at the moment. They'd probably talk to the locals, who would be making up all sorts of stories.

One of the TV interviewers shouted over to them but Gardener turned his back again. Returning to the station and setting up an incident room was now at the top of his list. He mentioned it to his partner, who asked PC Richmond to move the crime scene tape to let them out.

Thirty minutes later, Gardener and Reilly were pulling into Leeds Central Police station in Leeds. They went straight up to the fourth floor where Gardener spotted PC Patrick Edwards and PC Paul Benson. He collared them both and drew them in the direction of a free room. They were experienced officers who knew the drill, and Gardener didn't waste much time on telling them what to do.

Back in Gardener's office, desk sergeant Dave Williams was waiting for him.

"Morning, sir."

"Dave, how are you?"

"I'm okay, I'm not having the morning you're having by the sound of things."

"Lucky you," said Reilly.

"I'm guessing you have something for us, Dave," said Gardener.

"I do, sir, but it's not good news."

"When is it ever?" added Reilly.

Williams laughed. "I've run a check on everything you gave us. Both phones were pay-as-you-go burner phones and both are now out of service."

"Do you have any dates of when they went out of service?"

"The one in Hemel Hempstead, six months ago."

"And the other?" asked Reilly.

"Couple of days back. The last known call was almost certainly to the girl at the estate agent."

"I know it's a burner phone but can we get anything from it?"

"I can try," replied Williams.

"Use Gates and Longstaff," said Gardener.

"They're geniuses with this stuff," said Reilly.

"I'm guessing there is further bad news, in the form of Hemel Hempstead."

"You guess right. The premises do exist, on an industrial estate, but it belongs to a parcel delivery company, and has done for years. No one has ever heard of WEB Enterprises."

Gardener sat down. "Doesn't surprise me. Okay, Dave, keep digging – you might turn something up. If you leave all the paperwork with me, I'll get Sarah Gates and Julie Longstaff on to it."

"If anyone can unearth stuff from phones and computers it's them two," said Reilly.

"That reminds me, we still have Katie Tunscroft's computer, Sean. Can you bring it in and we'll get them to look at it."

Reilly and Williams disappeared, leaving a very anxious Gardener to wonder about what Fitz might find with the body.

As Reilly returned, Gardener's phone chimed. It *was* the man in question requesting their attention immediately, if not sooner.

* * *

It took them another forty minutes to negotiate the town centre before they finally arrived at the mortuary in the Leeds General Infirmary in Great George Street. Neither man spoke when they entered the building and their footsteps echoed through the empty corridors, leaving Gardener with a real feeling of trepidation.

Reilly opened the door and they found Fitz in a pristine office with a fresh coffee and the sound of an opera coming through speakers at low volume.

Fitz glanced up and smiled. "Coffee's on, help yourselves."

Gardener was astounded. "It's not like you to give up everything so easily. Are you feeling okay?"

"If I don't, he'll only ransack the place," said Fitz, glancing at Reilly.

"What it is to be loved," replied Reilly, doing as he was told. He also went through the drawers for any spare biscuits.

"So, what's the urgency?" asked Gardener, taking a seat.

"You need to see for yourself."

"Why can't you just tell us?" asked Reilly, turning around from the filing cabinet.

"You won't believe me," replied Fitz. "You'll think I've lost it."

"Of course we won't," said Gardener.

"No more than we already do," smirked Reilly.

"Well is it male or female?" asked Gardener. "Surely you can at least tell us that much."

Fitz stared at them. His expression was grim. Gardener noticed the lenses of his glasses still bore spots of whatever he'd been working on.

"What the hell have you found?" Reilly asked.

Gardener could feel the day growing longer by the second. Fitz rose from his chair and led them through to the mortuary. There was only one body on the steel gurney, which Gardener took to be theirs.

"In answer to your question of male or female," replied Fitz, "both."

"Both?" asked Reilly. "Are you having a laugh?"

The elderly pathologist pulled back the sheet.

Both detectives glanced at the gurney, but it was Reilly who spoke first.

"What in God's name is this?"

Chapter Nine

"I'm afraid God won't help you, gentleman," said Fitz. "This is definitely *not* one of His creations."

"I don't think my brain is working here, Fitz," said Gardener. "What exactly are we looking at?"

"An abomination," said Reilly.

"One corpse, four different bodies," said the pathologist.

Fitz then remained silent, allowing them to process the information their eyes were feeding them. The head, arms and legs of the unwrapped body all had a different shade and skin texture to each other, and all of those were male. The torso was female.

Gardener concentrated on the head, because that's really the one thing that might be of use to him and the team when it came to identification. Judging by the moon-shaped face, whoever he was he had been a large man; one would almost say rotund, with wobbly jowls, a neck like a rooster, and a grey combover. He had brown eyes, a bulbous nose and a hair lip.

Another indication that the arms, legs and torso did not belong to the head was an obvious one – thick, dark blue sutures connected them all. They were cumbersome. Whoever had sewn the joints had taken very little care; they simply wanted the job finished. Where each of the limbs met the torso, the flesh was heavily bruised. Some of the flesh had curled where it had hastily been rejoined, and the whole thing had a hideous Frankenstein monster appearance.

Each of the body parts was showing some age. In the case of the torso, it was wrinkled, and the breasts were flat. The pubic hair was grey. The arms and the legs were also wrinkled, with veins standing proud, but the short hairs were dark.

The smell was something else, quite putrid, reminding Gardener of a bag of rancid chicken he had once found in the boot of a car at a crime scene.

"What do you make of the stitches?" Gardener asked Fitz.

"I'd be very surprised if it was a surgeon or a nurse. Professional stitches are usually small, neat and subtle."

Gardener nodded. The answer was no less than expected.

"Best guess on where you'd find stitches like these?"

"Maybe a pathologist, but I can think of two other areas I'd be looking at first: butchers and farmers."

"What the hell's gone on here?" asked Reilly.

"We're almost into the realms of science fiction, gentlemen," said Fitz. "If we were watching a film, none of us would be surprised."

"What about the clothes, Fitz?" asked Gardener.

"No such luck," he replied. "Corpse was naked underneath the polythene."

Gardener was disappointed. Clothes might have helped.

"Have you kept that for us?"

"Yes, I'll bag it up and have it sent over," said Fitz. "There is another problem."

Gardener glanced at the pathologist as if he'd lost his mind.

"Christ!" said Reilly. "Isn't this bad enough?"

"The body parts had been frozen prior to wrapping them up."

"Pardon," said Gardener.

"Frozen," repeated Fitz.

"That's what we thought you'd said," replied Reilly.

Gardener leaned in closer. "How do you know?"

"I suspected because the body is damp and the flesh is a little rubbery," continued Fitz. "When flesh is frozen, the water inside the cells freezes and expands. This ruptures the cell membrane. On thawing, the water and other cell contents leak out of the ruptured membranes, causing a change in the look and feel of the flesh.

"How and when the body was thawed will also be important. On first thawing the body looks damp, as the water from the surface cells leaks out. When it's allowed to dry – in air, under a lamp, or using heat – the body starts to look wizened and slightly mummified, as the cells lose their water content. We're not at that stage, yet.

"How much the body dries out depends on the conditions and time it's been left to thaw and dry. Bodies do not thaw at the same rate all over, so organs such as the liver, heart, lungs etc. will take longer, which again depends upon the conditions."

"How did you actually find this out?" asked Gardener.

"Under a microscope. To be absolutely certain, I need to organize a biochemical test – maybe the SCHAD would be very useful."

"What's that?" asked Reilly.

"It's an enzyme in the liver, which is involved in the metabolism of fats. A SCHAD measures the short chain 3-hydroxyacyl-CoA dehydrogenase activity, but I'm not clear how it is affected by being frozen. I will have to make some calls, but this is my initial assessment."

Gardener was still fascinated by the corpse, so much so that his brain was slow to activate. There were so many questions he needed to ask to understand everything.

"Might be a stupid question," said Reilly, "but why would you freeze a body?"

"Freezing causes a substance to change from a liquid to a solid, which occurs when the molecules of a liquid slow down enough that their attractions cause them to arrange themselves into fixed positions as a solid. A phrase you might be familiar with is Cryonics, which uses temperatures below −130 °C, called cryopreservation."

"What the hell is that?" asked Reilly.

"It's an attempt to preserve enough brain information to permit the future revival of the cryopreserved person," replied Fitz. "Cryopreservation can be accomplished by freezing, using a cryoprotectant to reduce ice damage, or by vitrification to avoid ice damage.

"Procedures can only really begin after the patients are clinically and legally dead. Which might be within minutes of death. But it's not considered possible at the moment for a corpse to be reanimated after undergoing vitrification, without damage to the brain. In the future, things might be different."

"But that isn't what's going on here, is it, Fitz?" asked Gardener. "Four people have, at some point, been killed, cut up, and sewn back together, and then frozen. Why would you do that?"

"Where would you do it?" asked Reilly.

"Well, the where could be anywhere," said Fitz, "but I suspect you'd need somewhere big, probably remote. A barn for example, out in the middle of nowhere, to allow you to continue your work uninterrupted."

"Which brings us to the farming community," said Gardener.

"True," said Fitz, "but the fact that they've been frozen as well means you need access to possibly some industrial unit, like a walk-in freezer. It would need to be big enough to store four bodies."

"Which could point us back to butchers," said Reilly.

"How do you think they were detached?" Gardener asked Fitz.

"Probably quite simply – butchery. Sharp knives and a saw for the bones, whether they are butchers' tools, kitchen knives or surgical tools. Cut the flesh, tendons etc., down to the bone. A shoulder, possibly a hip might be dislocated to keep the joint whole. The cervical spine –

neck – is a simple straight joint – cut through a cartilage disc. When you have all the parts, sew them back together with strong thread, like we do after a post-mortem."

"You make it all sound so simple," said Gardener. "Still doesn't actually tell us why. Why would you kill four people, cut them up, rejoin them and then freeze them?"

"Well, as for killing and cutting up and rejoining," said Fitz, "you can see why. They've all been rejoined but not to their original bodies, so the killer must be playing some kind of a game, and he or she is making it much harder to identify them, making your life hell."

"I don't somehow see a 'she' being involved," said Reilly.

"Maybe not in the actual killing perhaps," said Fitz, "but no reason she couldn't be involved in the joining together."

"I'll go with that, Fitz," said Gardener.

"But if there was a male and female involved, they'd have to really trust each other," offered Reilly.

"I don't disagree, Sean," replied Gardener. "You wouldn't want to be falling out with someone after you'd carried out a task such as this. But I still don't see the need for freezing."

"Unless…" added Fitz.

Gardener glanced at him. "Unless what?"

"Unless you wanted to make it difficult to calculate *when* the original crime was committed."

Reilly whistled through his teeth. "Jesus Christ!"

Gardener remained silent for a moment or two, trying to work through the implications, and what and how he was going to tackle such a crime. With what Fitz had said, where was he even going to start? If someone was trying to disguise when it was done, the field was wide open, especially as each body part belonged to a different person.

"I've just thought of something else that will cause us a problem," said Gardener.

"Only one?" said Reilly.

"Don't worry," said Gardener, "the brain hasn't stopped but there are too many questions to process. What I wondered was, when these people were killed, were they frozen first and cut up and rejoined afterwards…"

"Or cut up and rejoined first and frozen afterwards?" questioned Reilly. "I see where you're coming from."

"Exactly," said Gardener. "If all of this was done years ago, where are we going to start?"

The SIO turned to the pathologist.

"Have you even come anywhere close to a normal post-mortem?"

"Not yet," he replied. "Obviously, I suspected some foul play so I wanted to check out the dampness first, but that was after I called you two. The next thing I need to do, to be quite honest, is lay out the body parts – arms, legs, torso and head – and have a fast-track DNA test done on each, as well as toxicology and any other test I can think of, including fingerprints. If I can find out what blood group they are, and if I can identify any evidence of deep-rooted problems, there may be some medical records somewhere that might help."

"At least that will give us a chance to marry them all up to their correct owners," said Gardener, which was a chilling enough statement.

"Because we now know there are going to be three more," said Reilly, finishing off how terrifying it was all becoming.

"Almost certainly," said Fitz. "What we're seeing here is perhaps only the beginning."

"And unless any of these people have a criminal record," said Gardener, "DNA won't really be of any use to us." Gardener then glanced at his partner. "I'll be honest, Sean, I don't even know where to start with this one."

"And you think I do?"

"Well, I'd hate to pile on even more pressure," said Fitz.

"But you're going to," said Gardener.

"There can't possibly be any more," said Reilly.

"I wish I could say for you that there wasn't. Follow me."

Chapter Ten

Both men followed the elderly pathologist back into his office. Reilly immediately made for the coffee machine and poured one for all of them. Gardener took a sip and placed his cup on the desk.

Glancing at Reilly, he said, "If this turns out to be a cold case – and I'm sure it will – just how far back are we going?"

"What worries me is how we're even going to identify them," replied his partner.

"As I mentioned, gentleman," said Fitz, "I will be doing a fast-track DNA test, so there could be *some* light at the end of the tunnel."

"I'm guessing here on the correct procedure," said Gardener, to Fitz, "besides you, I think we might also need to use the college of policing experts, throw it open to the policing family. There are different levels of SIO, each with their own specialist subjects: kidnap, murder, serial, sexual etc."

"There's bound be one or two medical men in there that we can drag into this nightmare," said Reilly.

"Each body part needs to be treated as a scene," said Gardener, "which means we have four suspected murders."

"Maybe I can find a consultant surgeon to study how they've been attached," offered Fitz.

"Not to mention how they were *de*tached from their original owners," added Reilly.

"Clearly a priority," said Gardener, "is to identify the four people and look for any connections between them."

"It won't be easy," said Reilly.

"But before we even consider all that," said Gardener, sipping more coffee, glancing at Fitz, "you said there was more."

"I'm afraid so."

Fitz donned a fresh pair of gloves and reached behind him to a set of filing trays. When he turned to face the two detectives again, he had with him three A4 laminated sheets of paper, and an object in a separate bag. He placed them on the desk. Leaving the bag where it was, Gardener studied the object.

"It's a chess piece," said Reilly.

"The queen," added Fitz.

"How interesting," said Gardener. "So what bearing does this have on the case?"

Reilly leaned in closer. "It obviously means something to somebody."

"To whom?" asked Gardener. "The killer, or the person who's been killed?"

"The *four* people who have been killed, you mean," said Reilly.

"Or is it relevant to only one of them?" Gardener glanced at Fitz. "Where was it?"

"Inside the mouth."

"Here we go," said Reilly.

"So if it was inside the mouth," said Gardener, "is it relevant to the head, or is it relevant to the torso because that is female and the chess piece is a queen?"

"My guess would be the torso," said Reilly, "unless someone is trying to tell us something about the head and the person it belonged to."

"Like what?" Gardener asked.

"Maybe that he was gay, and the killer didn't like gay people."

"Bit extreme," said Gardener, "but it wouldn't be the first time someone has killed a gay person because they didn't like them."

"That could mean all three of the males were gay," said Reilly. "Perhaps they were part of a secret club."

"Maybe you should read the first laminated piece of paper," said Fitz.

Gardener leaned over and did as he suggested. It was simply a one-line message.

Old Mother Hubbard – Fuck all in the cupboard, so she's gone hard!

Gardener glanced up at Fitz.

"That suggests the killer is talking about the torso. And is Hubbard the name? If it is, where will that lead us? The owner of the shop is called Wendy Hubbard, and the person who wanted to view the shop is called Hubbard, whose first name we don't yet know."

"So is this the wife?" asked Reilly. "Or the mother?"

"Or someone else altogether?" added Fitz.

"I doubt the person who wanted to view the shop is really called Hubbard," said Reilly, "so it might *actually* be a coincidence; there might be no connection at all between the owner and the viewer."

"Maybe the second page might offer a clue," said Fitz.

Before studying it, Gardener asked, "Where were these laminated sheets found?"

"Can't have been inside the mouth," offered Reilly.

"No," said Fitz, "they were wrapped up inside the polythene. They've obviously been laminated to stop them getting wet as the body thawed."

Gardener and Reilly both leaned in and read what was written on the second sheet.

Debra Gosforth

DOB: 16/01/69

Description: approximately five feet five inches, with long ginger hair. Tubby with bucked teeth, glasses, and a mole on her left cheek. Debra had an accident many years previously in which she broke her ankle. The joint never fully recovered, leaving her with a limp.

Background: Debra came from Armley. Born into a poor family as an only child. Her father was a criminal, often out on the rob. Debra regularly missed her schooling for one problem or another. Her mother died from breast cancer when Debra was five. Her father was killed whilst driving the getaway car during an armed robbery on a bank in Armley one year later. No family could be found to take care of the child.

Date Missing: 16/01/85

"What the hell is this?" asked Reilly.

"Something the killer left," said Gardener, "but who exactly is he or she talking about?"

"Looking at the date of birth and the date the person went missing," said Reilly, "I'm guessing it's not the female torso attached to that body out there."

"Definitely not," said Fitz. "The person who went missing was sixteen, she would now be fifty-three. That torso out there is seventy if she's a day."

"But when was that?" asked Gardener. "If Old Mother Hubbard was seventy when Debra Gosforth went missing that would suggest she may have been born in the Twenties. If she is a recent victim and she was seventy now, that would suggest she was born in the fifties. Where exactly are we going to end up with this case?"

"A lunatic asylum," said Reilly.

"Are there any around here?" Gardener asked.

"I'm talking about us," said Reilly.

Gardener studied the notes again before asking, "Has Debra Gosforth actually been killed? Or did she simply go missing? Is what we're seeing here, revenge for something that happened to Debra, suggesting that three more people were involved in that crime? These are questions for the incident room," said Gardener. "At least we have a name."

"Be no less challenging," said Reilly.

"So what's the third piece of information trying to tell us?" asked Gardener, leaning over.

> *The location of your next surprise will depend on your ability to decipher the meaning of the following numbers:*
>
> *653, 6123, 23 9 4 5 12 1 14 5*
>
> *Had you done your job properly, these animals would have been locked up years ago.*

Leaning back and sighing, Reilly said, "Those numbers could mean anything."

"Well, the statement about us having done our job properly definitely indicates a revenge of some kind."

"But there's a lot going on here, boss," said Reilly. "We have four bodies, each one a different person, all of whom need to be identified."

"We have a missing girl," said Gardener, "probably dead."

"From nearly forty years ago," added Fitz.

"We know there are going to be three more bodies," said Gardener, "possibly indicating that four people may have been involved in Debra Gosforth's disappearance."

"And we have someone who knows about it now, who, according to him or her," said Reilly, "is doing our job for us."

Gardener remained silent for a few seconds, studying the cryptic clue they had been left.

"Cracking this code is going to be important to us. It's going to lead us to the location of the second body."

Reilly nodded. "And how long has that body been there – wherever there might be?"

"That's just what I was thinking," said Fitz. "This is the first body we've found, and we can assume it's been put in the shop very recently, because it's only just started to thaw."

"But any others we find may have been on location for quite some time," said Gardener.

"Which means they could be in a much worse state of decay," said Reilly, "making identification even harder."

"Exactly," said Fitz. "With this body I can make a start and it might be relatively easy to learn things about it. Depending on the length of time that the other bodies have been left, or thawed out, my job might be made much harder."

Gardener nodded. "At least with this one we can have some decent photographs we can use. Is it possible I can have a very good clear photo of the head, and a retinal scan for our meeting at the incident room?"

"Which is when?" asked the pathologist.

"A couple of hours?"

Chapter Eleven

Gardener had had one hell of a day and his head was fit to bursting, as if someone had tried to squash the contents of an entire rubbish dump into a small pedal bin. So much had happened since the discovery of the corpse that he wasn't quite sure where to start.

He and Reilly were in the office ahead of the first incident room briefing. Gardener finished his bottled water and studied Reilly, who was reading a newspaper behind an empty cup and plate.

"Are you ready?" Gardener asked.

"As ready as I'll ever be," said Reilly, still reading the paper.

"Something caught your eye?"

Reilly glanced over. "I was just reading about a missing eighty-five-year-old man by the name of Winstanley."

"Eighty-five?" said Gardener. "Mind you, I think I might go missing if I was called Winstanley."

"Yeah," said Reilly, "happened a couple of days back. He took a walk into the centre of Ilkley to pick up some stuff; never came back."

"Sounds a bit off," said Gardener, thinking of his own father, Malcolm. "Men of that age just don't go missing."

"That's what I thought."

"Does the article say anything about the ongoing investigation?" asked Gardener. "I assume there is one."

"I've not really read it all," said Reilly. "Apparently, they're talking to everyone and thinking of dragging nearby rivers."

"Well good luck with all that," said Gardener. "Anyway, what surprises me more is, you actually being able to read."

Reilly smiled. "It's only very recent. I've been taking night classes, so I have, so I can write my resignation myself. Then you'll be sorry."

Gardener laughed. "Only for the police canteen. Think of the massive drop in revenue."

"The whole station will probably go under."

Gardener rose and collected some files, heading for the door. In the corridor, Gardener mentioned to Reilly that he had invited DCI Briggs to the incident room meeting. The pair of them entered to find a full turnout, an eager team ready to impart what they had found, though whether any of it would help them was another matter. As yet, the team had no idea what he and Reilly had uncovered at the mortuary.

Edwards and Benson had done a good job of setting up the room. Desks with chairs had been brought in, with at least four whiteboards, one of which was only partially filled. Gardener was about to change all of that. HOLMES had been called and briefed and were in the next room. The team had divided into their usual pairs: Longstaff and Gates, Anderson and Thornton, Sharp and Rawson. Drinks and snacks were present on the tables. Given the time of night, he couldn't blame them.

DCI Alan Briggs was sitting at the back. He'd held the senior position for some time, having transferred from Liverpool. Gardener had been in line for the promotion when the position became available, but his wife's death had removed the possibility.

The DCI was physically overbearing. Little could be seen of his face due to his thick black beard and moustache. He usually spoke extremely fast without fluffing any of his words – which gave him an air of great confidence. Gardener had to admit he was very fair and very good at the job.

Gardener started the meeting with a brief outline of what they found at the shop earlier in the day, from the call to finding a body enveloped in polythene.

"You couldn't see *anything*?" asked Briggs.

"No," said Gardener, "and it had been sealed up at the back. There was no way we wanted to play around with that, so we left it to Fitz."

"Have you seen Fitz since?"

"*Have* we?" said Reilly.

"That sounds ominous," said Briggs.

"It sounds like it's getting worse as it goes along," said Frank Thornton.

"I'll come back to that," said Gardener, "but first things first, all of you guys have been circulating Morley since this morning, are there any witness statements that might help our plight?"

"We got something from a woman called Maureen Lyons," said Sarah Gates. "She frequents one of the coffee shops around there on a daily basis. I think she's lonely. Anyway, she's noticed a rag-and-bone man on the streets during the last week. She'd never seen one before... or at least not for some time."

Julie Longstaff took over. "He's been pushing a hand cart that she thinks is more in the keeping of an old-fashioned market barrow. She particularly remembered seeing him on Thursday."

"Scattered across the top were what appeared to be a bundle of old rags and a bit of furniture," said Gates. "That might back up what you were saying about the ground in the passageway behind the shop revealing tracks from very thin wheels."

"Did she see him go that way?" asked Gardener. "Into the alley behind the shop?"

"No," said Gates. "She came out of the shop, saw him, and was then suddenly sidetracked by a friend, Mary Pringle, who was coming the other way. Once she got talking to Mary, the pair of them wandered off down Queen Street."

"Did this Maureen Lyons have a phone?" asked Reilly. "Did she take a photo?"

"Not from that generation," said Longstaff. "She's seventy, doubt if she even knows how to use one."

"Marvellous, isn't it," said Briggs. "Everywhere you go now you can't escape mobiles, and people taking pictures and bloody selfies. The time we want one, our only witness draws a blank."

"I wouldn't worry too much, sir," said Gardener. "There's plenty of CCTV around Morley; we're bound to spot him on one of them. I think it's the handcart that's important. Did she give you a description, did she elaborate?"

"The only thing she said was it had a roof on it," said Gates.

"A roof?" repeated Reilly.

"Actually," said Dave Rawson, "we can add something more to that."

"Yes," said Colin Sharp, "we have a description of both: said rag-and-bone man and the cart. He's approximately six feet tall with long, straggly grey hair, beard and moustache. He was wearing an old boilersuit, contaminated by every stain imaginable, and large rigger boots. He was well-built, stocky, and had a deep, gravelly voice."

"Christ!" said Reilly. "Who was the witness, Sherlock Holmes?"

"Pretty good, isn't it?" said Gardener.

"Here's the interesting bit," said Rawson. "All that information came from the woman who lives in the first house, next to the alley leading to the back of the shop. Her name's Brenda Blenkinsop. She gave him two bags of clothes and went back into the house for two more."

"When she came back out," continued Sharp, "he had the first lot laid out all over the cart."

"But she'd already spotted a roll of blue polythene that looked as if it might be a carpet," said Rawson.

"She asked him what it was," offered Sharp.

"Go on," said Reilly, prompting an end to the silence that had descended.

"She said that he said, it's a body," said Rawson. "And then he started laughing."

"Got some nerve, hasn't he", said Bob Anderson, laughing himself.

"Best way to put someone off the scent," said Thornton. "What is it they say, in plain sight? It's always the best way to hide something."

"What happened then?" asked Gardener.

"She didn't really know," said Sharp. "She offered him a cup of tea but he declined saying he had a lot to do. He threw the other two bags on top and started to open them."

"So what did *she* do?" asked Reilly.

"Went back in the house at that point," said Rawson. "She said she wanted to do some shopping and she left him to it."

"Did she go shopping?" asked Gardener.

"Yes," said Sharp, "and we know what you're going to ask, but she left via the front door and when she glanced down the passage, he wasn't in view anymore."

"But he could still have been there," said Gardener. "He could have been outside the back of the shop."

"I take it she doesn't have any CCTV at the back of her house?" asked Reilly.

"No," replied Sharp, "we checked."

"What did *she* say about the cart?" asked Gardener.

"Her description wasn't as good as the one she gave us for him," said Rawson.

"Two wheels, two handles, four posts on the base, and a roof," said Sharp.

"But she reckons it wasn't a cheap affair," said Rawson. "If anything, it looked handmade, well put together."

"She notice any colours or anything written on it?" asked Reilly.

"Not that she can remember, just that it was a sturdy affair, not cheap or flimsy."

Gardener thought about that. "Might lead to something."

"But surely an old-fashioned totter would have been noticed around the place before now," said Reilly, "especially with something as distinctive as this cart."

"Unless he's just moved into the area," offered Briggs.

"So," said Gardener, "who is the mystery rag-and-bone man? Did anyone else pick up any information on him?"

No one had.

"Run a list of totters in the area and check them out," said Gardener. "He could be completely innocent and the roll of blue polythene on his cart *might* have been a carpet."

"And pigs might fly," said Reilly. "I might have agreed on his innocence up to the point of a roll of blue polythene being mentioned. But that's a step too far for my liking."

"You're probably right, Sean. Either way he's given us a very good reason for intensifying house-to-house inquiries. Maybe we'll pick up some more witness statements about him. We need to find him and talk to him.

"Add to that," continued Gardener, "joiners and woodworkers. Maybe the cart is handmade, and someone out there made it specifically for our rag-and-bone man's specifications."

"We might also want to try builders merchants," said Reilly, "especially with the roll of polythene. We have some samples from Fitz. Maybe that was bought locally. There might be a batch number that will pin it down."

Gardener nodded, noting down all that had been covered on one of the whiteboards before turning back to the team.

"Moving on, did any of you have the chance to interview the staff of Crossley's on Queen Street, in association with Katie Tunscroft's mysterious contact by the name of Hubbard?"

Thornton and Anderson had conducted the short interviews, but no one at the estate agents knew the contact, nor could anyone remember speaking to him.

"Seems odd," said Gardener. "Did you get the feeling that any of them were holding back, perhaps not telling the truth?"

"Not really, sir," said Thornton. "There're only three staff apart from the boss and Katie Tunscroft. It's a small enough place, I can't imagine any of them have anything to hide."

"There is another possibility," offered Bob Anderson. "Maybe the killer's local. He or she could have been watching Katie on a regular basis, knew when she was in the office and when she wasn't. Perhaps he or she only made the call when they knew she was in."

"And if Hubbard only ever called her mobile," offered Thornton, "then no one else is ever likely to have spoken to him."

Gardener accepted the point. Although they were building up a picture there was still very little to go, and so much more to give them. He decided now would be a good time to deliver Fitz's shocking results.

Chapter Twelve

Gardener nodded to Reilly, who picked up the file that Gardener had brought in with him. He opened it and withdrew the contents. As Gardener told them all what Fitz had found, Reilly pinned the various photos to the whiteboard. No one interrupted and when Gardener had finished, he was met with a wall of silence, not to mention confusion.

Briggs crossed the room, staring at the whiteboard.

"What are we dealing with here?"

"Judging by what we've heard and seen," said Anderson, "someone who likes puzzles."

"And games," offered Longstaff.

"Jesus, that's a bit gross," said Sharp.

"Look at all that cutting and rejoining, when and where has all that been done?" asked Thornton.

"Under cover, obviously," said Rawson.

"But who by?" asked Benson. "And is there more than one involved?"

"I like the fact that you're all thinking about it," said Gardener, "and I doubt very much you're going to ask a question that Sean and I haven't already asked ourselves. *We* also wondered if there was more than one perpetrator. The thing is, we need to go right back to basics with this. Let's bring the rules of the murder manual into play." Gardener suddenly stared at Patrick Edwards, the youngest member of the team, "Which are what, Patrick?"

To give him credit, the young man stumbled initially but recovered quickly.

"What, why, when, where, how, and who?"

"Well done, Patrick. Most of those questions are, at the moment, unanswerable," said Gardener. "We don't really know what happened other than the fact that we have one corpse that's made up from four different bodies."

"Although we don't know why it happened," said Reilly, "revenge is a possibility."

"When did it happen?" asked Rawson. "We can pretty much guarantee that the dumping of the body is recent but when did all the other shit take place?"

"Yes," said Longstaff, "if that note about the missing girl is anything to go by, this could be something that happened forty years ago?"

"That would back up why the body was frozen," said Gates.

"All good ideas," said Gardener, "none of which help with the *when*."

"How it happened is obviously still a mystery," said Briggs.

"Which leaves us with who," said Gardener, "and we don't have an answer to that either. So I think it's time we put some actions on the board to be getting on with first thing tomorrow."

That brought a sigh of relief from the team, judging how late in the day it was now.

Gardener glanced at Gates and Longstaff. "Julie, Sarah, you two are the best I know when it comes to IT, computers, and the world of electronics. We have Katie Tunscroft's computer and her mobile. We know she's been in touch with someone who calls himself Hubbard so can you go through her computer and her emails and see if you can run this character to ground?"

"Did you say the phones were burners?" asked Gates.

"We did, Sarah."

"Brilliant. That could be a real minefield."

"Is it true that you can't trace them?" Briggs asked the girls.

"Not quite," said Longstaff. "There *are* some things we can try but don't hold your breath. It can be notoriously difficult."

"But we'll certainly have a go," said Gates.

"Thank you," said Gardener, turning his attention to Patrick Edwards and Paul Benson. "I'd like you two to check the shop and the neighbours closest to it. Pay particular attention to the lock. Has it been forced, or has it been made to look that way? I know it's a bit like locking the stable door after the horse has bolted, but if it has been forced, one of the neighbours might recall hearing a noise."

"Have the SOCOs finished with the place?" asked Benson.

"I believe they have, Paul," said Gardener. "But I also want you looking into the polythene. As Sean said, we have a few samples from Fitz so check out the builders merchants and anywhere else that may sell it. See if there are any numbers on it that might tell us something about the manufacturer. If we strike lucky with that we might find out where it was sold, which could narrow down the area."

Gardener waited until Reilly wrote the action down on the board before continuing. His eyes rested on Dave Rawson and Colin Sharp.

"Fitz said he was going to fast track the DNA samples so we should have the results tomorrow. Can you guys call and see him and make a start on the DNA database, and ask him if he has anything on fingerprints? I appreciate that none of the four that make up the corpse might have a criminal record."

"That's doubtful," replied Rawson. "You don't get yourself cut up for being a Sunday school teacher."

"Or a vicar," replied Sharp.

"Stranger things have happened," said Reilly.

"Maybe they have," said Briggs, "but how far back are we going? Have these people been cut up recently, or when that poor lass went missing?"

"Great question, another one that we can't answer – yet," said Gardener, "but we have to make a start somewhere, so it might as well be there."

"That should keep us busy forever," said Rawson.

"That's not all," said Gardener.

"Didn't think it would be," replied Rawson, laughing. "What else have you got for us?"

"I asked Fitz for dental plates. We can perhaps make a list of all the dentists and email the plates off and see if we strike lucky with that. At least if we can identify the head, it would be a help."

Sharp made notes.

"But there is something else you can try," said Gardener, "something quite new."

"Go on," said Sharp.

"There's been some very interesting work done on retinal scans recently," said Gardener. "I'm sure you all know that the back of the eye is as unique as a fingerprint. There's a case ongoing with an SIO from another force and I was quite impressed when he told me about one of his DC's going into Vision Express and searching through their database to see if the person they had on record had ever had an eye scan there."

"So that's all the opticians as well, sir?" said Sharp. "Best ring my wife and tell her I won't be home tonight."

"Or for the next month," laughed Thornton. "He must really love you two."

Gardener smiled, glancing at Frank Thornton and Bob Anderson, two very experienced members of the team. Once they had their teeth into something they wouldn't let go.

Anderson stared at Thornton. "You had to open your mouth, didn't you? Look at the grin on his face, looks like he's got something much worse for us to follow."

"Butchers and farmers," said Gardener.

"What about them?" Thornton asked.

"Judging by what Fitz said about the stitching used to reconnect the body, it was clumsy, cumbersome; those were two areas he suggested looking at."

"Christ," said Anderson, glancing at his partner, "for a minute there I thought he was serious."

"Essentially, what you're asking is," said Thornton, "how would you go about finding someone that can't sew very well?"

Bob Anderson suddenly started laughing. "That's going to be 95% of the male population and maybe 60% of females!"

"You might have hit on something there," said Gardener.

"How do you mean?" asked Rawson, smiling, obviously enjoying the fact that he and his colleague hadn't come off worst in the deal.

"You might have a go at it from the other side," said Gardener.

"You mean there is another side?" asked Reilly.

"Maybe," said Gardener. "Maybe we should be looking at what material they used to do the sewing. Is it unusual in any way? What kind of a needle have they used?"

"Might be worth asking Fitz if he can say what size it might have been?" offered Briggs.

"Where would someone get the materials from?" added Gardener.

"It might be a bit easier," said Briggs, "if you try and look for someone who is willing, and able, to sew body parts together."

"Oh right," said Thornton, "because Leeds is just full of people like that. The universities have no end of doctor Frankensteins."

"You said it," Gardener pointed out. "You're putting your thinking caps on now. But let's be honest, no one starts off with killing loads of people and sewing them together. Whoever they are must have practiced on something: dead animals, sewing skins or leather together. I'd be looking at recent past reports of those kinds of things being found or reported."

"I appreciate it's a wide-open field," said Briggs, "all of it a long shot – but worth the time of an enquiry team."

"He also made a suggestion about path labs," offered Reilly.

"Whoever put this back together wasn't bothered about how it looked," said Gardener. "The kind of stitching used signifies people in those fields: butchers, farmers, medical students, anyone sewing leather, or path labs."

"I'd probably steer away from paths and funeral homes," said Briggs, "as they are usually very skilled. I once viewed the body of a man that had been decapitated after it had been prepped for family viewing – I fully expected to see the body with a scarf or high collar. Not a bit of it, open-necked shirt, you'd never have known his head had been off."

"Okay, chief, we get the message," said Anderson, "but checking out that lot won't be easy."

"I agree," said Gardener, "but it needs to be done. The photos make for uncomfortable viewing but nothing they're not used to. What we're watching for here is body language. No one is going to admit they've done this, and they may not want to drop anyone in it if they recognize what's going on."

"Okay," said Anderson, "we'll make a list in the morning and plan out a route of some description."

"Whilst you're doing that, can you make out a list of rag-and-bone men?"

"Why?" asked Thornton. "You reckon they stitch people up as well?"

"No, you pillock," said Gardener, "but they might. I was thinking more of checking out the CCTV in Morley and seeing if we can spot the rag-and-bone man with his cart, see if we can get some decent images that we can print off and show to any of the existing totters and see if they recognize it or him."

"*We* should check all the CCTV in Morley," said Longstaff. "He may have been captured by more than one camera."

"We might be able to plot his route," added Gates, "see where he started and finished."

"If it helps," said Reilly, "I noticed CCTV at the corner of Queen Street and Brunswick Street."

"Can you tell if it covered the alley leading to the back of the shop?" Gardener asked.

"Not from where I was standing but once we check it out, we might have more luck."

"If it does," Gardener pointed out, "we might be able to see exactly what time he went in and came out. Sounds like it was during daylight hours, so the images on the cart might be pretty good."

"There's another camera on Queen Street, at the junction with Queensway," said Sharp, checking his phone.

"Check out that one as well."

Gardener glanced at his watch. "I'm sorry, guys, I know it's been a long day but I'm really eager to cover all the possible actions tonight, so we do have more."

Chapter Thirteen

Following a ten-minute tea break, the team resumed, and Gardener continued.

"I've given quite a bit of thought to this case today," said Gardener. "We have to give some real consideration as to why the bodies have been frozen and for how long – for a month or two, or perhaps as long as forty years. No one knows how far back we could end up going here. I think facial recognition is going to play a big part in this. And we have to make use of a powerful tool at our disposal. The press."

"You don't like the press," said Briggs.

There were one or two raised eyebrows, not to mention the odd snigger. They all knew what Gardener thought about the tabloids.

"In fact," continued Briggs, "it's very well known what you think of the press by the lack of press conferences you give."

"You're right," said Gardener, "but in this instance, I believe that if we release a photograph of the head – the face, to the press we might well yield some results."

"I can see where you're going," said Briggs. "If the head belongs to someone recently deceased, it's likely that more than one person will recognize him."

"Whereas, if it's from forty years ago, God forbid," said Anderson, "we might have an old boy with a good memory."

Gardener nodded. "It's usually a bit of a last option but something might give."

"At least if we get a name," said Reilly, "there's no telling where we might end up, and it will have been worth it."

"Besides which," added Gardener, "I won't have to deal directly with the press. We can use the press office."

"I thought there'd be a catch," said Briggs.

Gardener smiled. "Well, I'm warming to the idea."

"Okay, Stewart," said Briggs. "Send me a copy of the photo. We'll get the tech boys to clean it up a little and release that, and I'll try to make it front page."

The idea was met warmly and most of the team nodded and spoke between themselves before Gardener turned to yet another topic.

"I think we need to concentrate on the clues our killer has left behind. Let's have some feedback." Gardener pointed to the one-line rhyme they had found on one A4 sheet. "Old Mother Hubbard. Here we have the name Hubbard again. What does it mean? Is it referring to the torso because that's female?"

"I don't know much about the rhyme," said Reilly, "but didn't it refer to an old housekeeper who lived in a cottage?"

"All I know is she must have been hard up because when she went to the cupboard to feed the dog it was bare," said Anderson.

"And you've got grandkids," said Gardener. "You must have read it dozens of times to them."

"I have," laughed Anderson. "Doesn't mean I'm paying attention. I just want them to go to sleep."

That comment lightened the mood.

Gardener continued. "Which is what the line is suggesting: Old Mother Hubbard – Fuck all in the cupboard, so she's gone hard! Is the killer trying to tell us that the torso belongs to someone called Hubbard?"

"Which possibly means," said Briggs, "that the killer has made a play on words for his own name?"

"Almost certainly," said Gates. "Whoever contacted Katie Tunscroft is not called Hubbard."

"But it's possible that the torso might *not* belong to someone called Hubbard," suggested Longstaff. "Maybe he has a thing about nursery rhymes."

"Or maybe it just rhymed with what he wanted to say," offered Benson.

"So," said Gardener, "the head might give us an identification, but let's assume for now that the killer *is* referring to the torso – in this instance. But another part of the puzzle is the chess piece in the mouth. It's the queen. What's the meaning behind that?"

Reilly offered an explanation. "Does it refer to the torso or the head?"

"Sean and I discussed the possibility that the person whose head we have here may have lived some kind of a secret life that the killer knows about and disagrees with."

"But is a secret life bad enough to kill someone for?" asked Gates. "That suggests that whoever the head belongs to might have been gay, and the killer is homophobic, but what's been done here has been done to four different people."

"Which suggests more than homophobia," offered Longstaff. "I'm inclined to agree with Sean, it sounds like revenge for something. It's way over the top for a homophobic killing."

"But if it was," said Rawson, "it would have to include all four for the same reason."

"Very probably, but I think it might be a stretch to kill four people because of their sexuality," said Gardener. "The key here will be identifying the owners of the separate body parts, which eventually might lead to a connection. Might make our lives easier if that connection was homophobia. But I seriously doubt it will be."

"Well by the time we have identified all of them," said Anderson, "if the connection is not homophobia, it might be really obvious what else it is."

"I hope so," said Gardener. "I don't think there's a lot we can do on the chess piece itself. There could be any number of meanings."

"Maybe it's personal to the killer," said Thornton, "and maybe nothing at all to do with the scene. Perhaps just trying to throw us off the scent."

"Maybe," said Gardener, "but the same cannot be said for the cryptic message; that is definitely something for us to work out. I think our killer likes puzzles, we already have a rhyme and a chess piece. But what is the cryptic puzzle trying to tell us?"

Gardener pointed to the board.

The location of your next surprise will depend on your ability to decipher the meaning of the following numbers:

653, 6 1 2 3, 23 9 4 5 12 1 14 5

Had you done your job properly, this animal would have been locked up years ago.

"The numbers could be anything," said Rawson, "may even be just a series of random numbers."

"I doubt they're random," said Gardener. "It's just another part of the game. Look at the line above. If we find out what the numbers mean, will it lead us to another body?"

"Because we suspect there will be more," said Reilly.

"He's taunting us," said Gardener. "We have to work out what the numbers represent before we find another piece of the puzzle, in other words, another body."

"And we need to find them quickly," said Briggs, "so we can match them all up and find out who the hell is behind this, and what they are up to."

"I agree with the boss," said Longstaff. "These are not random numbers. They're important."

"Probably the most important bit of the puzzle we have," said Gates. "I think Julie and I would like to have a crack at decoding this."

Longstaff nodded. "I don't know how, but it looks interesting."

"But he's also telling us something else," said Gardener. "Whatever happened years ago, our killer is saying that we didn't do our job properly. And that someone who should have been locked up went free."

"Christ, if all of this happened when Debra Gosforth went missing, it's a long time to harbour a grudge," said Patrick Edwards. "It's before I was born."

"Which makes it all the harder to crack," said Gardener. "Every piece of evidence we pick up needs to be fed into HOLMES. It might just highlight something similar that's happened in the past and hopefully point us in the right direction."

"Let me take care of that, Stewart," said Briggs. "You lot have enough on your plate. We may even need some operational support officers, despite police budgets."

Gardener wrote down most of what they had discussed on the board before turning back with one more point.

"Okay, guys. It's late, go home, get yourselves a good night's sleep and crack on early in the morning. There's a hell of a lot to go at here and I'm not expecting miracles. I realize fully that we have probably missed the *Golden Hour* principle but I honestly believe this case will be a slow burner, particularly as we have what looks like a missing teen from nearly forty years ago. But, before you go, does anyone have any theories on Debra Gosforth?"

"There's some interesting stuff on there," said Anderson, pointing to the note, "but I reckon there is some vital stuff being left out."

> *Background: Debra came from Armley. Born into a poor family as an only child. Her father was a criminal, often out on the rob. Debra regularly missed her schooling for one problem or another. Her mother*

*died from breast cancer when Debra was five. Her
father was killed whilst driving the getaway car
during an armed robbery on a bank in Armley one
year later. No family could be found to take care of
the child.*

Date Missing: 16/01/85

"You're right, Bob," said Gardener. "We have a name
and some information about the parents, so that might be
easy enough to check on."

"Especially the bit about the armed robbery," said
Reilly.

"Yes," Gardener agreed. "Sean and I will have a look
into this but the most disturbing aspect is that no apparent
family could be found and the girl went missing."

"Missing from where?" asked Briggs.

"Exactly," said Gardener. "That's what we need to find
out."

"Who wrote this stuff?" asked Colin Sharp. "If you
look at the rhyme about Mother Hubbard, and the cryptic
clue, they look like the same type face. But the note about
Debra Gosforth is hand-written, so that's different. Are
two different people involved here?"

"Maybe," said Gardener, "or was the handwritten note
written forty years ago by someone who *had* found out
exactly what was going on?"

"But surely that means there is some connection to the
killer here," said Rawson, "because he or she obviously has
access to both sets of notes."

"They're all good points," said Gardener, "and all I
really wanted was one or two early thoughts. Sean and I
will start searching the archives tomorrow while the rest of
you investigate the other actions. But we have to keep one
thing in mind. Whilst we're investigating a recent crime
scene, we need to keep one foot in the past."

Chapter Fourteen

Following an uneventful weekend of little other than arguments with his wife and family, Patterson found himself back in the shop earlier than usual on Monday morning. He'd laid out the trays of fresh meat, pies and pasties, sausage rolls and pork pies. Emily was well under way with the meat for the hot sandwiches when he suddenly heard a scraping sound in front of him.

He jumped, coming face to face with *him* again. Fuck me, not first thing on a Monday, thought Patterson. As usual the customer was dressed in his shabby overcoat, grey trousers and Wellington boots.

"Good morning," said the totter, standing erect at the counter with his hands behind his back.

"Is it?" said Patterson.

"Oh dear, someone got out of the wrong side of bed this morning?"

"Wish I'd been lucky enough to sleep in a fucking bed," said Patterson, jumping slightly, moving his head and rubbing his neck – the crick a constant reminder of his sleepless night on the couch.

"I don't think I'll inquire any further."

Good, thought Patterson, then I won't have to tell you to fuck off and mind your own business.

"Is Emily in, please?" asked the totter, straight to business.

"Is it important?" asked Patterson.

"What do you think?" asked the totter, before adding. "Might I recommend something to you, young man?"

"If you must."

"*How to Win Friends and Influence People* is a very good book, one that seems to have passed you by. I'd suggest you find a copy and give it a go."

"Emily," shouted Patterson, staring at the back room, completely ignoring the suggestion, because he didn't feel it dignified a reply.

Emily came rushing through.

"Good morning, dear lady."

"Oh, hello, love, how are you this morning?"

"All the better for seeing you."

Patterson slipped into the back room. "Excuse me while I stick my fingers down my throat."

"Somebody should," said Emily.

"With a bit of luck they might drag his tongue out and cut it off, do us all a favour."

Emily laughed and Patterson returned with a fresh tray of devilled kidneys. "I heard that."

"Sounds like your ears are as big as your mouth, then," said Emily.

"I'm beginning to like you, my dear," said the totter, producing a bottle of rosé wine from behind his back.

"Is that for me?" said Emily.

"Certainly isn't for him," replied the totter, nodding toward Patterson.

"Oh, we are all full of ourselves this morning," said the butcher.

"Well thank you very much," said Emily. "To what do I owe this pleasure?"

A couple of barking dogs at the door drew everyone's attention. Two people had met in the street but their dogs were not as friendly as they were. Both pulled at the leads, telling the dogs to calm down: not that that did any good.

"I appreciate your kindness," said the totter.

"And I yours."

Patterson glanced at the ceiling, rolling his eyes.

"I wondered if you might be free on Wednesday evening?" asked the totter.

"Ooh," said Emily, obviously taken aback.

Before she could answer, the totter continued. "I'd like to take you out for a bite to eat. There are some lovely local restaurants, and I would very much value your company for the night." Before she could answer, he went on. "I can, when the occasion demands, clean myself up." He laughed. "I wouldn't want you to think I dressed like this all the time."

Patterson waited patiently for her to turn him down flat.

"Wednesday would be lovely," said Emily, stunning them both into silence.

It was Patterson who was nearly flat, on his back. He simply stared at Emily open mouthed.

"Close it before someone throws you a fish," said Emily.

"In that case, I shall tether the horses and make sure the cart is up to scratch."

Emily put her hands to her mouth. "A horse and cart? How romantic."

Before anything else was said, another distraction at the door caught their attention in the form of Andy Blanchard, who almost fell through it, sweating like a pig, red-faced, nearly doubled over, breathing heavily. Patterson put his tray on the counter and skipped around toward Andy.

"Are you okay?"

"Just let me get my breath back."

"Would you like this seat, young man?" asked the totter, pointing to the one next to the counter.

Andy glanced up at him, still doubled over, leaning on the counter.

"No, no, I'll be fine once I get my breath back."

"Whatever have you been up to, Andy?" asked Emily.

"Been for a run."

"Where? London?" asked Patterson. "Via Liverpool, Manchester and Spain?"

Andy laughed. "I think I might have overdone it."

"You want to be careful, son," said the totter. "A bit of exercise is one thing."

Andy finally stood up and his breathing calmed a little. "I know what you're saying. Just having a rough time of things at the moment and I find running is a distraction."

"So long as you're okay," said Emily.

"I will be," said Andy. He turned to Patterson. "I just wanted a quick word."

Patterson stared at him. "Is it private, like? Do we need to go through the back?" Patterson then glanced at Emily. "Only these two need a room."

"Behave yourself, Patterson," said Emily. "You're always the same when you're not getting any."

"I hope I haven't interrupted anything," said Andy. "Anyway, no, it's not private. I just wanted to let you know I'll be moving out of the flat above the shop."

"Well, it's your flat and your shop," said Patterson. "I hardly think you need to give me notice."

"I realize that. I'm just being courteous. But I know a young couple who need somewhere to live. They're struggling at home and they just want to get a place of their own. And I think they need it more than I do."

"What a lovely thought," said Emily.

"All credit to you, young man," said the totter.

"So where are you going to live?" asked Patterson.

"Don't worry about me," said Andy, "I have enough places I can use."

"So long as you'll be okay," said Emily. She turned to the totter, "Do you know he's a lovely man. We've known him years. I wish he'd get himself a nice young lady."

Andy blushed.

"I think you've embarrassed him, dear lady," said the totter.

Patterson stepped up to his rescue. "Hey, have you heard the news about the murder on Brunswick Street?"

"Murder?" said Andy.

"Aye, a murder. It was awful, they reckon," Patterson said.

"Who reckons?" asked Andy. "Who is they?"

Patterson shrunk a little. "Well, everybody."

"The locals, you mean?" said Andy. "I wouldn't go listening to them too much; they'll tell you anything."

"It's a bit more than gossip," said Patterson. "Body cut into pieces, laid out all over the shop floor. Young girl who found it fainted and had to be taken to hospital."

"Who told you that?" asked the totter.

"Never you mind."

"I do mind," he replied. "This is Morley, not Los Angeles."

"I think he has a point," said Emily. "That does sound a bit over the top."

"I'm only telling you what I was told," said Patterson, hands in the air.

"If the body was cut up and laid out all over the shop," said Andy, "I'm pretty sure the whole street would still be closed off."

"Not to mention Scotland Yard probably involved," said the totter.

"Watch a lot of *Midsomer Murders*, do you?" asked Patterson. "You seem to know a lot about procedure."

"If I do, it doesn't come from that program."

"You've let your imagination run away with you, Patterson," said Emily.

"I think someone's probably been taking you for a ride," said Andy. "I'm not saying it were nothing, but I don't quite think it were quite that bad."

Patterson leaned over the counter and rearranged all the trays, hiding his embarrassment.

"Anyway what's got you so hot under the collar that you have to run yourself to death?" Patterson asked.

Andy stared at the floor, and then at the group. "Just the usual, that time of the year. My dad and all that."

Emily put her hand to her mouth and the totter stared on oblivious. He obviously wasn't aware of the story, which meant either he wasn't local, or had not lived here long.

"Ooh, I never thought. It must be nigh on forty years since he went missing, around this time as well."

Andy simply nodded.

The totter removed his cap and held it close to his chest. "I'm so sorry. Did something happen to him, or did he simply vanish and never return?"

"Vanished and never returned," said Andy.

"And you have no idea what happened to him?" asked the totter. "How sad, and terrible for you when you were growing up and maybe needed him the most."

"Yes," said Andy. "But I know he's out there somewhere. I just know it, in here." He pointed to his chest.

Before anyone else could add anything, Andy turned to Patterson.

"Oh, before I forget, save us a fillet steak for me tea and a steak pie for my mother. She's quite partial to your pies."

"Just one steak?" queried Patterson. "Can't see that filling you."

"What you trying to say? I'm a fat bastard," laughed Andy.

Patterson laughed with him, feeling a little uneasy about everything they had discussed.

"You know what I mean."

"Aye, you're right," replied Andy.

"Two, then, is it?" asked Patterson, ready with the knife.

"No," replied Andy. "Best make it three."

Chapter Fifteen

Andy let himself in through the back door. Despite being late in the year, the door was open a little to allow his mother's cat to come and go as it pleased. Although the door housed a cat flap – because Andy had fitted it himself – the cat had refused to use it from day one.

Andy's mother, Betty, lived in a small house on Troy Hill, next to a building that resembled a village hall and had the name Observer Mews above the door. Betty had lived there all her married life, and it was the house that she and her husband, Robert had bought when first married.

Andy carried with him two large carrier bags full of shopping from Lidl, which he deposited on the small kitchen table. Two things hit him immediately: one was the voice of Ken Bruce from BBC Radio 2; his mother would not listen to any other station. The second was the mouth-watering aroma of apple and cinnamon pie. Nobody baked a pie like Betty Blanchard.

Today must have been a good day.

Betty had good and bad days due to a condition called myelodysplasia: a type of rare blood cancer, which meant she didn't have enough healthy blood cells. She had to have blood transfusions once a fortnight and for now that seemed to be controlling things. She was told by her doctor that there were many different types of MDS. Some stay mild for years, and others were more serious. Though Betty wanted to be strong for her son, in private moments she suspected that she didn't have much time left.

"Anybody home?" shouted Andy.

Betty came through from the parlour into the kitchen.

"There's no need to shout, you big lummox, I'm not deaf."

Andy laughed. Betty was a small woman – probably only a third of his size but she ruled the roost. She had silver-grey hair tied up in a bun, and wore small wire-rimmed glasses. Her complexion was still healthy despite her seventy-nine years, and her MDS.

"Have you been baking?" Andy asked.

"Whatever gave you that idea?" she laughed. "For a builder, you're not the sharpest tool in the box, are you?"

"No, you take that prize."

In the sink, Betty deposited a cup and saucer before glancing into a cupboard to her left.

"You'd better have saved some for me," said Andy.

The kitchen was homely with an AGA against one wall, which was why the place was always warm. Beams crossed the ceiling, with pans hanging from hooks. Andy had put up a number of shelves that now housed the crockery, and jars full of tea, coffee, sugar, flour, and whatever she could find.

"More than my life's worth if I hadn't."

"Must be a good day, eh, Mam?" shouted Andy, drawing her closer and giving her a squeeze.

"Put me down, lad, I don't know where you've been."

"Definitely a good day."

"Aye, not bad."

"No dizziness?"

"No," she replied, reaching up and pulling the pie stand out of the cupboard.

A knife lay across the top. Betty made all her own pastry, and Andy would have backed it against anyone's, even the big shops. She never weighed anything, it was all done by guesswork, but it was perfect every time.

"You cut the cake and make the tea," said Betty, "and I'll put the shopping away."

"I don't mind putting it away."

"Do as you're told. You're not too big for a clout."

Andy laughed, knew better than to argue. Betty set about the bags and nimbly began putting the shopping away.

"How's Olive next door?" asked Andy.

"She's okay. We're off to the bingo tonight."

"Are you gonna win?"

"I doubt it, but a couple of milk stouts should soften the blow."

Andy was still pleased that his mother made the effort to meet with friends as often as she could. They had the odd night out – once a week they usually traipsed into the town to one of the cafes for dinner. Another day a minibus would pick them both up and take them to a day centre.

Tea made, and shopping put away, the pair of them went into the parlour. Andy sat and had his pie and sipped his drink before anything was said. The room was homely with another small table and chairs and a Welsh dresser, full of chinaware and solid silver cutlery. Andy wondered if she used any of it.

Set up on a small round table in front of the window was a chessboard. The game had been in progress since the day Andy's father had gone missing. Robert had made his move before going to work, leaving Andy with three possible options. Even now, he still wasn't sure which one was best. Every time he visited his mother, Andy would glance at the board, sometimes for as long as five minutes.

"Made your move, yet?" Betty asked.

"Can't do that, Mam."

"Why not? He wouldn't mind."

"Unfair advantage," Andy replied. "He wouldn't see me make it."

"It wouldn't matter to him. He'd probably still remember his game plan." Betty appeared hesitant over her next sentence. "If he ever comes back, that is."

"He will," said Andy, cutting another piece of pie.

Betty leaned over and placed a hand on her son's when he'd finished putting the pie on his plate.

"You might have to let it go, love. It's been nigh on forty years."

Andy didn't reply. Although his father had taught him to play the game when he was six, it wasn't until Andy was twelve that he really felt the benefit of the lessons his father had bestowed upon him. Robert had always felt that chess would be good training for helping his son to solve the problems that may develop in his life – because it had always worked for him.

Andy had actually used that training and philosophy to help out a work colleague many years back on a building site. They were in the middle of Leeds on a lunch break and Andy could see that his friend, Tom had a problem, and asked if he could help.

"I don't feel as if I have any control over my life at the moment. My parents telling me one thing, my friends are telling me another. Wife's going through money like there's no tomorrow and I don't think she has a great deal of respect for me. Everything keeps changing and I'm not sure what I should be doing next."

Andy nodded his head. Reaching into his bag he produced a miniature chessboard, asking Tom if he played. Tom nodded, but said he wasn't very good.

Andy set it down on the table between them and motioned for Tom to start. They casually exchanged a few turns without any real intent, before Andy spoke.

"Who are you?"

"What do you mean?" asked Tom.

"In this game of chess, who are you? Which piece do you feel most represents you?"

"At the moment," said Tom, "I feel like a pawn. I'm limited by where I can go and what I can do, and don't have much ability."

"Who would you rather be?" Andy asked.

"That's easy," replied Tom. "The queen. She can move in any direction, and I reckon she's the most feared piece on the board."

"Are you sure about that?" said Andy.

"Why?"

Andy sat back for a moment and then said, "I had a very similar conversation with my dad when I were about twelve. I'm gonna tell you now what he told me, and I want you to listen... carefully. You don't really want to be the pawn, or the queen. To be the person *you* were meant to be, you need to be the player moving the pieces around. Stop being pushed around by others. Take charge. There're too many people in the world whose lives are dominated by the decisions of others: their boss, their parents, peers, the media, government decisions. You're better than that, step up and take charge! We weren't born to be pieces shuffled around on a board, we were born to positively influence and impact the world around us."

Tom remained silent, and then his eyes suddenly lit up. He nodded his head, moved his final piece, and smiled. "Checkmate."

Andy laughed. A couple of years later they met again on another site, and Tom appeared to be a completely different person. Andy asked him how he was doing. He told Andy that he had never forgotten that game of chess, or the knowledge Andy had given him. He'd left that game and spent the afternoon six inches taller, determined to change the world. That's what he had done, and he'd never been happier.

Andy glanced at his mother, his eyes moist.

"Have *you* ever let it go? Have *you* ever given up on him?"

"I wouldn't say given up, love, but if he were still around, why hasn't he come back? Why has he left us in such limbo?"

Andy stood up and collected the pots, stopping briefly before stepping into the kitchen.

"There'll be a reason," he replied. "Dad never did owt without a reason."

Betty stared back. "If you say so, love. But I can't for the life of me imagine what that would be."

Chapter Sixteen

Fitz was sitting behind his desk, a coffee in hand, listening to the gentle tones of an opera in the background. The clock on the wall informed Gardener and Reilly as they entered that it was 4:30pm, and the SIO felt as if they had not achieved a thing during the last couple of days, though in all fairness it had been the weekend, a time when the wheels of industry usually ground slowly. He was hoping the pathologist would have something positive for them.

"Have you any good news for us, Fitz?"

"I have news, gentleman, quite how good it is..."

The sentence remained unfinished, which, to Gardener's way of thinking, was not good. Fitz leaned forward and opened a file on his desk, extracting some paperwork.

"I said when we started, I wanted to do every possible test I could think of, which might help you both when making an identification. The first thing I did was disconnect the limbs and lay them out on separate tables. I did the SCHAD test to determine whether or not the bodies *had* been frozen. They had, but that's all I can tell you."

"At least we know for definite," said Gardener, "not that it will get us anywhere."

"I also fast tracked the DNA results," said Fitz, "which I emailed over this afternoon. They need to be fed into the system to see if they are on record. But that may not get you anywhere, either."

"Particularly if the crime turns out to be a cold case," replied Gardener, sipping his water. "I can't imagine, with what's happened to these people, that they are not criminals."

"They have to be," said Reilly. "They must have upset someone enough to have paid the price they did."

"But have they ever been caught for anything?" asked Gardener. "Whether they're in the system for something else is another matter."

"With our luck, it's unlikely," said Reilly. "You know what these people are like, they can commit crimes for years and go undetected. A certain Radio 1 DJ springs to mind, look what he got away with."

"I'm not sure he went undetected, Sean. I think a lot of people knew but were too afraid to say or do anything."

"Is that what we're dealing with?" asked Reilly. "When we get to the bottom of this, is it likely we'll be looking at high profile people?"

"Maybe," said Fitz.

"Granted," said Gardener, "but we have to find out who they are first." He turned to Fitz. "So, you've done a SCHAD test, determined they were frozen. You've fast tracked the DNA so you can hopefully marry up the other bodies when we find them, what else have you found out?"

"I think I've discovered two things of importance that might help."

"Anything is better than nothing, Fitz," said Gardener. "If you have two more things we didn't know before we walked in here then we will have learned something."

Fitz sat back, adjusting his spectacles, pushing them further up the bridge of his nose.

"I believe whatever happened to this lot probably did so in the Nineties, or maybe even earlier, and for whatever reason, our killer chose to freeze them at that point, but only decided now to release the bodies."

"What makes you think that?" asked Gardener.

"It's an educated guess at the moment," said Fitz, "given that Debra Gosforth went missing in 1985. That's a reasonable amount of time for someone to do their research and set about a revenge mission."

"Wonderful," said Reilly, finishing his last biscuit. "I had *some* hope before I came in here."

Gardener laughed, pointing to Fitz. "When has he ever given us hope?"

"Just you hold your horses, young man," said Fitz. "Because I suspected this as possibly being from the Nineties, I thought one of the tests worth doing was for HIV."

"How the hell did you manage that?" asked Gardener.

"Why did you even think of it?" asked Reilly.

"It was pretty rife around that time," said Fitz. "If one of our people was into something he shouldn't have been, we might hit the jackpot. The greatest risk while performing an autopsy on cases of acquired immunodeficiency syndrome is not the case itself, but the pathologist's lack of regard for potential risk and concern for a safe technique.

"Care needs to be exercised when handling blood, mucosal surfaces or tissues of patients suspected of being infected with HIV. The other thing is, cases may also harbour many other potentially transmissible pathogens such as hepatitis B virus, Mycobacterium tuberculosis, herpes simplex virus, cryptosporidium and other respiratory pathogens. Anyway, I won't bore you with the details but one of the bodies definitely had the HIV virus."

That made both detectives sit up and listen. "Which one?" asked Gardener.

"Whoever the head belongs to."

"That's a result," said Reilly.

"Especially considering you're releasing a photo to the press," said Fitz. "If someone recognizes him, your case might come on leaps and bounds."

"If he had HIV, wouldn't there be records somewhere?"

"There are quite a lot of pitfalls with that one. The main one I can see is, he might not have known he had it. He would only have known if he had visited the doctor for any number of problems and a blood test was taken. It also depends on when he had it. They didn't start making records straight away. We didn't know anything about it. In fact, for quite some time, we didn't even know what it was, or what we were dealing with."

"So if he didn't know he had it, we might be back at square one," said Reilly.

"Possibly," said Fitz, "but it has to be worth checking. I appreciate patient confidentiality is a big thing where patients and doctors are concerned, but this *is* a murder case."

Gardener nodded. "You don't need to tell us, we still have problems with that one. Thank you for this, Fitz, but we need to know a lot more about the bodies, and for that we need the rest of them. Releasing the photo of the head to the press might be our best move."

"At least if he's recognized, we can build a picture," said Reilly.

"That might help us with the others," said Gardener, "and any possible personal records."

"Have you released the photo?"

"Briggs has," said Gardener. "Hopefully it'll be in today's or tomorrow's editions."

"So what else did you find out?" Reilly asked Fitz.

After more note consulting, he glanced upwards. "In the torso, I found evidence of cancer cells."

"Really?" asked Gardener.

"And they were very advanced," said Fitz. "I think it might be fair to assume that whenever the killer took the female, she probably wouldn't have lived much longer anyway."

"That might help, there should be records we can follow," said Reilly.

"We still need to know who she was," said Gardener.

Reilly nodded, obviously appreciating that they had something to go on.

"But I have found out something even more interesting, that wasn't present in her system, but was in everyone else's."

"Go on," said Gardener.

"Methanothorox."

Gardener's vision narrowed, as if he had been seeing the world through 16:9 widescreen, and someone had changed his view to 4:3 letterbox.

"And you two know all about that stuff, don't you?" added Fitz.

"Not that stuff again," said Gardener.

It was almost the first case he had ever been involved in and became the closest thing he had ever come to experiencing the famous locked-room mystery, involving the death of a dental receptionist killed by the chemical which had been ingeniously injected into her packet of facial wipes.

"That might work in our favour," said Reilly. "The only people we know who use that are farmers."

"Good point, Sean," said Gardener. He turned to Fitz. "Can you think of any reason why our torso didn't have any traces?"

"Only one," replied Fitz. "It's my guess the killer *knew* she was dying anyway: he or she would have known quite a lot about the victims. She would have been on some medication, which she would have needed. Perhaps the killer stopped all drugs, simply allowing the cancer to eat her, which would have been pretty painful. Shows you what you might be up against, gentleman. Whoever this is, he or she has really been harbouring a grudge for quite some considerable time. What they have done would have taken some serious planning, so the chances of letting down their guard and making a mistake will be quite slim."

Chapter Seventeen

Following the meeting with Fitz, a drink and a catch-up, Gardener and Reilly immediately headed into the incident room. Having been there almost an hour, Gardener felt that despite his team's efforts, the brick wall was growing.

Edwards and Benson had spent most of their day researching polythene. Like other synthetic plastics, polythene was not readily biodegradable, and usually ended up in landfills. However, there were a number of species of bacteria and animals that were able to degrade polythene. When exposed to ambient solar radiation, the plastic produced two greenhouse gases, methane and ethylene. In short, they had drawn a blank.

Gardener went on to inquire if they had discovered anything at the shop. Benson said the door appeared to have been forced. Whoever had done that, in their opinion did have keys, and had done it for show. A local carpenter who had shown up to work on the nearest house gave them the benefit of his experience, verifying what they had thought. The nearest neighbour who had previously given a description of the rag-and-bone man and his barrow, never actually heard anything, nor did she keep that close an eye on the shop.

So another blank had been drawn.

When Gardener asked about HOLMES, Patrick Edwards had said there were a number of hits that needed to be thoroughly checked – plenty of stuff involving bodies being cut up. Strangely enough, two cases of bodies being rejoined together had been reported in Russia sometime in the Nineties, but nothing in the UK.

Benson said quite a lot of bodies having been wrapped in polythene had come up but nothing bearing any close resemblance to what they had here.

Sharp and Rawson had had their hands on the DNA results that Fitz had sent through. They checked against the database and found no matching criminal records, but there was still some mileage left in that one.

Earlier in the day, the pair of them – armed with a list of dentists and opticians – scoured Morley. Of the places they had so far spoken to, the dental and retinal scans had come back negative; nothing matching what Sharp and Rawson had. That side of the investigation was on-going, but it was a big job.

Gardener made a comment that the further they delved into the case, the less likely they were to find that any of the victims would be current. It definitely appeared to be a cold case, which would make life very nearly impossible.

Briggs confirmed he had sent the head-shot photo to all the local newspapers, as well as the nationals. The locals promised it would headline in the morning. The nationals had yet to reply. And as a further measure, he had sent it through to Interpol. He didn't feel so confident about that one, but it was worth a try.

Thornton and Anderson had both spent some considerable time putting together a list of all farmers and butchers in the area, as well as craft shops, and anyone else that sold thread, which they had put into a spreadsheet, and sectioned up into areas to make a start on. Both men felt Operational Support Officers were needed and Gardener agreed, especially with what Fitz had told them.

They had also researched Old Mother Hubbard. The first published version of *The Comic Adventures of Old Mother Hubbard and her Dog* came out in 1805 and was attributed to Sarah Catherine Martin and associated with a cottage in Yealmpton, Devon.

They could see absolutely no connection with the modern-day murder. Apart from suggesting that the female torso belonged to someone called Hubbard, the killer seemed to be simply feeding them a line.

Chapter Eighteen

"Even though we've only been on this case a couple of days," continued Gardener, "and despite knowing the mountain we'll have to climb, I felt almost as soon as we found out about Debra Gosforth, she was always going to be the biggest challenge, if the information we had was true. And there was no reason to think it wasn't.

"If you want to trace someone, there is quite a lot you can do; know your data. Get as much information as you can about the person you are trying to trace – internet searches; Google, Bing. Social Media. Electoral roll. Certificate trawls and index searches. Probate & Wills. Companies House. Look for people they know. Very few of these will work for our search, apart from the last one.

"There is no doubt that what's happened in Morley recently has a connection to something that happened forty years ago and involves a missing child."

"Maybe more than one," offered Anderson. "We've come across one body, and we know there's probably going to be four, so what's to say that each scene is going to be any different to this one?"

"Who's to say we won't be looking for four missing children?" said Thornton. "As well as four victims?"

Gardener suspected they were right.

If they were dealing with a serial killer, there's every chance the MO would be the same on all of them.

"You're no doubt right," said Reilly, "and the worst of it is, we're not going to be in time to prevent any of it. What's happened has already been done, and a long time ago."

However distressing the news, Gardener continued. "Sean and I have spent most of the day trawling the police archives, but we at least had something to go on if the killer was telling the truth. We found a reference to Debra's parents, and the house in which they lived in on Salisbury Terrace in Armley."

"Not far from Morley, then," said Rawson. "At least the killer's kept it local."

"We jumped in the car and paid a visit and found a neighbour, a lady by the name of Annie Stokes. She knew the family, but as she pointed out it was a long time ago, so the details might be sketchy."

Reilly took over. "Annie Stokes reckons Debra's mother was a nice enough woman, but she lived well under the shadow of her husband, who was a bit of a wrong'un."

"That's backed up by the armed robbery on one of the local banks," said Gardener. "After the mother died, the father was offered help with Debra, but he always refused it – said they could manage."

"And manage he did," said Reilly, "in a fashion. The wee girl was always fed, and in clean clothes, but the father never worked, so Annie Stokes reckoned he had the time to do those things."

"She always attended school," said Gardener. "The neighbour told us at Armley Primary on Salisbury Terrace."

"But as we all know – according to the killer's note – it all went wrong," said Reilly. "The neighbour knew the father had been killed in a car crash, which she thought was odd because they never had a car."

"Although she suspected he was a bit dodgy underneath," said Gardener, "she'd never really had any proof."

"Here's where it gets interesting," said Reilly. "The next thing Annie knew, the church was somehow involved. The story she got was that Debra would be placed in a convent, but she didn't know which one. She met the clergyman involved, but from what she could remember he was very vague, and people of that generation rarely argued with a man of the cloth."

Gardener took over. "She couldn't really tell us much more, so we visited the school, which was basically at the bottom of the street, and we were given the name of the headmistress at the time. Her name is Elizabeth Holmes, and she now resides in Baildon. We didn't manage a visit because we had to go and see Fitz."

Gardener studied his notes.

"So, I need someone on that tomorrow. We contacted Mrs Holmes and asked if we could go and see her." Gardener smiled at the next bit. "I don't think she gets many visitors because there was a mention of tea and freshly baked scones." He stared at Reilly. "My colleague is deeply disappointed that it won't be us that's going to see her."

"Yes," said Bob Anderson, "but who is?"

"As a matter of fact, you and Frank are."

"Get in," shouted Thornton, glancing at Reilly. "Don't worry, we'll take a doggie bag."

"You'd better," said Reilly.

The rest of the team laughed. Thornton and Anderson were now marked men, they knew the punishment if they didn't bring something back for him.

Gardener glanced at the whiteboard, made notes and then pointed to another topic.

"Burner phones, have we had any luck?"

He'd left Gates and Longstaff chasing those, as well as checking out Katie Tunscroft's computer.

"Basically," said Gates, "nothing positive has come up."

"No," said Longstaff. "All the emails the killer sent have gone through a dozen servers, or more, so it's very difficult, if not impossible, to follow. We haven't picked up anything concrete from that yet."

"And whoever has the burner phone knows exactly how to cover their tracks," said Gates. "A burner phone number *can* be traced. All mobile phones – including prepaid ones – and burner apps, go through something called a cellular carrier or virtual number operator."

"That means your identity can be tracked through call logs," said Longstaff, "data usage, approximate location, and text messages."

"But," said Gates, "the average customer who buys a burner phone number can take steps to add layers of privacy."

"There really are all sorts of tricks you can get up to, to make life awkward for the likes of us," said Longstaff.

"You can have a friend buy a phone and dispose of it by leaving it active on public transport," said Gates.

"Choose a dumb phone over Android or iPhone smartphones," said Longstaff. "Use prepaid phone plans to avoid a phone bill."

"Some people use cash and refuse to touch a receipt," said Gates. "You'll like this one, refilling or topping up prepaid minutes on a burner phone is a perfect use for cryptocurrency. It's number three on this list of real-world problems that crypto solves. Several services like Bitrefill accept cryptocurrency."

Gardener raised his eyebrows. "I think we get the message. What you're actually trying to tell us, is that after spending the weekend trying to track the killer, you haven't actually got anywhere."

"I wouldn't say that," said Longstaff. "We haven't managed to trace where the phone was bought or who has it."

"But we can tell you something," said Gates. "We had the number, and the IMEI number, which is unique to every handset. From that, we discovered the provider was EE. We gave them all the details we had. They told us the phone had been bought around six months ago and has been switched off until recently."

"Why was that?" asked Bob Anderson.

"Probably to make sure that if there was any CCTV where it was bought, he or she couldn't be traced," said Longstaff. "It would have been wiped and reused after a month. It was prepaid, so no top ups were required, and the phone is now completely out of service. Interestingly, all phone calls to Katie's phone came from the West Yorkshire area – nowhere else."

"How did you find all this out with a burner?" asked Reilly.

"Because we're good," replied Longstaff. "That's how we keep our job."

Reilly threw his hands in the air, which Gardener found amusing. He was happy with Gates and Longstaff, a good addition to the team, and if they wanted to keep their secrets he was good with it so long as they produced results.

"I take it you're staying on that tomorrow," said Gardener, "to see what else you can find?"

"Yes," said Longstaff, "and we also intend to start work on the cryptic message first thing in the morning. See if the killer is as clever as he or she thinks they are."

"It might not be about being clever," said Briggs, "they're already a step ahead of us. It might be more about seeing how clever *we* are."

Gardener nodded, once again made notes, and then asked, "Anything on the chess piece?"

Gates nodded. "We had a look, but again, there isn't much to tell. We could tell you quite a bit about the game of chess and where it originated but we don't think the killer is really using the pieces for that."

"No," said Longstaff. "We think the queen perhaps refers to the torso. It's considered the most powerful piece in the game. She is allowed to move in any direction and in as many squares as she wants."

"History has proven that many reigning queens could be ruthless when it came to battles and wars," said Gates, "since she can move freely across the board many players favour this piece over all others."

"That it?" asked Reilly.

Gates nodded. "Like I said, I don't think there's any real hidden meaning here. Maybe the killer is trying to tell us something about the woman in the mix up of body parts."

"Maybe she was a matriarch of some description, a powerful figure."

"She would be if this all connects back to the church," said Gardener. "A mother superior perhaps?"

"That might tie in with the convent idea," said Sharp, "that the neighbour offered up."

"Okay," said Gardener, glancing at Anderson and Thornton, "when you go and see Elizabeth Holmes tomorrow, see if you can press her about the convent. Annie Stokes *believes* the girl went to a convent, can Mrs Holmes confirm that, or is she telling a different story?"

Gardener made notes on the whiteboard before turning. "At least we're making some progress."

"How did you two get on with Fitz?" asked Briggs.

"Now that's a conversation worth hearing, so it is," said Reilly.

Gardener briefly mentioned the dreaded M word.

"Pardon?" questioned Patrick Edwards.

"Not that stuff again," said Briggs.

"What exactly is it?" asked Sarah Gates.

Gardener noticed Longstaff on her phone; she was almost certainly checking it out, so he saved her the bother.

"It's nasty stuff," said Gardener. "Despite wearing gloves, methanothorox absorbs its way into your skin: odourless, colourless, and untraceable in a dead body until recent times. Toxicity levels go off the scale. Symptoms include anxiety, restlessness, dizziness, headache, nausea, hypersalivation, vomiting, you name it. Muscle weakness and fasciculation may develop, and then progress to generalized flaccid paralysis, including ocular and respiratory muscles, and eventually death.

"Methanothorox is an organophosphate insecticide; mainly used to kill insects. They work by damaging an enzyme in the body of the insect which is critical for controlling nerve signals in the body. Many organophosphates are potent nerve agents. Even at relatively low levels, and may be hazardous to human health."

"Insecticides and nerve agents," said Rawson, "all in the same explanation. Where the hell are we going with this?"

"If the case *is* going back forty years, then this insecticide at the time would have been undetectable as the cause of death," said Gardener.

"So someone knew his onions," added Reilly.

"You'd think so, Sean," said Gardener, "but what puzzles me is, once again, the killer has waited forty years to give us the bodies. Technology moves on a lot in that time. Even if he or she knew their onions back then, and we didn't, they must have known that today we'd have an easier job tracing it."

"Maybe so," said Briggs, "but he or she isn't bothered whether we trace it or not."

"I'm not even sure the killer is bothered about being caught," said Reilly. "They're on a mission. He or she is taking revenge for something and once they've finished, they'll either disappear, or we will have caught them: either way, I don't see it being a problem to the killer."

"I'd like to know who makes the insecticide," said Gardener, "where it's principally made, is it controlled, and are there records of who buys it and when? How far back do the records go? The list will almost certainly include farmers, but we need to know who else uses it and why."

"I know we can't rule anything out," said Briggs, "but I can't see it being a woman."

"What if the woman has nothing to lose?" Reilly asked.

"What do you mean?" asked Longstaff.

"What if she's discovered she had an incurable medical condition and decides she has nothing to lose by bringing the problem to light now? Maybe tying up loose ends before meeting her maker."

"Fair point," said Briggs.

"But she might still need a man for the physical stuff – hence the reason for the rag-and-bone man."

"We have a bit more on him," said Gates.

"Do tell."

"CCTV footage shows the rag-and-bone man going into the alley behind the shop mid-morning, and you can quite clearly see the polythene," said Longstaff. "The camera shows him leaving around two o'clock, without the polythene."

Gates took over. "He goes back up towards the junction with Queen Street but he stays on Brunswick and then goes out of view of the camera. That takes him to Station Road, and the railway station."

"The railway station?" Gardener was disappointed. "If he came in and went out on a train he could be anywhere by now."

"We've already been to the station," said Longstaff.

"There is nothing on camera at the station with the rag-and-bone man or the cart," said Gates, "and nothing that we've looked at that shows he took a train anywhere."

"Does that mean he has a van?" asked Reilly. "Does what he needs to and then disappears?"

"That's the obvious solution," said Briggs. "He wouldn't be able to move the barrow around on a train, unless it was collapsible, and it certainly doesn't look like that."

"Maybe you guys need to go back, check all the vehicles in the car park, see which ones appear on the camera on the day in question and follow them up," said Gardener. "See who owns them, if only for elimination purposes."

Gates nodded. "Will do."

"Better still," said Gardener, "in view of how much work you ladies have, let Colin and Dave tackle that task." He turned to Thornton. "Nothing else on the rag-and-bone man?"

"Of the totters we've spoken to," said Thornton, "there is no one new in the area and no one knows him or the cart."

"Maybe not," said Rawson, "but another member of the public has seen him. A woman who lives in the flats on Queen Street opposite the butcher, confirmed she saw a well-built man pushing a barrow past her place."

"She thought he was a rag-and-bone man and ran back into the flat to offer him some old clothes," said Sharp. "When she came back out, he had disappeared, but she couldn't see how that was possible. She came down the stairs and on to the street and stared in all directions but he was nowhere to be seen."

"Was there any further CCTV down there that captured him?" Gardener asked.

"No," said Sharp.

"Does that mean he's local to that area and he's hidden the cart somewhere?"

"Possibly," said Rawson. "I'm thinking out loud here but there was mention of a butcher, so maybe we should call back and check the buildings, see what's behind there. Might give us a chance to check out the butcher as well."

"Good idea," said Gardener.

He suddenly realized how late it was, quickly wrote down the information on the white boards before running through everyone's actions for the next day.

Chapter Nineteen

Early Tuesday morning, Sarah Gates and Emma Longstaff were seated either side of a desk, with coffees and croissants. The station was quiet, either because the rest of the team had yet to arrive, or they were out following their own actions. Neither Gates nor Longstaff had spotted Gardener or Reilly yet.

Longstaff had a copy of the cryptic note on the desk, and both were studying possible meanings. They had already discussed the idea of the numbers replacing letters, and whether or not that would tell them anything – should they manage to crack it.

> *The location of your next surprise will depend on your ability to decipher the meaning of the following numbers.*

653, 6123, 23 9 4 5 12 1 14 5

*Had you done your job properly, this animal would
have been locked up years ago.*

"It doesn't matter whether it's letters, numbers, arcane symbols, lines and dots, or weird alien squiggles," said Longstaff, taking a sip of the coffee, croissant in hand. "If you're asked to replace each letter in the alphabet with another symbol, you're dealing with what's called a simple substitution cipher. What we need to do here is try to get inside the killer's mind. What are they actually thinking? What are they trying to tell us? Will this translate to words, or is it strictly numbers?"

Gates had already bitten into the almond croissant and rolled her eyes at how fantastic it appeared to taste.

"I was doing some research last night on code cracking," she said. "Apparently it was the Spartans who pioneered cryptography in Europe. They used a device known as the scytale."

"Bloody hell," said Longstaff. "What was that?"

"Military commanders used it. It was like a tapered baton. And wrapped around it was a spiral strip of parchment or leather which contained the message. Words were written lengthwise along the baton, one letter on each revolution of the strip. When unwrapped, the letters of the message appeared scrambled and the parchment was sent on its way. The receiver wrapped the parchment around another baton of the same shape and the original message reappeared. Not sure any of that will help us here. And then there was a lot of stuff done at Bletchley on that Enigma machine."

Longstaff laughed. "I watched that film last, *The Imitation Game*. I wondered if that might help."

"Did it?"

"Did it, buggery," said Longstaff, finishing the croissant. "So, do these numbers represent a word, or a series of words?"

"Maybe they could be a phone number?"

"Or the name of one of the victims?" asked Longstaff.

"I'm not sure it'll be that simple."

"Maybe not," replied Longstaff, "but whoever is doing this has entered into some kind of contract with us. I think they want the bodies found because of what happened years ago, justice needs to be served."

"Agreed," said Gates. "But for what?"

"That's what we need to find out."

The pair of them threw their empty cups and wrappers in the bin and settled down to see if they could decipher the message. Both trawled the internet for nearly an hour, entered the term 'cracking codes' into a variety of search engines and came up with very little of any use.

Finally, Gates sat back and sighed, rubbing her temples.

"I can't make any of these numbers cross to words: none that make any sense, anyway."

"In which case," said Longstaff, "are they simply numbers that don't actually represent words?"

"It's looking that way," replied Gates. "If that's the case, what the hell do they mean?"

"Is it anything to do with the chess piece? Is there anything in chess that signifies numbers?"

That set them off on another internet search. By the time they had finished, all they had was a very good idea of where and when the game originated and something fascinating about the author H.G. Wells, who apparently claimed that chess addiction is a real thing. As he once put it, 'The passion for playing chess is one of the most unaccountable in the world. It is the most absorbing of occupations, the least satisfying of desires, an aimless excrescence upon life. It annihilates a man. There is no remorse like the remorse of chess.'

All Gates knew was it was beginning to annihilate them too.

"Okay, nothing there," said Gates. "So let's assume this cryptogram is more about the numbers than anything else. You're good at numbers, what do you think here?"

Longstaff left the room and reappeared with two more drinks and sat down.

"You need to establish a pattern, and for that there is a routine that you need to follow. Firstly, determine if the mathematical distance between the numbers is the same by subtracting each number from the number that follows it."

"Christ, that sounds complicated."

After twenty minutes, they went on to the next step.

"Look for a pattern in the differences between the numbers you found in step one," said Longstaff. "If there is no obvious pattern in the differences…"

"I know," said Gates, "on to the next step."

That yielded nothing.

"Okay," said Longstaff, beginning to visibly droop in her seat. "Return your attention to the original number pattern, and look for a common denominator."

Nothing.

"Okay, next step," said Longstaff, ready to scream, or laugh, whichever was easier. "Look for a pattern in the numbers as they are written. This means that instead of looking at a mathematical solution, look for a code."

"Give me an example," said Gates.

"You might be given the following sequence: 1, 12, 121, 1213, 12131. Here the next number, 121314, is in the pattern of digits as they are written, not in the way they are mathematically manipulated."

Still nothing.

"This is getting us nowhere," said Longstaff. "What the hell have they done with this puzzle?"

"There's always a chance it's just a complete random mess," said Gates, "in which case we really are on the road to nowhere."

"That's it," said Longstaff. She suddenly clicked her fingers in a lightbulb moment.

"What's it?"

"You just said road."

"I know, road to nowhere."

"Maybe not," said Longstaff. "The first two sets of numbers look familiar. Is this a case of where two roads meet, which could produce a location?"

Gates jumped up and scurried to one of the cupboards. After searching the shelves and drawers she returned to the table with a map.

"Let's have a look, but where do we start?"

"Only one place I can think of," said Longstaff. "Morley. That's where we found the body in the shop. Then work outwards from there."

It didn't take long before Longstaff stabbed the page with her forefinger. "There," she shouted.

Chapter Twenty

Gardener was about to take a sip of water when Gates and Longstaff charged through the door like a pair of advancing rhinos, almost knocking Reilly over in the process.

"Where's the fire?"

"What's got you two so revved up?" Gardener asked.

"We think we've cracked the code," said Gates.

"Really?" said Reilly.

The four of them took a seat around a table and Longstaff laid out what she had, explaining the process they had gone through, and the fact that it had yielded nothing.

"Then Sarah mentioned us being on the road to nowhere."

"And that's what did it," said Gates.

"What did?" asked Reilly.

"Road to nowhere," repeated Longstaff. "Roads."

"Explain," said Gardener.

Longstaff pointed to the paper in front of her. "653 and 6123. Put letters in front of them and you have A653 and B6123. Where they meet is a roundabout."

"Wide Lane intersecting with Dewsbury Road," said Gates.

"Just outside Morley," said Longstaff.

"What do the rest of the numbers mean?" asked Gardener.

"It's the reference for Google Street View. If you go to that intersection on the street view, the rest of the numbers make sense."

Gardener glanced at Reilly. "It's the best we've had so far."

"So what's there?" asked Reilly.

"Mostly roads and fields," said Gates. "There's a farm on one side of Wide Lane, and a MacDonald's on the other side."

"Nothing else?" asked Gardener.

"Not that we can see," said Longstaff.

Gardener thought for a moment. "Is it the killer's style, an open field?"

"Not sure we know enough about the killer at the moment," said Reilly, "to see if they actually have a style."

"True," said Gardener, grabbing his hat. "Time to find out, though."

* * *

They arrived within twenty minutes, noticing the MacDonald's as they pulled into Wide Lane. On the left, heading towards Morley town centre there were hedges obscuring the fields. Gardener noticed a pair of wrought iron gates leading to possibly a farm or a farmhouse. On the right there was another field, and a layby.

Reilly parked the car on the layby, both officers jumped out. Gates and Longstaff pulled up behind.

Gardener glanced into the field. It was big and barren, with trees and bushes covering the extreme left and right. He turned back to stare at the wrought iron gates leading to the farm. He couldn't really see anything there.

They heard a voice from the right. A small squat man wearing a padded jacket and a trilby was walking a dog. He had a ginger moustache, and a round face and thick lips.

As soon as he stopped to talk, the dog lay down. "What are you lot up to this week?"

"What do you mean?" asked Reilly.

"There were a bloke here last week, spent two or three days here."

"Doing what?" asked Gardener.

"Couldn't rightly tell you. He were from the water board or something. Had one of them 4x4 vehicles parked up here, and one of them little tents erected on the road."

Gardener flashed his warrant card and introduced himself and Reilly, informing the man they were from West Yorkshire Major Incident Team. The man introduced himself as Trevor Walker and seemed visibly shaken at the mention of police.

"Can you describe him?" Gardener asked.

Walker pursed his lips. "Let me see. About six feet tall, short dark hair and clean-shaven. Face were a bit lined, brown eyes. He wore one o' them hi-vis jackets and large rigger boots, safety helmet. He had thick tortoiseshell glasses and walked with a limp. He was well-built, the type you wouldn't argue with."

"Did you talk to him at all?"

"I just said good morning and he nodded. But we did talk at some point. Why?"

"What did he say?" asked Gardener.

"Summat about a leaking water pipe, which he thought were in one of those fields. Reckoned it was causing a drop in pressure at the farmhouse."

Gardener glanced at the field. It was bone dry.

"I know what you're thinking," said Walker. "I never noticed any water, either. I thought I might have seen something."

"Did he show you any credentials?" asked Gates.

"No," said Walker, "but I never asked him for any either. Has he done summat, like? Is he wanted for something?"

"If he was a water board official," said Reilly, "did you notice any logos on the vehicle, any phone numbers?"

Walker scratched his head. "Not that I can think of."

"Did you notice his registration?" asked Longstaff.

"No," said Walker. "Didn't think I needed to."

"Did you ever see him in the field?" asked Gardener.

"Come to think of it, no. In fact, I only really saw him on the first day, and not much on the second. Tent were here yesterday but not now. What's this bloke done?"

"Who owns the field, do you know?"

Walker turned to his right and pointed. "Joe Proctor. Like as not he'll know what's going on."

"Is there anything in the field, do you know?" asked Gardener.

"Not much," said Walker. "On the left, over there" – he pointed again – "you can't see it from here but there's a large stable for two horses, and on the right just a tatty old lock-up on its last legs."

That was enough to set alarm bells ringing for Gardener.

"Thank you, Mr Walker. You've been very helpful. Can you leave your details with one of my officers and we'll send someone round to take an official statement?"

Walker was once again flustered, desperate to know what was going on.

Gardener tipped his hat to Walker, and then turned and asked Reilly to follow him into the field. As he strolled to the right-hand side, Gardener wasn't too pleased about the weather conditions. The sky was grey and threatening. Once past the clearing, they saw what Trevor Walker described as the old lock-up.

It was really an old wooden shed, larger than normal, with a raised V-shaped corrugated roof, still attached, that had seen better days. The framed timbers had holes in them. Gardener approached and peered through the holes but he couldn't see anything.

He stepped around the sides, though difficult due to overhanging branches. He noticed side windows that had never been cleaned, covered in moss, with no way of seeing through.

He came back to the front. Both wooden doors had swelled with age and the paint was flaking. One very noticeable thing, however, was the hasp and staple and the padlock: all were new.

"What do you think, Sean?"

"I think we need to look inside. Given the description and what this big bloke was up to, and what we found at the shop in Morley, we have a very good reason to enter the premises."

"Should we get the farmer?" asked Gardener.

"He could be anywhere."

"Just what I was thinking."

"We don't have a key, and there's not much time to find the farmer, who might or might not have one, and I'm asking myself who installs a brand-new hasp and staple and padlock that's worth more money than the fucking shed?"

"You have such a way with words. What are you thinking?"

"That we have a screwdriver in the car. Won't take two minutes to undo the screws on the hasp to gain entry."

"All yours," said Gardener.

Reilly left. Gates and Longstaff approached.

"This looks interesting," said Longstaff.

"That's what we thought."

Reilly returned and set about his duty. Two minutes later, everything was discarded to the floor and Reilly stepped back.

Gardener opened both doors. They creaked, and caught on the ground underneath them, but the view inside was worth it. The smell was something else. Gardener stepped back and grabbed a handkerchief for his nose.

"Fucking hell," said Reilly.

Gates and Longstaff kept their distance.

Unlike the body they had found in the shop in Morley, there was no polythene. The corpse was naked, nailed to a home-made cross that was very rugged and well put together.

The MO was exactly the same: four different bodies, different skin textures and colours; rough stitching. However, the condition of the body was a little different. It was slightly wizened and starting to mummify. He remembered Fitz saying that might happen depending on how long it had been exposed to air, which had obviously been longer than the first.

Gardener moved in closer. He noticed another chess piece sticking out of the mouth, but all he could see was the head of a horse, which made it the knight, if he was not mistaken.

He glanced around the shed. Behind the corpse he saw an old wooden barrel. He pointed it out to Reilly, who donned a pair of gloves. Reilly lifted the lid and peered inside. He reached in and retrieved a manila envelope, sealed.

Gardener figured it might well conceal the journal pages and maybe the cryptic note. There was no doubt they were staring at victim number two.

Something even more disturbing was the number of containers at the back of the shed. He stepped around the corpse toward the blue drums with faded labels. They were chemical drums but nothing he recognized.

Each of the drums had a number of labels. One of the labels was red, with the code 'CSL4'. Another label claimed, 'Danger – Toxic if ingested'. And another was marked 'LD50'. Additional labels included two symbols: one was a flame over a circle and the other was a skull and crossbones.

The final code was about twenty digits long, made up of numbers and letters split between upper and lower case. Gardener had an idea what might be inside the containers, but for now he played his hunch and made a phone call.

Fitz answered quite quickly and Gardener described what they had found.

"It's all very dangerous stuff. Those labels determine the level of toxicity. LD stands for lethal dose," said Fitz. "LD50 is the amount of a substance, given all at once, which causes the death of 50% of a group of test animals. The LD50 is one way to measure the short-term poisoning potential – the acute toxicity – of a material.

"It is usually expressed as the amount of chemical administered, for example milligrams per 100 grams for smaller animals, or per kilogram for bigger test subjects of the body weight of the test animal. LC stands for 'Lethal Concentration'. LC values usually refer to the concentration of a chemical in air but in environmental studies it can also mean the concentration of a chemical in water.

"Depending on how the chemical will be used, many kinds of toxicity tests may be required. Since different chemicals cause different toxic effects, comparing the toxicity of one with another is hard.

"We could measure the amount of a chemical that causes kidney damage, for example, but not all chemicals will damage the kidney. We could say that nerve damage is observed when 10 grams of chemical A is administered, and kidney damage is observed when 10 grams of chemical B is administered. However, this information does not tell us if A or B is more toxic because we do not know which damage is more critical or harmful."

Gardener pretty much stopped him there but asked one question about the chemical itself. Is it likely that when analyzed, they were going to find the dreaded methanothorox?

Fitz thought it very likely.

"I think I heard enough of that conversation to know which way you're thinking," said Reilly.

"Okay," said Gardener, "we need everyone here: the team, SOCOs, PolSA. I'm not sure what the weather is going to do so a call to the Met Office will help, and we'd better have a marquee. Once we've sorted that out, we'll go and see what the farmer has to say."

Chapter Twenty-one

Joe Proctor was in one of the largest barns on the farm, situated behind the farmhouse: an open construction with a roof on but the only thing large enough to accommodate the combine, which was currently in need of repair. He'd been putting the job off for a month or two. Luckily, they had managed the harvest before it gave up the ghost.

Proctor cupped his hands and blew into them. That was a total waste of time. When did that ever warm anyone up? It was bloody cold. He wore a pair of fingerless mittens but they were no help. He was sure the ends of his fingers were turning blue.

Proctor gripped a spanner in one hand and a magnetic lamp in the other. He'd basically climbed into the bowels of the combine to find out exactly which hydraulic pipe had burst a seal. It had been easy to determine what was wrong with the vehicle because of the pool underneath. Which pipe was another matter. He had however discovered, in the last few minutes, that there was more than one burst seal. There were at least four that would need fixing.

He heaved himself back out of the vehicle and put the lamp and the spanner on a bench. It was time he had a cup of tea. Vicky, his wife had gone into the centre of Morley. Benjamin, his son, was out dry stonewalling. If he was lucky, Chloe, his daughter, might be in the kitchen; luckier still if she made him a bacon sandwich, so he could sit and think about what to do with the pipes. To do the job properly they would all need replacing. He could of course repair the bloody things, but that obviously hadn't worked last time.

Joe suddenly figured he was turning into his father: repair, or bodge, but never spend money you didn't have to.

The last conversation Joe Proctor ever had with his father, Ken, had ended with an argument. It was the usual story, young blood, and new ideas versus traditional methods. Joe felt that the farm was stagnant because his father was sticking to the old methods. He wanted to move forward in every area: crop rotation, new equipment, the latest pesticides. Ken didn't trust them, using the age-old argument as his reasoning; there was nothing wrong with the old methods. They worked. No need for change or to spend money unnecessarily.

Joe's mother, Jean had it from both sides. She listened to the debate – saw the pros and cons in each argument. She pleaded with Ken to cut Joe some slack. He would eventually be the future of the farm, as Ken had to retire at some point. He agreed, but until then however, he said he would have the last word.

If Joe didn't like it, he could go and work somewhere else. Each of them knew that that would not be an option. Joe wouldn't walk away from his inheritance. And Ken wouldn't give it up easily, so the stalemate continued.

The day came and, as ever, things went far from smoothly, particularly when the ancient combine broke down again; the belts were old and cracking, the engine tired, and the bearings noisy. They'd had quotes, none of which had impressed Ken. Joe said they should cut their losses and buy a new one. Ken nearly had a stroke when he saw the prices. The old one would do – they would have it serviced and repaired. Joe argued that they may have those jobs done but everything else on the vehicle was still twenty years old.

That same night, as evening wore on, Ken said he was going in for his evening meal and then out for a game of bowls with the lads. It was one of those warm, glorious summer nights. Ken left home before Joe had finished working but he hadn't particularly wanted to see him because of the argument they had had in the afternoon.

Joe came in for his evening meal around nine o'clock, totally bushed, complaining to his mother that the machine was not worth repairing. She listened sympathetically, apologizing for Ken, saying she would have a talk to him.

Joe said she was wasting her breath, and Ken wasn't worth wasting breath on. If he continued down the route he was going, Ken would end up dead, through a stupid and pointless and unnecessary accident. But that was *his* funeral, and Joe had had enough. He was finished with arguing. He would never speak to his father again until he changed his attitude. His mother asked him to take that back, as he would only regret saying it. Joe said he doubted it.

But it did come back to haunt him. Ken never came home, and Joe found him three days later in a ditch. The post-mortem revealed a very low level of alcohol. There were no drugs in his system, and the likelihood was, judging by the massive trauma his body had suffered, mixed with internal bleeding, he had been the victim of a hit and run. There were no CCTV cameras, no witnesses.

The police spoke to everyone connected to Ken, including his friends at the bowling club. They had all said that he was in fine spirits and had drunk very little that night, citing feeling out of sorts because of an argument with Joe. He loved his son dearly and he did not want to argue with him, only to make him see reason.

No one was ever charged. Joe was seething and full of regret, as his mother had said he would be. He vowed he would find out who was responsible, and he would get even with them.

A voice calling his name brought him back to the present.

"Joe? Where are you," shouted Vicky.

"In here, t'other side o' combine."

Vicky appeared: a typical farmer's wife with straw-blonde hair, carrying more weight than was good for her but there was no substitute for good food, and if you couldn't eat good food when you owned a farm, when could you?

"You're not still trying to repair that thing, are you?"

"No, tried that last time. Anyway, I'm ready for a cuppa and a bite to eat."

"That might have to wait."

"Wait? Why?"

"If I'm not mistaken, the police are all over Renter's Field like a rash. I've no idea what's going on but you'd better get out there fast and find out."

Chapter Twenty-two

Bob Anderson and Frank Thornton found the home of Elizabeth Holmes quite easily. She lived in a cottage in High Fold, off the Hawksworth Road. Lovely in summer, not so nice in winter thought Anderson, a little out of the way, with quite a hill to drive up.

The cottage was painted white, the grounds built on three different levels, each one accessible by stairs and railings. The garden was immaculate. She had apple and pear trees; in one corner Anderson spotted what he thought might be a blueberry bush, all of course now bare because of the time of year.

The door opened and Elizabeth Holmes introduced herself, inviting them into a warm hallway and through to an even warmer living room. The walls were brick tipped, decorated with dried flowers, and the floor finished in parquet. There were four wingback chairs upholstered in a dark tan leather, and a log burner nicely crackling away.

Both men introduced themselves and displayed their warrant cards. She invited them to sit. On a table in the middle, she had tea in a pot, with plates and cutlery, and a cake stand with rich fruit scones. Anderson smiled to himself when he thought of the devastation Reilly might cause to such a scene.

Elizabeth Holmes was sprightly for her advancing years. She had grey hair tied up in a bun, with a round face, blue eyes and glasses. She wore a two-piece navy and white suit, the skirt full-length.

"How lovely to see you, gentlemen," she said, pouring tea. "Please help yourself to scones. I do like to see a healthy appetite, and you certainly look as if you have one, Detective Anderson" – she glanced at Thornton – "but I fear you need a bit of building up, young man."

Anderson smiled as he thought of how she'd greeted his partner. He hadn't been called a young man in an age.

When everyone was settled, she spoke again. "So, you've come to see me about young Debra Gosforth?"

"We wondered if you could remember anything of what happened at the time," asked Anderson.

"Dreadful business," replied Holmes. "Such a young girl to suffer that kind of a tragedy."

Elizabeth Holmes jumped up and left the room. Anderson glanced at Thornton but no explanation had been given so they had no idea what was happening. She returned very quickly with a large photo.

"It's a school year photo," said Holmes. "I believe it was the year Debra's mother died, but before her father went. It's not very good but you can see her."

The ex-headmistress pointed to a thin dark-haired girl kneeling on the front row. "That's her. Oh, when I think of the life she must have had, the things she must have seen for one so young."

"May we keep this?" asked Anderson. "We can take a copy and return it to you."

"No need, dear," said Holmes, "that is a copy. When I found out you were coming to see me, I popped out and had a copy made. Thought you'd need one."

The log fire made a spitting sound. Elizabeth Holmes jumped to her feet, opened the door to the burner, and threw on a couple of more logs. By the time she had closed the door and returned to her seat, the flames had taken hold.

"Do you know how her mother died?"

"Breast cancer. Another tragedy. Diagnosed too late. They're much better now at catching it sooner."

"And what was Debra like?" asked Thornton, finishing his scone.

As he placed his empty plate on the table, Elizabeth Holmes grabbed a pair of tongs and put another on it.

"She was a quiet, reserved type of girl. She had a small group of friends that stuck mainly together. She wasn't boisterous, from what I remember, joined in activities if invited but never pushed herself."

"What was she like after her mother died?" asked Anderson, helping himself to another scone before it was thrust upon him.

Elizabeth Holmes topped up their cups with more tea.

"Surprisingly, not much different. There were times when we found her sitting on her own just staring into space but I think that was only to be expected. She was a very intelligent child. According to some of her teachers, she never asked many questions but the ones she asked were good, showing above-average thinking. She thought about things a lot."

"Did you meet the father?"

"Yes, once. He came to the school shortly after his wife died and he had the decency to explain everything. He said he would do everything in his power to make sure Debra didn't suffer. And outwardly, she didn't appear to. She was always well-dressed, clean, smelled nice. She appeared well fed, so I believe he was as good as his word."

Elizabeth Holmes took a sip of tea before continuing.

"I found it very hard to believe what happened to him. Debra was missing for a short while and we read about it in the papers. The social service people came to see us to say that she was being cared for and they were trying to locate family members to help."

Anderson put his plate down and said that the scones were lovely but he was full and couldn't manage anything else, but he knew a man who would and could he please take one to pass on. Holmes was delighted by the comment and suddenly produced a brown paper bag, from where, Anderson had no idea, where she put not one but two scones inside. Reilly would be pleased.

"We have spoken to one of her neighbours who believes she was taken into a convent," said Thornton. "We wondered if you knew about that, and perhaps which one?"

"Convent, dear?" questioned Holmes, with a confused expression. "We never heard anything about a convent."

"What did *you* hear?" asked Anderson.

"Well, Debra did return to school after a short period, perhaps a week or so. You could certainly see a difference and none of us knew what would become of the child. She was staying with neighbours, but I'm not sure I can remember which one now. It was a long time ago."

"I get the impression, Mrs Holmes," said Anderson, "that you're going to tell us there was no convent."

"Yes, dear," she replied. "At the start of the second week of her return, a priest came to see us."

"About Debra?" asked Thornton.

"Yes. He said that they had located family in Ireland and that Debra was going to stay with them, and that she would continue her education over there."

"Can you remember his name?" asked Anderson.

Elizabeth Holmes remained silent for a few seconds. "Yes, I can. That was the one thing I do remember about the whole affair. He called himself Jeremy Cleeves."

"Sounds like you didn't believe it."

"I did then, not so sure over the years."

Anderson made a note and then asked, "Did he have papers to prove as much?"

"It was a different time back then, Detective," said Holmes, "but, yes, he did. They all looked genuine enough. He even had the names of the social workers who had visited after her mother had died. All the papers were in order. He was a lovely man, as I remember, very gentle, very calming. He talked about the tragedy and said they

119

had moved heaven and earth to make sure Debra would be cared for and well looked after."

"Can you remember where in Ireland?" asked Thornton.

"He did say, dear, and I do remember because it was such a strange name. Rosscarbery he called it – said it was about an hour south of Dublin."

"But you don't remember an address?"

"No, but I believe it was on one of the papers he had with him. I *can* tell you it was not a convent."

"When exactly was she moved?" asked Anderson. "Can you remember?"

"At the end of that week."

"Did you manage to check any of what he was saying?" asked Thornton.

"To be honest, I didn't. People didn't argue with the clergy in those days, did they? Or now, come to think of it."

"This may sound strange, Mrs Holmes, but did you ever hear from Debra again, or any of the people involved with her moving?"

Elizabeth Holmes shook her head, with a very genuine expression of sorrow.

"No, I'm afraid I didn't. I did what people always do in life. Got on with it, feeling slightly better that she was going somewhere with people who loved her."

Anderson removed a photo from the folder he had brought with him. It was the head shot of the victim they had found in the shop in Morley.

"Do you recognize the gentleman in this photo?" asked Anderson. "It wouldn't be the priest, would it?"

She studied the shot. "This is the gentleman in the paper this morning. I believe you're looking for information about him."

"Very observant, Mrs Holmes, yes we are," replied Anderson. "Do you recognize him?"

She passed back the photo. "I'm afraid not, Detective Anderson. Whoever he is, he's not the priest who came for Debra."

Chapter Twenty-three

Having closed off the crime scene, spoken to the SOCOs, PolSA, and the rest of his team, and given them their immediate actions, Gardener and Reilly were now sitting in Joe Proctor's kitchen. Vicky was sitting beside Proctor. The room was homely if a little cluttered with a large table and eight chairs in the middle of a tiled floor, a cooking range across one wall, which heated the room adequately, shelves containing tins were fixed to every wall with an assortment of herbs, spices, flours and perhaps everything else a farmer's kitchen would need.

The aroma of bacon hung in the air, and Proctor had an empty plate in front of him. Everyone had a mug of tea and Reilly had managed to snaffle a piece of homemade parkin cake to go with his drink.

Proctor was short, a little over five feet five, with thick dark hair, little of which could be seen because he was wearing a flat cap. He had brown eyes, a round nose, square teeth, and his complexion was very rugged, as Gardener would have expected. Proctor was dressed in work gear of overalls and Wellington boots. Although his frame was thin, he was quite muscular, which Gardener suspected was down to all the outdoor work on the farm.

"What's all this about?" asked Proctor.

"Stay calm, love," said Vicky.

"I am calm, but these lot are all over my land without an explanation and every minute I'm sitting here is costing me money."

Gardener waited until he'd finished. Quite satisfied that he had, he made his opening statement.

"I do have to advise you, Mr Proctor, that you are being questioned under caution and that anything you say may be taken down and can be used as evidence."

"Am I under arrest?"

"No, only caution."

"What's the difference?"

"If you were under arrest, we wouldn't be sitting here asking questions in a civilized manner without a solicitor. You have the right to free legal advice, and you can ask me to leave whenever you like."

Proctor nodded, obviously taking the wise words of his wife.

"Can I just confirm for the record, Mr Proctor," continued Gardener, "that you own the field we are searching?"

"I do."

"What type of a farm do you have here?"

"Mixed," replied Proctor.

"What does that entail, Mr Proctor?" asked Gardener.

Reilly had taken to making notes.

"We grow crops and raise cattle."

"How does that work out for you?"

"In general it works out well but it's not without its problems."

"Such as?" asked Reilly.

"Mostly knowing what fields to hold off. Some fields are more accommodating to the environment than others, so each year we have to shift things around."

"How long have you been here?"

"All my life. I were born here and took it on after my father passed."

"Do you run it alone, or do you have help?"

"We all help," said Vicky.

"Who's all?" asked Reilly.

"Me," said Vicky, "and we have a son and daughter who chip in. They're both out at the moment. Not sure where Chloe is, but Benjamin is in one of the fields repairing walls."

Gardener changed topics. "The field we've been in looks quite barren. Do you actually use it for anything?"

"No," said Proctor.

"We rent it out," said Vicky, "which is why we call it Renter's Field."

"Are the stables yours?"

"Yes, but the horses are not ours," said Vicky. "They belong to a man called Corbett."

"What do you know about Mr Corbett?"

"Not a lot," replied Vicky, glancing at her husband.

Gardener picked up on it, but Reilly beat him to the question. "What does that mean?"

Proctor now bore a sheepish expression.

"I would advise you not to hide anything from me, Mr Proctor," said Gardener. "What do you know about the man who rents the stable? Do you have a tenancy agreement with him, and if so, can I have the details, please?"

"It's not that straightforward," said Proctor. "He needed somewhere for his horses and we have a cash arrangement. Nothing goes through the books."

Gardener nodded. He wasn't interested in the financial side of it, more about the man himself.

"Do you know where he lives?"

"To be honest," said Proctor, "no. All we know is he pays the rent on time, in cash, and we've never had cause for complaint, and he treats them animals like they were his family – really looks after them."

"How often do you see him?"

"He's here every day," said Vicky. "Comes first thing in the morning and later in the evening. So if you want to know more about him, he'll be here around six o'clock."

Reilly made a note.

"How often do *you* visit the field?"

"Rarely," said Proctor. "Benjamin checks on it now and again."

"Where is Benjamin?" asked Reilly.

"Like Vicky said, repairing walls."

"We will need to speak to him," said Gardener. "Can you call him and get him back here, please?"

"Look what is this about?" Proctor asked. "Has something happened? If it has, we have a right to know."

"Who owns the lock-up on the right?" Gardener asked.

"Me, well, technically it's mine."

Reilly rolled his eyes. "Why technically?"

"My father signed a lease years ago. The field is ours, as is the lock-up, but we actually rent them out."

"Is that a cash arrangement as well?" asked Gardener.

"No," said Vicky. "We had nothing to do with it."

"When you say he signed a lease, how long was this lease?" asked Gardener.

"About a hundred years."

"Pardon?"

"I know," said Proctor. "Madness, isn't it, but that's what he did, for reasons known only to himself and there's nowt I can do about it."

"Must be a bit frustrating," said Reilly.

"Not really. They're paying good money so why should I care."

"So, do you have any paperwork for the lock-up and the field?" asked Gardener.

Vicky disappeared into another room and returned very quickly with a file. Leafing through it, she finally drew out a contract, passing it over to Gardener.

The file stated that a man called Richard Monarch of MCC Holdings signed a ninety-nine-year lease in 1990.

The company was located on an industrial estate at Thorp Arch Trading Estate, near Wetherby.

Gardener noticed a phone number and immediately called it. The number was out of service. He informed his partner.

Gardener was unhappy: another brick wall. The shop in Morley that was apparently owned by someone in Hemel Hempstead who didn't exist came to mind. He wondered about the connection.

Vicky passed over another file with the bank details. Gardener studied it; as she had suggested, it was paid for monthly and came direct from a bank account under the names Richard Monarch and MCC Holdings. So why was no one answering their phone? He passed the papers to Reilly and asked him to arrange for two of the team to investigate immediately.

"Have you any idea what's in that lock-up, Mr Proctor?"

"No," said Proctor, "I don't go in there and I can't remember the last time I did."

"So you wouldn't know why such a dilapidated building had a brand new hasp and staple and padlock on it?"

"No good asking me, I've just told you I can't remember the last time I were in there."

"Have you ever seen Richard Monarch?"

"No."

"So he isn't like Mr Corbett, he doesn't come here every day?"

"If he does, I've never seen him," said Proctor.

"Nor me," said Vicky.

"Any idea who *has* put the new security on the door?" asked Reilly.

"No," said Proctor.

"Come on, son, you're not helping yourself here," said Reilly. "We need proper answers to our questions."

"You haven't answered mine yet, have you?" said Proctor.

"I think you have the wrong idea, son," said Reilly. "We're not actually here to answer *your* questions."

At that point, the situation defused because Benjamin walked through the door and introduced himself. He was very stocky, around six feet tall, muscular, had a rugged complexion like his father, and when he spoke his voice was rather gravelly. He took a seat at the table. His mother poured some tea and explained who and why the two officers where here.

"I don't know about the padlock either, but I saw it there yesterday."

"Do you know Mr Corbett?"

"Yes. In fact I was talking to him yesterday and he happened to mention the lock; said he noticed it when the horses were out for a trot, but it was nothing to do with him."

"You haven't questioned it?"

"I thought it were Dad's doing."

"But you didn't ask?"

"No. By the time I got finished yesterday it were quite late and I forgot."

"Are you gonna tell us what this is about?" said Proctor. "I'm fed up now. You turn up mob handed, you're all over my field, you storm in here like the SS and you bombard me with questions about my land. You want to see records and yet you don't have the decency to tell me why. I think that's a bit rich."

"He does have a point, officer," said Vicky.

"Can I also see the farm accounts, please?" asked Gardener.

"Why?"

Gardener leaned forward. "Can you please just show me the invoices for the last six months?"

"No," said Proctor, "not until you tell me why."

"You need to calm down, Joe," said Vicky.

"He has a point, Mam," said Benjamin, defending his father.

"I'm sure they have good reason for all of this," replied Vicky, "and I'm sure they'll tell us when they can."

Once again, Vicky left the kitchen, returning a few minutes later with a reasonably thick folder. She passed it to Gardener, who glanced through it. Eventually, he pulled out a sheet of paper and passed it back to Proctor.

"You have an invoice here for something called Menox. Can you tell me what that is?"

"It's a pesticide. We need it for treating the animals."

"That's probably a trade name," said Gardener. "Do you happen to know if there's another name for it?"

Proctor nodded. "I were speaking to one of the drivers once, he mentioned something called methanothorox."

Bingo. "Is it licenced?" asked Gardener.

Vicky said it was, and from another file she produced the necessary paperwork, the COSH sheets, and the licence.

"Can you tell me where you keep it?"

"Locked up in one of the barns."

"Can you show us?"

Gardener and Reilly rose from the table and everyone went outside. They followed the Proctors around the back of the house. The barn was unlocked, and Gardener noticed six new drums stacked against the wall, all of which were different to the ones they had found in the lock-up, though still blue. He examined them more closely. All the lids were sealed. The labels were different but he suspected the drums in the lock-up were much older.

He turned to Proctor. "Do you have any empty drums of this stuff?"

Proctor led him to another section of the barn. Two old drums were up against the wall.

"Why are these in a different place?" asked Gardener.

"They're empty. Company who makes this always asks for the old drums back again. I like to hide them out of sight until they come, despite the fact that it's usually locked up anyway."

"And can you account for those two?"

"Aye," nodded Proctor, "wife keeps records."

Gardener changed subjects. "What were your movements last week, Mr Proctor?"

"Why, did summat happen then like summat's happened now?"

Vicky suddenly put her hand to her mouth. "Oh my God, is this anything to do with that body found in the shop in Morley last week?"

"Oh, Christ," shouted Proctor, taking a step forward. "Is there a body in our lock-up?"

Gardener thought now was the time to break the news, despite Proctor having suspected. He explained there *was* something in there, along with drums of chemicals and that, until Gardener had completed his investigation, the field, the stables and the lock-up was off limits to everyone. He then asked a question about the possible water board van.

"Water board? What the hell are you talking about?"

Gardener explained what Trevor Walker had told him.

"No problems here wi' water, or in that field," said Proctor. He knew nothing about any van.

Gardener suspected as much.

Vicky said she had seen the vehicle and the tent but she didn't actually see anyone around, or anyone on the land.

"It's a working farm," said Proctor. "We're all busy, we don't get to see every field every day."

Gardener accepted what he'd been told, for now. Realizing there was little else to be gained, he said he would send two officers round later for official statements, and to speak to Chloe to see what, if anything, she knew. He also wanted the Proctors to stay local in case he needed to talk to them again.

"Furthermore," he added, "I will be taking all the empty barrels in the lock-up, and I'll be posting an officer outside the barn behind the house, because I would like one empty drum from here, and one of the full ones for analysis."

Chapter Twenty-four

The wind rattled around the eaves. The place was old, draughty, like its occupant. A house would have been a better option, but houses attracted people and people were nosey. Neither was needed right now.

On the desk was a leather-bound journal, A4 size, plenty of pages, mostly full – covering everything that had happened. The diary had been started in 1985… well, that was pretty much the start of everything. Not that anyone was to have known how it would turn out.

Missing children, misdirection by most of those involved; blackmail, deceit, all of which then resulted in missing policemen. The very people who should have been all over it didn't take it seriously. It had to be a mistake, they'd claimed in the early days. No evidence, they said.

A mistake!

Three years it had taken to investigate those bent bastards responsible. Three years of hard work, interviewing, running around, going back time and again, taking statements, speaking to the most important people of all, those it was happening to, building a case, and for what?

There was enough information to sink the whole diocese; the people you're supposed to trust, not supposed to argue with, because they speak God's word – human beings of the highest order in which you should put nothing but your trust.

Fat chance!

The Black Angels they called themselves. That had only been discovered much later. They certainly had the black bit right. What they did was as dark as it came, beyond all redemption.

Still, they've all paid the price, except one, but his time was coming. And soon!

A hand closed the journal, the reader extremely grateful. Had it not been for the large, full book, nothing would have come to light.

Actually, that wasn't quite true, had it not been for Isabella Moorcroft, none of it would have come to light. A huge debt of thanks was owed in her direction, such a pity it couldn't be delivered in person.

Chapter Twenty-five

"There's a gentleman downstairs to see you, sir, by the name of Gerry Drake."

Desk Sergeant David Williams had tracked Gardener and Reilly through the station and into the incident room.

"He says he recognizes the picture in the paper."

"Does he now?" said Reilly.

"That's good news," said Gardener. "Can you show him into a room and give him a cup of tea and we'll be there in a few minutes?"

Williams nodded and left. Gardener turned to Reilly. "Looks like the media have helped us for a change."

"Be interesting to know who our victim is... well, one of them at least," said Reilly. "Have we heard anything from Fitz?"

"No but he promised to have something for us by the time we hold the briefing a bit later."

Reilly nodded. "Right, let's go and see our man."

Both officers entered the room. Drake was sitting at a table with a coffee and some biscuits on a plate. He rose as soon as Gardener came through the door.

"Mr Drake?" said Gardener. "Thank you for coming in so promptly."

"It's no problem, sir."

Gardener detected a scouse accent. Drake was mid-fifties, didn't carry any excess weight, with a good head of silver hair, and wire-framed spectacles. He was dressed in a suit jacket, white T-shirt and blue jeans.

"Please," said Gardener, "take a seat. I believe you have some news about the gentleman you've seen in the paper?"

"I do," said Drake. "I'm pretty sure it's him. Not seen him for a long time."

"What do you do, Mr Drake?"

"An accountant, like the man in the paper."

Gardener nodded. He produced a sheet of paper from a manila folder. Reilly took it and wrote the details down.

"We're going back a few years now," Drake said. "I married my wife over in Liverpool and she's a nurse. Got a well-paid job here at Jimmy's hospital. She's still there, only she's not a nurse anymore. She reckoned I could get a job anywhere, doing what I did. Anyway, I managed to get a firm to take me on, and it looks like she was right, cause now I own the place."

"Well done. Where are your offices?" asked Gardener.

"In the Corn Exchange."

Gardener withdrew the photo of the head from the folder and passed it over.

"So you think you recognize him?"

"Pretty sure it's him. The name is Richard Monarch."

Gardener suddenly shivered. He glanced at Reilly, who remained silent. Second time he'd heard the name. He figured what Drake would have to say could prove very important.

"Sounds like *you've* heard of him as well," said Drake. "Not that that surprises me. Where the hell is he now?" Drake appeared to think about that and then said. "Stupid question, really. I don't suppose you know, which is why you're looking for him."

"What can you actually tell us about him, Mr Drake?" asked Gardener.

"The last time I saw Monarch was years ago, maybe even as far back as the early Nineties. From what I remember he worked quite closely with a lawyer. They shared the same building and according to rumour they were a right shady pair of bastards." Drake paused. "Sorry about the language."

Gardener smiled. "Sounds like you've had dealings with them."

"Not me personally, but the firm that took me on used to bellyache about them all the time. We eventually took a lot of their clients because those two didn't like paying money out, but they certainly knew how to charge, without doing much for it. Check your records, they were in trouble with the police on more than one occasion, but nothing was ever proved."

"Can you remember the name of the lawyer?" asked Reilly.

Drake's expression changed, became a little more intense as he thought. "I remember it being quite short, Shot or Trot or something like that."

"Where was their office?" asked Gardener.

"It certainly wasn't in the centre of Leeds because they wouldn't have wanted to pay the high prices for office space. If memory serves me correctly, it was somewhere on Roundhay Road. I think they rented a couple of rooms above a shop, a travel agent, I think." Drake suddenly corrected himself. "No, not Roundhay Road, Street Lane.

That's about as much as I remember. It was years ago, but I certainly remember his face."

"Any idea where the lawyer is now?" asked Reilly.

Gardener suspected he was one of the Morley four but it had been worth asking the question.

"With any luck he'll have gone missing with Monarch. I'm assuming Monarch's gone missing 'cause you're looking for him, and I haven't seen him for years. Mark my words, when you get to the bottom of this, them two will have been up to something together."

Gardener nodded. Reilly had finished writing.

"Can you remember anything else about Monarch, anything that you think will help us?"

Drake shook his head. "I'm not sure. I know the business above the travel agent went down the pan about six months after I last saw him. I remember that because we had a number of new clients and they told us. Apparently, there was no one at the helm and there were a number of outstanding debts. There were plenty of rumours that apart from being a dodgy accountant, he frequently visited places of ill repute. And I'm not just talking whorehouses either."

"What else?" asked Reilly.

"I can't really say, officer, because I can't prove any of it and as far as I'm aware it was only hearsay."

"Go on," said Gardener.

"Something to do with children, who also subsequently went missing. And that's all I can tell you."

Chapter Twenty-six

Harry Corbett and Emily were sharing an evening in the Kasa Rosa restaurant on Fountain Street in Morley. The décor of emulsioned walls and tiled floor was basic but spotless. Kasa Rosa was next to the Pizza Bello, outside of which was a spare patch of land where Harry's footman had parked the horse and cart and had decided on a pizza instead of joining them.

Harry had picked Emily up exactly as planned outside her house at the agreed time, and helped her into the beautiful white cart with black and gold rimmed wheels and gold carriage lamps, which were lit. She sat on plush red velvet seats and the interior was actually heated. She had no idea how.

Once seated inside the restaurant they had sampled tapas of lamb in sherry sauce, moved on to the starter of fresh Shetland mussels in chilli and garlic, before enjoying a main of lobster thermidor.

Harry told her all about his horse and cart and his love of horses in general. Emily couldn't believe the difference in his appearance. His hair was dark, cut short, and he was dressed in a suit that probably cost most people a year's rent. Before the main course she made a reference to his appearance in the shop, which reminded her of one of the characters in the classic sitcom, *Steptoe & Son*. He remembered the program well, finding his disguise and her story amusing.

"Perhaps I'm not really what I appear to be, my dear."

"I can see that. So why the big secret?"

He said he lived in a house on Scotchman Lane, past the golf club.

"That's where Patterson lives."

"I know," replied Harry.

Emily suddenly remembered the area. "The only house beyond the golf club that I know about is a large, white mansion with black and gold wrought-iron gates, with a paved drive and white columns at the front door.

He never replied, which she took as being positive.

"Oh, my word, Harry. Do you live there on your own?"

"I do live on my own, yes," said Harry, "but I allow myself the luxury of a butler and a footman."

Emily was shocked and asked him what he did for a living.

"I made my money working the land." His reply was guarded, almost as if he was embarrassed. "I started with a small market garden, selling vegetables and salad. When I saw my opportunity, I bought more land and went into fruit, selling directly to consumers and restaurants.

"I took on staff, bought more land, took on more staff. We grew a variety of different plants, with the emphasis on continual production throughout the year."

"And is that what you still do?" asked Emily, over coffees.

Trade in the restaurant had grown quiet, but it had not been really busy all evening.

"No, I'm retired now. I still have weekly meetings with the accountants and the solicitors and the managers. I prefer to keep myself hidden nowadays."

"Why?" asked Emily. "If you don't mind my saying, you're a good-looking fella."

He blushed. She found it sweet.

"Why the disguise?" she asked.

"The business grew so quickly and so well," replied Harry, "that I won award after award, year after year. There was far too much publicity for me. I couldn't deal with it. To be honest, I'm very reserved. My life wasn't my own. People recognized me all over the place. I was often invited to lunches, sometimes to speak after dinner. It was all too much. I value my privacy, my dear, so I find it easier to change my appearance and walk amongst everyone unnoticed."

"Do you have anyone in your life, a wife perhaps?" asked Emily, though she felt she shouldn't have done. She couldn't for a minute think Harry was the type of man who would two time, or cheat on his wife.

"I did," he replied. "She died of bladder cancer ten years ago."

"I'm so sorry."

Emily touched his hand and he physically jumped – perhaps not because he was appalled but simply unused to the closeness.

"Despite the money we had, I simply couldn't do anything about it. I took that very badly. I'm not used to failure."

"It was hardly your fault, Harry. There was nothing you could do, and you shouldn't blame yourself."

He smiled, changing the subject.

"I've enjoyed tonight, Emily, my dear. It's the first time I've entertained a lady since my Kath died."

"Thank you," she replied. "I find it very flattering and it's been a great honour."

"You're very kind and considerate," said Harry. "How the hell did you get mixed up with that idiot, Patterson?"

Emily laughed heartily. "He's not normally like that, you know, but he's not been himself for a while."

"I'll take your word for that. Has he not said what's bothering him?"

"No," replied Emily, "and I've no idea what it could be. Can't be the business, that's doing very well. He's not tight with money. He pays well and there are lots of perks. I can only think it's the kids, or his marriage."

"Well, either of those can cause problems."

"He can be quite sarcastic," said Emily, "upsets people on a regular basis, so maybe his wife has chewed his ear off. The things he says to customers are not really acceptable but they always come back because the produce is first class."

"Proctor's isn't it?" asked Harry.

Emily nodded.

"I believe there was an incident there yesterday, in one of his fields."

"I heard about that, any idea what it was?"

"No," replied Harry, "but it must have been bad; police all over the place. They spoke to me because I keep two horses there."

Emily glanced up. "Why do you keep them there? Your place must surely be big enough."

"It is," replied Harry. "It's very isolated and perfect for what I need, as is Proctor's farm. I'm only keeping them there temporarily because I only recently bought the horses and they have to be kept in isolation for a health problem, but after this week, I'll be able to transport them to my own stables."

"I'm sorry to hear that," said Emily again, the second time in as many minutes. "What was wrong?"

"They were not looked after, showed signs of a fever and a discharge from the nostrils. Thankfully now, they are well on the mend. As healthy as they probably ever have been, so I can move them soon."

"What were the police asking about?"

Harry waved his hand. "Something and nothing. They wanted to know who owned the lock-up at the other end of the field. Had I seen someone in a 4x4, with a roadwork blockade and a tent? The usual stuff when something serious happens."

"Had you?"

Harry nodded. "I saw the vehicle and the tent and the roadwork fences, but not the person running it all."

"Do you know who owns the lock-up?"

"No, afraid not. I only go there to tend to my horses."

"So if you rent space from Proctor, how come you don't buy your meat direct from him?"

Harry blushed again. "Because you don't work there."

It was Emily's turn to blush.

Harry checked if they had finished, signalled the waiter, and paid the bill with a very generous tip before escorting Emily outside. She had no idea what was coming next but was more than surprised at what did.

He glanced at his watch before opening the door to the carriage. He helped Emily into it and then asked his footman to see that she arrived home safely.

"Are you not coming?"

"I'm so sorry, my dear, but no," said Harry. "I really do have some urgent business to attend to. Brian will look after you. And I will come and see you in the shop later in the week. Perhaps we can do this again?"

She nodded, smiling but disappointed. She thought better of asking what his business may be.

Harry turned to Brian. "Can you return for me later in the evening?"

The footman nodded. "At the agreed time and place?"

Harry nodded. "Yes, please."

Chapter Twenty-seven

The team had assembled in the incident room for a briefing. Gardener had a lot to tell them. He hoped they had in return. He glanced at his watch: 8:30pm. He didn't want to keep them here any longer than necessary but things had to be discussed.

Sharp and Rawson said that there was nothing further on the rag-and-bone man. Speaking to witnesses in the area revealed that only two of them had seen him very briefly and had paid little or no attention. He'd been spotted on Station Road but no one knew where he had gone, which brought into play the possibility that he had some form of transport other than the cart.

Sharp mentioned that vans seen in the area and on the station CCTV were still being checked but they had nothing concrete as yet.

"What about dental and retinal scans concerning the head? That reveal anything?" asked Gardener.

As he spoke, the door quietly opened and DCI Briggs took a seat at the back of the room.

"Nothing," said Rawson. "Of the opticians we've checked, they have said that records only really go back a short time in terms of years."

Gardener suspected there wouldn't be anything on the scans. The more information they gathered, the more likely it was they were dealing with something cold. He had however, been hoping for something on the rag-and-bone man because he now suspected there was nothing genuine about him. The rag-and-bone man at scene one was probably the water board man at scene two – though he had yet to fill the team in on that one – which could mean that the man might have a number of different vehicles.

He turned his attention to Thornton and Anderson.

"How did you get on with Elizabeth Holmes?"

"Very well, sir," said Anderson.

"Yes," said Thornton, smiling, "she certainly knows that the way to a man's heart is through his stomach."

Gardener rolled his eyes, he knew what was coming.

"Are you trying to wind me up?" said Reilly.

"As if," replied Thornton.

"But those scones were to die for," said Anderson. "So soft, so crumbly."

"So delicious. With jam and fresh cream," said Thornton.

"And do you know something?" said Anderson. "She made us have two each. We were near stuffed."

Reilly glanced at Gardener. "Tell 'em, boss, they didn't go there for scones," he said scowling at Anderson.

Gardener noticed even Briggs was laughing. Anderson jumped up and passed a brown paper bag to Reilly.

"Calm your passions, my friend, I said we wouldn't forget you."

Reilly's face beamed as he dipped into the bag.

"I don't care what they say about you, I keep telling 'em, they're all wrong."

"Can we get back to the meeting now?" asked Gardener.

Anderson returned to his seat and told them what Elizabeth Holmes had said, which was very unsettling.

"What she said was," continued Anderson, "a clergyman came to the school for the girl, but he never mentioned a convent. He said Debra was going to family in Ireland, and he had papers to prove it."

"According to Holmes," said Thornton, "they looked pretty genuine. His story checked out. He took Debra but she was never seen again."

"I don't suppose she had a copy of the papers?" asked Gardener.

"No," said Anderson, who then produced the school year photo for the whiteboard.

"Have you made any headway trying to locate a copy of the papers?" Gardener asked, though he figured that would be a needle in a haystack.

"No, not yet," said Anderson. "We've been through the proper channels. The local council and the social services are on it."

"Doubt it will give us much," said Gardener, "but I'd still like to see them. I think when we finally uncover this lot, we're going to discover a grave miscarriage of justice where missing girls are concerned."

"Girls?" asked Thornton. "Do you mean there is another?"

"I'll come back to that," said Gardener, eager to continue with the current discussion.

Anderson said that he and Thornton had made a list of the local convents anyway; there was always a chance that she *might* have gone into one. There were three in Armley, none of which had a record of a Debra Gosforth being there. There were others to check but it still remained a big task with possibly nothing positive to be gained.

"What about this so-called clergyman, Jeremy Cleeves?" Gardener asked.

"Another big job," said Anderson. "Not sure where to start but we will be on it first thing in the morning. There must be a register somewhere. Maybe the papers Cleeves carried with him were false, and the family in Ireland didn't exist."

"Which then begs the question, what *did* happen to the girl?" asked Gardener.

"Could be anything," said Gates. "There was every chance that human trafficking could have been going on then."

Longstaff nodded. "But probably in much smaller numbers."

"I think we need to give as much priority to the missing girls as we do to the victims that are turning up," Gardener added.

He glanced at the whiteboard, and the photos of the body they had found earlier in the day on Joe Proctor's land.

"So," said Gardener, "we have a second body, and some more clues: the MO is exactly the same but for the polythene, suggesting the same person is responsible, and the clues they have left also take the same format."

He briefly explained the condition of the body and everything they had found at the scene before moving over to a table where he had a manila folder with Fitz's findings. He emptied out the contents onto the desk. As before, there were two laminated pieces of paper and a chess piece.

"From what Fitz says, the second body is made up from the following: the torso is male and shows evidence of HIV, which matches the head from body number one, but he's still doing a fast-track DNA test. I have photos here of the latest head." Gardener stared at Anderson and Thornton. "Can you take this to Elizabeth Holmes, please, see if she recognizes it as the man who took Debra Gosforth?"

Gardener then continued. "The arms show evidence of cancer, which matches the previous torso. One of the legs on this body has at some point been broken."

"So it's obviously the same four people," said Sharp. "Maybe the photo of this head will give us a lot more to work on."

"Hopefully," said Rawson.

"Anything on fingerprints?" asked Sharp.

"Nothing as yet," said Gardener.

Gardener then made notes on the whiteboard. However, before pinning the page that resembled a hand-written journal to it, he slipped it into a projector and shone it on the wall so they could all read what it said for the first time.

Name: Lisa Small

DOB: 09/06/71

Description: incredibly tall and gangly for her age, reaching almost six feet. Despite having an eating disorder, she had a very pleasant nature but was a timid individual. She had fair hair cut quite short and severe, but the most beautiful piercing brown eyes.

Background: Lisa was born and bred in Bromley, Greater London. Both parents passed when she was only two years old. Her mother had leukaemia; her father had thyroid problems, which eventually caused a blood disorder. The only family that Lisa had was an aunt called Marion, living in Guiseley. Her aunt had never married and appeared to be the spinster type. She had a number of cleaning jobs and worked for a number of charities. Marion asked if Lisa could be taken into care six months after she took over her welfare. She knew nothing about children and could not cope with her eating disorder and constant hospital attention.

Date Missing: 21/02/85

"As you can see," said Gardener, "we now have the name of another child, and the same thing appears to have happened again. Lisa Small had no family to speak of when she tragically lost both parents."

"We have *something* to go on," said Paul Benson, "we need to check out whoever this Marion woman from Guiseley is and see if she's still alive."

"There must be someone who remembers her if she was a cleaner and worked for a number of charities," offered Edwards.

"It's always possible," said Briggs, "but just look at the dates and see what kind of a tall order we have here. Small was born in '71. If she lost her parents when she was two, that made it '73. At two and a half she was taken into care, wherever that might have been, and went missing in '85. Whoever this Marion is, she would have been in her twenties or thirties for her to have been any kind of age to look after a child, and that could make her in her seventies or eighties now."

"Which means she could have passed on herself," said Gardener.

"Or she may not be of sound mind, and be in a nursing home," said Thornton.

"It's another needle in a haystack," said Gardener, "but we need to follow it up. Especially if she *was* taken into care. There must be a record somewhere. The big question now is, do we have a child abduction ring involving the church or the schools or the social services?"

"Jesus," said Briggs. "If the church is involved, there's no saying we'll get anywhere. You know what them lot are like for closing ranks."

Gardener nodded. "I know. But it still has to be investigated. And it's on my watch, and I for one will not allow the church to pull rank."

"Good on you, Stewart," said Briggs, "and I'll back you all the way but be prepared for a rough ride."

"Does the killer have a personal connection to any of them?" asked Patrick Edwards.

"In what way, Patrick?"

"I was just wondering whether or not he or she might have been one of the children that was abused in some way and managed to survive it all?"

"It's a very good point," said Gardener. "It's possible that when we start piecing it all together, we may find your theory is correct."

"It's almost a certainty that the bodies turning up today have something to do with it all," said Colin Sharp.

"I think that's a given," said Gardener, "that they were all involved in whatever happened to the children. But they're not all clergy."

"They're not?" questioned Rawson. "Does that mean you've found out something?"

"Yes," said Gardener, "but I'll come back to that. I want to move on to the chess piece." It was in a clear evidence bag. "This one is the knight, or the horse, so if we can have someone looking into that, we may find it's a vital clue."

"Or another red herring," said Reilly. "It might be worth seeing if there are any local chess clubs, check them out."

Gardener nodded. "Good point."

He placed the bag on the table. No point dwelling any further on that one. He figured the cryptic puzzle was going to prove far more interesting. He placed it in the overhead projector.

> *The king is in his counting house — at last!*
>
> *Well done, Detective. Legally, a guardian is your advocate for the next one. 1985 was a good year for the news, so trot along, and keep an eye out for hawthorns. As opposed to being a thorn in your side, the little shrub will help you enormously.*

"'The king is in his counting house — at last'."

"I know what that comes from," said Anderson. "I've read it to my grandkids enough times. It's a well-known nursery rhyme, *Sing a Song of Sixpence*."

Gardener picked up on it. "A nursery rhyme again. The last one was Mother Hubbard, which we felt suggested the torso might belong to someone called Hubbard, but it was also the name the killer had used for him or herself. Do you know all of it, Bob?"

"No, I've only read it a couple of times."

"Okay," said Gardener, "might be something, might be nothing, but I'd like someone on it. Check out the rhyme for hidden meanings, or is it something that simply fits in with the killer?"

Gardener turned to the board and made notes before addressing the team again.

"However, Sean and I believe it is referring to something else, and I'll come back to that because I want to press on with other things connected to what we're hearing and seeing at the moment, namely the puzzle, or the personal note, because that's what I feel it is this time."

Gardener read the first sentence. "Well done, Detective." He turned to the team. "He or she is praising us here for a job well done. We've followed the clues, we've found the body." Gardener pointed to the next sentence. "Legally, a guardian is your advocate for the next one. What do they mean by that?"

"Well," said Longstaff, "an advocate is someone who speaks in favour of you, aren't they?"

"Yes," said Gates, "but they're also someone who pleads on behalf of another, especially in a lawcourt."

Another reference to what Gerry Drake had told them, thought Gardener.

"Yes, but look at the next bit," said Thornton. "A guardian. In other words, a protector, or a keeper."

"A guardian is also someone who had legal custody over someone who is incapable of managing their own affairs," said Briggs.

"Once again," said Gardener, "all of this points to either members of the church—"

"Or members of the bar," said Reilly, "lawyers, solicitors."

"It could mean something else," said Rawson.

"Go on," said Gardener.

"1985 was a good year for the news, it says. Is the killer referring to the newspaper, *The Guardian*?"

"That's interesting," said Sharp. "Maybe we should speak to them, see if they can find any old microfiche from that year and see if anything sticks out."

"That'll be my eyes if we have to look through that lot," said Rawson.

Sharp sighed and nodded, "I didn't say it would be easy."

"Good points made there, gentlemen," said Gardener. "Another action for tomorrow."

He also knew that 'trot along' was another big clue, something that he needed to share with them soon.

"And what's that supposed to mean?" asked Longstaff. "'Keep an eye out for hawthorns. As opposed to being a thorn in your side, the little shrub will help you enormously.'"

"Might mean we'll find the next body in a patch of grassland," said Gates.

"Christ!" said Edwards. "Another crap job, who the hell do you talk to if you want to find out where all the patches of shrub land are in Yorkshire?"

"It's funny you should ask that, Patrick," said Gardener.

"Oh, don't tell me," replied Edwards. "I'm about to try and find the answer to my own question."

"That's what we like about you, son," said Reilly. "You catch on pretty fast."

"There's something else we need to check out," said Gardener. "Sean and I spoke to a man called Trevor Walker at the scene of the lock-up in the field. He said a 4x4 was parked at the side of the road, with a small tent, and some road works set up on the road in front of the field. Proctor's wife backed that up, but no one actually saw anyone doing any work. Walker thinks the vehicle was connected to the water board."

Gardener checked the notes that had been made, giving the team the description of the water board man that Trevor Walker had described.

"Interesting," said Anderson. "The rag-and-bone man was well-built but didn't walk with a limp."

"He was probably putting it on," said Rawson. "It's obviously the same bloke."

"I don't doubt that," said Reilly. "Question is, is he the killer? Or is he the man with the muscle?"

"Either way," said Sharp, "it sounds like he's in on it, so we need to find him."

"I agree," said Gardener. "I don't think there is any CCTV in that area, but I'd like someone to pull off a list of the CCTV cameras within a ten-mile radius, ANPR cameras as well. Go through them. It won't be easy and I'm not expecting a result tomorrow, but we need to check the 4x4s, cross-reference any that come up on both and try and locate them."

The team made notes and Gardener was determined to have a word with Briggs to see if any more operational support officers could be found. The budget would go through the roof but that sometimes happened. It didn't mean you could cut corners.

Gardener turned and filled them in on what else they had discovered in the lock-up on the farmland that belonged to Joe Proctor – apart from the body.

"You found those chemical drums in his lock-up?" Briggs asked.

Gardener nodded. "But to be fair, they looked as old as the hills, and not much like the stuff he kept under lock and key."

"Maybe not," said Briggs, "but it's an easy enough job to pour new chemical into old bins. What did he have to say about all this?"

"He appeared shocked."

Gardener went on to tell them what Proctor had told them, especially about the ninety-nine-year lease.

"Ninety-nine years," said Anderson.

"And he knows nothing about it?" asked Thornton.

"I wouldn't say he knows nothing about it," said Gardener. "He knew about the lease but what he said was, it was before his time, so he didn't really know the ins and outs."

"But he's quite happy to take the money by the sound of it," said Rawson.

"We need to check out the chemicals found on Joe Proctor's land," said Gardener. "We've come across this stuff before and even though this may not be important, or be linked to Joe Proctor, I need someone looking into it. Methanothorox would almost certainly require a DEFRA number to be given to the retailer on purchase –

they've been doing that forever. I know all this could be some time back but I'd like to trace who bought it, where and when? We need to know who knew the chemicals were in the lock-up? When was it stored? What specialist equipment or knowledge would you need to handle it?"

Briggs nodded before asking, "Who is the lock-up registered to, officially?"

"MCC Holdings. They're on Thorp Arch Trading Estate and the name connected to all of this is Richard Monarch."

"We checked that out, sir," said Benson, "when you called us. There's nothing doing. There is not, and never has been, an MCC Holdings on that estate."

"We never thought there would be," said Gardener.

"Someone is well ahead of us," said Reilly.

"This has been well planned to the last detail and we're going to have our work cut out," said Gardener. "However, the name Richard Monarch has come up twice in this investigation."

The team mysteriously glanced at each other. He knew they had not heard the name before.

"We had a visit earlier today from a man called Gerry Drake. He recognized the photo of the head we sent to the papers."

"And he said it was someone called Richard Monarch?" asked Sharp.

"Yes," said Gardener, he then recanted what Drake had told them about the dodgy accountant and his dodgy lawyer friend.

Gardener continued, pointing to the message the killer had written. "'The king is in his counting house – at last.' The head belongs to Richard Monarch and he was an accountant."

"That could be why we had numbers as a clue," said Longstaff.

"Indicating something you've been saying all along, Stewart," said Briggs. "Whoever is behind all this has really done their homework."

"It's also someone who has harboured a grudge for a very long time," said Gates.

"Very likely," said Gardener. "The way I am reading all of this is, some girls have disappeared in the Eighties, our killer knows who they were, possibly even where they went, and certainly knows who took them. So now they've decided to unload everything."

"And the fact that they're frozen might suggest that they were all killed a long time ago," said Rawson.

"True," said Gardener. "He probably killed them all years ago, and it's very unlikely he did anything after that killing spree. It's not likely he's still killing people."

"But why wait this long?" asked Reilly.

Gardener sighed. "There's no way of answering that one unless we find this person, but I suspect when the job is finished and they've said what they need to, they're going to disappear."

"Unless there are others connected to this that we don't know about yet," said Reilly. "They might well have left other victims until now, for some strange reason."

Briggs rubbed his hands down his face. "This is a nightmare."

"And according to what Gerry Drake has been saying, the next person we're likely to find, whose body parts we may be able to identify, might be the dodgy lawyer, and possible partner to Monarch." Gardener pointed to the board. "Look at the verse. Drake wasn't sure about the name earlier. He said it was short, something like Shot, or Trot. But the clue here says, trot along. That's good enough for me. We need to be looking for a lawyer called Trot, who had offices in Street Lane.

"So," continued Gardener. "What we need to do now is try to find the office, see what it is now and who owns it."

"Find out if anyone from Monarch's company actually still works there," said Reilly. "That would be a massive bonus."

"If not," said Gardener, "we need to trace those that might have worked there at the time. Is there a name from the past that someone can give us, in the hope that they are still alive?"

"And who else were they in league with?" asked Briggs. "If we can find that out, then maybe we'll discover the identity of all four bodies."

"Still might not help us with who's killed them all," said Reilly.

"We also need to try and find the identity of the mysterious priest," said Gardener.

"I'll lay odds he's one of them four," said Longstaff, pointing to the pictures of the Frankenstein creation on the whiteboard.

Gardener nodded, glancing at his watch. He was eager to wrap things up for the night. They had been in the room nearly two hours.

"Okay," he said, holding up his fingers to count things off. "Continue checking all names: Richard Monarch, and someone called Trot. Who knows them and what were they up to? Did Trot go missing; is he still alive? Or is he one of this lot?"

"Or is he responsible?" asked Reilly.

"Good point," said Gardener, continuing. "Who did Monarch and Trot mix with? We will need to check police records and convictions for those two names. We need more information about Debra Gosforth, and now Lisa Small. We can continue to check out convents but it's unlikely that any of the children actually ended up in there. It's my bet that was a cover story – so what did happen to them? Maybe the police records will show us something.

"More detail is needed on the rag-and-bone man, and the water board man, who are probably one and the same. Butchers may still have to be considered because of the rough stitching, but that's a very difficult, not to mention awkward task: it's not as if we can simply ask to check the contents of the freezer."

"Give that task to Reilly," said Rawson. "He'll have a wail of a time confiscating everything in their freezers for his own."

Most of the team found that funny, even Reilly himself.

Eventually, when the mood had calmed, Briggs spoke.

"The worst of all this, is that when we do identify the four victims from the past, we can't actually do anything about it. They're already dead."

"I know what you're saying, sir," said Gardener, "but I don't actually think that is the worst of it."

"What is?" asked Rawson.

"What in God's name happened to these children? And the chances are, we can't do anything about that either."

Chapter Twenty-eight

Given his age, Edward Winstanley still cut a fine figure of a man. Slim, standing a little over six feet tall, he walked with a straight back and without the use of a cane. He had a good head of silver hair and dressed well because he had the money. He ate well for the same reason: enjoying very rich foods, including oily fish like mackerel and kippers. He never turned his nose up at an after-dinner brandy or port, or both in the same glass. He was prone to a touch of gout and did not suffer fools.

At the moment, none of that mattered. His wealth and his health were not going to save him from his fate, whatever the hell that was. As an ex-police superintendent, he'd seen off plenty like the man who was taking liberties with him now.

Winstanley glanced around his prison once more, unable to work out where he was. He knew it was winter, and the roof of what appeared to be an abandoned building was leaking. He was trapped in a cage, about the size of a shipping container, with a chair, a table, a bed and two blankets.

Throughout the time he'd been here he'd had to endure watching his captor construct a huge wooden frame, and wire up an electric circuit, all of which he figured was probably for his benefit.

That was not comforting.

Quite what was going to happen he had no idea, because whoever had him had barely spoken two words since he had been taken during a pleasant walk home in Ilkley. He remembered the deserted country lane: no people, no cars. A van drew up in front of him and the next thing he knew he was inside it, unable to shout because of the gag, unable to see because of the blindfold, and unable to move because of the ropes.

He'd worked out roughly how long it had taken to arrive at their destination, which was around thirty minutes, but he had no idea whether it was north, south, east, or west. He'd been dumped unceremoniously into a cage inside a building that was some size, and from what he had been able to ascertain, was very likely an old church, one that had long been forgotten, which could literally have been anywhere. The walls were crumbling. Most of the windows had been smashed. A few pews remained but you couldn't sit on them.

A door opened at the far end of the building and his captor stepped through it. He had a carrier bag with him. He walked across the rubbled area without a care in the world. But when you were his size there was probably very little that bothered you. He was dressed in jeans and a T-shirt and his head was completely covered by a balaclava, which was why Winstanley had no idea who he was dealing with – although there was some familiarity about his manner.

When he reached the cage he unlocked the door and slipped inside. He emptied the contents of the carrier bag on to the table: sandwiches, fruit, small buns and some iced coffee. They were not really to Winstanley's liking but beggars couldn't be choosers. At least they weren't cheap.

"Who the hell *are* you?" asked Winstanley.

He wasn't shackled or bound to anything but there was little point in him trying anything physical with the man. He wouldn't stand a chance. During the times he'd been alone he'd tried shouting, but no one responded. Perhaps it was somewhere remote and deserted.

"You'll find out soon enough."

"Have we met?"

The man nodded. "A long time ago. Whether you'd recognize me or not is immaterial, I certainly know who you are and what you were up to all those years ago."

"Up to? All those years ago?" repeated Winstanley. "What the hell are you on about, what am I supposed to have done?"

"Don't make me laugh. Conveniently forgotten your past, have you?" He snorted. "Mind you, forgetting what you did would be rather convenient, wouldn't it?"

"You obviously know what I used to do for a living?"

"Of course I know. Otherwise you wouldn't be here."

"So you know what I'm capable of."

"I thought it was just your memory that wasn't what it used to be. I didn't know you were delusional."

"Meaning what?"

"You're eighty-five years old, man, you're not capable of anything. And in case it's escaped your attention, it's *me* that's holding *you*. You have no access to the outside world. No one knows you're here. So seeing as we have time on our hands, I'll tell you exactly what *I* know, what you *should* know. Are you sitting comfortably?"

"Would it matter if I wasn't?"

"Not really."

The man sat down opposite and folded his arms.

"Help yourself to the food. Do The Black Angels mean anything to you?"

"The Black what?"

"I thought as much. I'm not going to beat about the bush here, I'll give it to you straight so you can understand where I'm coming from and why I feel like I do."

Winstanley removed the lid from the coffee and took a sip.

"They were powerful people, the diocese; and they were twisted, evil individuals. They called themselves The Black Angels, which gives you an idea of how bad they were. The ringleaders were a bishop – the Bishop of Leeds, no less, and a mother superior."

Winstanley stopped drinking the coffee.

The man continued. "Do you know what these people were doing? Stupid question that, I suppose. You know damned well that they were sacrificing young nuns."

"Sacrificing?" questioned Winstanley.

"Don't be stupid, man. You're the delusional one. Bishops and Mother Superiors didn't do things like that. How the hell would they get away with something like that? The families of the girls would be all over the case, not to mention the police."

"You'd have thought so, wouldn't you? But for your information, these people were very clever and they hid it very well. The young nuns were orphans, no families; no one who cared. So what would it matter if they went missing?"

"Is that what this is all about?" asked Winstanley. "You're trying to besmirch the good names of people who did God's work?"

"I'd hardly call it God's work. Over a three-month period, three nuns went missing from their convent. The fourth, Isabella Moorcroft, had actually discovered their little secret, because the other three were her friends. Fearing for her life, Isabella decided she somehow needed to leave. She felt she had to speak out, and the only people she could speak to were the police. Still with me?"

Winstanley did not reply, but his memory bank was working overtime.

"When the Bishop became the victim of a vicious assault, a newly promoted detective sergeant, and his constable, were sent to the convent by their superior officer, to investigate what seemed to be a random attack on the Bishop. Isabella suspected it would be the perfect opportunity. You must remember that, Edward."

Winstanley did, vaguely. "How do you know all this?"

The man continued without answering. "That detective sergeant was approached by Isabella Moorcroft and informed of the situation regarding the three missing nuns."

It was coming back in bite-sized chunks, and for the first time since Winstanley had been held captive, a grain of concern was creeping in.

Fearing for his life, when given the opportunity, Winstanley explained what he remembered of the situation.

"The newly promoted sergeant was a man called Robert Blanchard. He did bring the matter up with his superior officer," he said.

"Who then took it to you, Superintendent Winstanley, who informed him that it was highly unlikely that any of Isabella's claims were true," said the masked man.

Winstanley continued explaining that she was probably bored, and most likely inventing stuff to relieve her boredom and her loneliness now that her friends had moved on. A bishop being attacked did not prove anything, especially if they could not find who was responsible. At that point, no evidence had been brought to the table. The Bishop claimed there was no attack, and that he merely fell down some stairs after a little drink.

The official story from the diocese on the girls was that they had been transferred to other convents around the UK, and they had the relevant paperwork to prove it.

However, Blanchard wasn't so sure. Winstanley remembered finding out that he had spent his own time investigating it privately. Eddie Perrin, Blanchard's constable, had informed the inspector that Blanchard had written everything down in a journal and had returned to speak with the Bishop and the Mother Superior to *check* all of those facts, before submitting his final report.

But having spoken to the diocese, Blanchard suddenly failed to report for duty later that day and was never seen again. The subsequent investigation to trace his final movements drew a blank and the journal in question had never been seen by anyone, bringing its existence into doubt.

"Finally," said the man in the balaclava, "you've admitted your guilt."

"Guilt?" shouted Winstanley. "What guilt? All I did was my job."

"Rubbish. You did nothing. You lifted not one finger to help us. That's the reason you're here. Because you claimed you could find no evidence pointing to the diocese of their supposed guilt – the disappearance of the nuns, and the police sergeant. You let everyone accused walk free because a bent lawyer had done a perfect job. He probably had you in his pocket. You are as much to blame as the diocese, and you should be punished accordingly."

Winstanley didn't like the sound of the phrase 'punished accordingly'.

"Like I asked earlier, how do you know all of this? Most of that information is classified, how could you know? Unless…"

"Got you thinking now, haven't I? You're actually starting to wonder just what, if anything, happened to Robert Blanchard. *Did* he go missing? Or is he still out there somewhere, claiming justice?"

"Justice?"

"Come on, man, you're not stupid. You must have read newspapers around the time. Didn't you start to wonder where they all went to?"

"If I'd thought there was any evidence to substantiate your claims, they'd have all been locked up."

"Unless, like I said, they had you in their pockets."

Winstanley didn't comment.

"Closer to the truth, maybe? Well, let me tell you, The Black Angels did disappear. I took them. Like I did with you, I patiently waited and abducted them at the right moment. Once I had them holed up, like you, I questioned them – thoroughly. I'll give them credit where it's due, none of them opened their mouths apart from one. The fat accountant, Richard Monarch, he spilled the beans about what was going down. Pretty much told me everything. That's how I know so much, old man."

Winstanley flinched, aware of what might possibly be in store for him.

"You won't get away with this, you know. I'm a retired police inspector, my colleagues will find me."

"Of course they will, they're coppers. Thing you have to worry about is, in what state will they find you?"

"What do you mean?"

"Alive, dead or worse?"

"Alive would be preferable, what's worse than dead?"

"Somewhere in between, wishing you were dead."

The smooth way in which that sentence had been delivered, frightened the life out of Winstanley – the silky voice, the calm manner; the underlying threat.

"Why won't you tell me who are you?"

"You work it out."

The man finally turned and left the cage without any further comment.

Chapter Twenty-nine

Patterson pulled his car onto the drive, killed the lights, switched off the engine, and simply sat there for a few minutes, thinking, working things out. His head was spinning. Everything was a mess. Decisions had to be made. If only it was that easy.

Finally, he jumped out of the car, locked it, walked down the drive to the house and let himself in through the front door.

As he closed it, a voice echoed in the empty hallway, causing him to flinch.

"It's past sodding midnight, where the hell have *you* been?" asked Paula, his wife, in a Lancashire accent that said she wanted no nonsense.

He turned. Paula was medium height, slim, brown hair in a bob, with large tortoiseshell glasses. Her face was granite-hard but fraught with worry. The lines under her eyes appeared to have deepened more recently. Despite what he felt for her he was in no mood for an argument.

"Out," he replied.

"Where?"

"Does it matter? I couldn't sleep."

"Who with? It certainly isn't me anymore."

"Give me a break," shouted Patterson.

"Keep your voice down," shouted Paula. "You'll wake the kids."

"You keep yours down, then, and leave me alone. I've got enough on my mind without you adding to it."

Patterson pushed past her and stormed up the stairs.

Chapter Thirty

Gates and Longstaff were sitting in front of a computer terminal when Gardener and Reilly entered their office.

"What have you found?" asked Gardener.

"We're not sure yet," replied Gates.

"But if it's what we're thinking," said Longstaff, "we might be on to something."

Spotting two cups, and a saucer full of chocolate bars, Reilly reached down and grabbed a Kit Kat.

Gardener glanced at his watch. "Doesn't Laura feed you at home?"

"Breakfast was ages ago. Man needs to keep fuelled up for the day ahead."

"The amount of fuel you take on board should get you from here to New Zealand."

"You're only jealous."

"Probably," replied Gardener, turning his attention to Gates and Longstaff. "Okay, what do you *think* you have?"

"We've been concentrating on the message from the second scene," said Gates.

"The keyword is obviously 'hawthorns'," said Longstaff. "The first thing we did was speak to the County Clerk's office, who has public records of property, deeds and other useful information when searching for a property owner."

"We also tried a title company at the County Clerk's suggestion," said Gates. "Title companies can research property deeds and perform title searches. They can find you the owner of a property, and a title search will check for any issues with the property."

"What we really wanted was a list of all the houses in the area that had a house name containing the word hawthorn," said Longstaff.

"Good thinking," said Gardener.

"So we had to eventually speak to the land registry. They gave us access to a very helpful site."

"And bingo," said Gates, holding out a sheet of paper for Gardener. She pointed to a house that was number 60 on the list.

Gardener's skin prickled. Gates was pointing to an address on the A653 Dewsbury Road; more specifically, an unmarked road near Topcliffe Grange Farm Road, where the road bore a sharp right.

"The area that the house stands on belongs to Proctor's Farm," said Gates, "and it's called Hawthorn House, and it's the only house in this area with that name."

"If you think about the previous two properties where we found a body," said Longstaff, "the killer is obviously keeping everything local, and this is well within the parameters."

Gardener sat down. "Have you tried to make contact with the owners of the property, or the people that live there?"

"We looked for a phone number," said Gates, "but there isn't one."

"Unlisted?" asked Reilly.

"No," said Longstaff, "just no number."

"But this is where it gets really interesting. We did a Google Earth and a Street View search," said Gates. "If we're not mistaken, this property looks derelict, unused for years."

"Which would be perfect for whoever is doing this," said Reilly.

"That's just the point, though, Sean. Who *is* doing it? Proctor?"

"Or someone who has it in for him?" suggested Reilly.

"It would have to be someone close: someone who knows him," offered Gates.

"Could be the son," offered Reilly.

"You mentioned that this was where it got interesting," said Gardener. "How interesting: what else have you uncovered?"

"That the house belonged to a couple called George and Emily Strange, who bought it during the war," said Longstaff, "with family money from what we can gather. For some reason they turned it into a kind of halfway house for children who were being adopted. The children stayed with the couple until they moved on. George died in 1988, and Emily passed away in 1992."

"And it's been empty since then?" asked Reilly.

"Yes," said Gates, "when it was sold to Proctor, but someone has been leasing it since that point, just hasn't done anything with it."

Gardener's stomach lurched. "Who?"

"A lawyer by the name of Mark Trot, and his listed address is a place called Atlas Transport, somewhere in Birmingham," said Longstaff.

"And you're going to tell me it doesn't exist," said Gardener.

Gates nodded.

"What the hell is going on here?" asked Reilly. "We have a shop belonging to someone called Hubbard, a lock-up belonging to someone called Monarch, and now a house being leased to someone called Trot, all of whom appear to be dead."

"There's only one way to find out, let's just get over there," said Gardener. "I don't want to forewarn Proctor by calling him. After all, there might not be anything there."

"But if there is?" asked Reilly.

"Then it's a different ball game," said Gardener. "Okay, same as last time; two cars. Good work, you two."

It took them a little over thirty minutes to reach the house in question, which they found very easily. Reilly and Gates parked the cars respectively and jumped out.

Gardener surveyed the area. The house was large, possibly four bedrooms, and as Gates and Longstaff had said, in a state of dereliction. It was so bad that Gardener reckoned a strong wind would probably bring it down. Most of the roof was missing, and all the windows were smashed. There were holes in the walls.

The grounds in which it stood were jungle-like. Everything was overgrown, and as a result the house could not really be seen from the road. A small drive led to the building, which once had gates but only the two stone pillars remained. As Gardener approached the property, a large iron gate with no lock stood in place of a front door. Grey clouds floated overhead, and it was spitting with rain. Daunting and gloomy was how Gardener would describe it; perfect for a murder.

He turned to Reilly. "Why would Joe Proctor have a place like this on his land and not make more of it?"

"The same could be said for the lock-up. I'd guess the house is on a ninety-nine-year lease as well," said Reilly.

"Could be another property he knows nothing about," said Gardener. "What was his father up to?"

"Maybe he was desperately short of money and this was the only way to save the farm," said Reilly.

"Possibly," said Gardener. He turned to face the property. "Shall we go inside?"

"What, without a health and safety risk assessment?" asked Reilly.

"When has that ever bothered you?"

"Fair point," said Reilly, "and there's no need to bother Proctor here. I think we have enough grounds to suspect it's a crime scene."

"And that we may be able to save a life?"

"Yeah, right," said Gates, behind them.

Longstaff came from around the other side of the building. "There's no back door on the place, just a frame, but I never went inside the property."

Gardener put on a pair of gloves and some shoe covers and gingerly opened the iron gate, stepping inside. He didn't need to worry about contaminating the crime scene because he didn't need to go any further.

He glanced upwards, feeling even less happy about being inside. The place was a complete mess, rubble all over, on the ground, stacked against walls, which had more holes, and big craters in the floors. Most of the interior doors were missing. By far, the most disturbing aspect to the building's safety was the fact that the ceiling was actually missing, allowing them a view straight up to the roof.

Hanging from one of the beams in the rafters, dropping below what would be the ground floor ceiling, was a naked corpse. As they had now come to expect, it was made up from four different bodies. The heavy stitching was unsightly; the skin was highly discoloured with purple and black bruises, shrivelled up like a dried prune. The smell was indescribable, but blocked drains would go someway to being close.

Gardener turned. Gates and Longstaff were still standing outside.

"I guess we were right about the third scene," said Gates. "I can smell that from here."

"But that's not why we're staying out here," said Longstaff, smiling. "We just don't want to contaminate the crime scene, sir."

"You're all heart," said Reilly. He turned to Gardener. "Are we about done here?"

Gardener nodded. "Call the team and everyone else we need: PolSA, SOCOs, Fitz. This is beginning to feel like *Groundhog Day*."

Both officers stepped outside and back towards their cars. As they did so, another dog walker approached them.

She was female, middle-aged, with straight blonde hair and blue eyes. She was dressed in a waxed jacket, jeans and Wellingtons. Gardener glanced down; the black dog also had a coat on. He tipped his hat but didn't actually say anything.

"Is he finally selling, or tearing it down?" the woman asked.

"Who?" Gardener asked.

"Joe Proctor, it's his place, isn't it?"

"We're not sure, Mrs?" Gardener inquired, flashing his warrant card and introducing himself.

"Jenkins, Vera Jenkins. If you lot are police, I guess it's something more serious."

Reilly finished on the phone and joined his superior officer.

"You could say that, Mrs Jenkins."

"Only I saw health and safety here yesterday."

That drew Gardener's attention. "How did you know it was health and safety?"

"Well, to be honest, I just guessed. The gentleman never actually said that. He had a clipboard and a small voice recorder."

"Did you speak to him?" Reilly asked.

"Briefly," Vera Jenkins replied. "We managed a few words."

"What did he say?" Gardener asked.

"We talked about the house and the fact that it stands in the way of a piece of land that a transport company wishes to buy."

"He said that?" asked Reilly.

"Yes."

"Did he mention which transport company?" asked Gardener, curiously.

"No, sorry. We then got sidetracked with dogs. He patted mine, saying he had a similar breed at home. But he never really said much more than that. He was most pleasant when he asked if I would excuse him whilst he continued with his report."

Reilly made notes in his pad.

"Can you tell me what he looked like, please, Mrs Jenkins?" asked Gardener.

"Pretty tall," she replied. "About as tall as you; approximately six feet, with short ginger hair and moustache."

"Can you remember what he was wearing?"

"A fluorescent jacket over a sweatshirt and black jeans; black polished shoes and a hard hat. As I mentioned, he had a clipboard and a voice recorder, and a pen in one hand."

"You're doing really well, Mrs Jenkins," said Gardener.

"Better than most people we speak to," said Reilly.

"Anything else?" asked Gardener. By now Gates and Longstaff had joined them.

"He wore a wedding ring. He was well-built, a big bloke, looked as if he trained with weights. And something else, he had a high-pitched voice, which didn't suit his image."

Gardener smiled. "Did you see a car or a van?"

She thought for a moment. "Come to think of it, no."

"You've been a great help, Mrs Jenkins, if you could just give your name and address to one of my team here," said Gardener, pointing to Gates and Longstaff, "we'll send someone round to take a formal statement."

As Vera Jenkins was about to speak again, she was interrupted by sirens: police cars with flashing blue lights, two Transit vans, and an ambulance.

She turned to Gardener. "Bloody hell, what's going on?"

"I'm sorry, Mrs Jenkins, but I need to speak to my team. But thank you so much for your help."

Gardener tipped his hat again as he left.

He gave out the usual immediate actions to his team: house-to-house – though there weren't many around –

speak to everyone in the area, check out any CCTV. To PolSA and SOCOs he wanted the place checking with a fine-tooth comb and in particular he wanted to know if they came across any methanothorox. As he was talking to them, the Home Office pathologist arrived.

On exiting the car, he glanced at Gardener. "Number three?"

"Afraid so," he replied.

"Not hanging about, is he?" said Fitz, disappearing in the direction of the derelict building.

"Third different description," said Reilly, "of probably the same man. The physical build isn't something he can disguise."

"He's not really bothered, is he?" said Gardener. "So long as he can look and sound different. There is one thing, Sean, I don't think we're looking for a woman anymore."

"Not as far as the heavy work is concerned, no," said Reilly. "But there could still be a woman involved. So, what now?"

"We go and arrest Joe Proctor."

Chapter Thirty-one

Having arrested Joe Proctor, section 32 of PACE kicked in for Gardener, allowing immediate power to search the arrestee, the area where he was, and the area where he'd recently been. The barn and the house came into play, and anything Gardener found could be used in evidence.

He'd checked the satnav in Proctor's vehicle, which confirmed he was nowhere near the crime scenes on the days in question, but Gardener didn't put a lot of faith in that because the farmer wouldn't have needed it if he was travelling locally. Proctor had not been anywhere out of town recently, his last visit was to Thornton le Dale some four months back to the garage where *Bangers & Cash* is filmed.

One of the things Gardener was keen to discover was who had access to both remote buildings. Gates and Longstaff suggested that Google Earth might help, as they had very detailed overhead pictures of the world. They could probably zoom in on the barn, and any cars parked nearby, perhaps catch people walking to or from.

Gates thought asking Google to share images in the past may also help. Longstaff thought it was a good idea; Google passed over Britain nearly every year. The RAF took photos for Ordnance Survey on a regular basis. If someone tried hard enough, they would be able to bring up fifty or sixty years' worth of pictures of the barn and the house to see how they had changed, and who might be around them. Gardener said it was a hell of a slog for some poor DC but if they were up for it, he didn't want to dampen their enthusiasm.

It was approaching early evening before the detectives had an opportunity to interview Joe Proctor. It had taken time to make a search of Proctor's house, a further search of the barn, and the derelict wreck on Topcliffe Grange Farm Road. Also Proctor's lawyer had not been available straight away.

Gardener and Reilly entered the room and sat down. Gardener placed a manila folder on the table in front of him and immediately started the recording facilities. He once again read Joe Proctor his rights, went through the preliminaries, and introduced everyone in the room. Gardener knew the farmer's lawyer, a man called Alec Ferguson. He was around sixty years of age, had been doing the job all his life, and always dressed in very fashionable suits. He had short silver hair, tortoiseshell glasses and was relatively slim.

"You know why you're here, Mr Proctor?" asked Gardener.

"You've arrested me for murder. I told you on Tuesday I didn't do it."

Proctor did not seem as relaxed as Ferguson but then Gardener never expected he would be.

"We're not referring to the murder on Tuesday."

"Pardon?"

"We have now discovered yet another body on your land."

"What?"

"Your expression tells me it's news to you."

"Well of course it's news to me, unless you think I put it there."

Gardener remained silent.

"You do, don't you?" said Proctor, staring at Ferguson, as if expecting some help.

"Two bodies in four days on your land," said Gardener. "Is there anything you'd like to tell us?"

"Don't you think you ought to tell *us* a bit more, officer?" asked Ferguson.

Gardener outlined the events of the previous two days, to which the lawyer claimed their unauthorized entry to both properties was illegal.

"Hardly," said Reilly.

"You entered them without my client's knowledge or consent."

"We didn't need it, we had just cause," said Reilly. "We may have encountered life in danger."

"It's hardly likely, given the state you're finding the bodies in."

"Maybe not," said Gardener, "but we can't assume anything. The first time we do, and we're too late to save a life we'll have the press and the public all over us."

Proctor chose to answer them, claiming that he knew nothing about the bodies, he did not put them there and he did not know who they were. He also reiterated that he did not *personally* know who leased either of the buildings; only the fields that they stand in are his. He once again repeated – for the benefit of the tape – that it related back to his father and the ninety-nine-year leases, and he didn't know the ins and outs.

"Why?" Gardener asked. "It's your farm."

"It wasn't always my farm," replied Proctor, "and I never signed the leases."

"I know," said Gardener, "your father did. When were they signed?"

"Sometime in the Nineties."

"You don't know for sure?"

Proctor appeared agitated. "I will have done at one time, but it was a long time ago and I can't remember now."

Gardener opened the manila folder and produced copies of both contracts so there could be no mistake. Judging by Ferguson's expression he had not seen them before.

"What was your father up to, leasing off farm buildings?" asked Reilly.

"You'd have to ask his father that question," said Ferguson.

"You know we can't," said Gardener.

"All I can tell you is, the money comes in regular as clockwork. I have no idea why someone would want them for such a period of time, or what they have been used for. Why should I care? If the money stops coming in then I'll have a problem."

"You might not have had a reason to care in the past, but you've got one now," said Reilly.

"Can you remember something that might have happened in the Nineties that made your father sign a mysterious deal?" asked Gardener.

"You don't have to answer that, Joe," said Ferguson.

He chose to. "I'm not really sure," replied Proctor. "The only thing that comes to mind is that my mother suffered some kind of serious illness around that time. Maybe my dad was short of money and this was one way of financing whatever treatment she needed. But I'm guessing."

"What was wrong with her?" asked Reilly.

"I don't know."

"Your own mother was ill, and it needed a lot of money to save her and you don't know what it was?" asked Reilly.

"No. My parents were like that, as most were in those days. They tended to keep things from us that they thought would affect us. The running of the farm was paramount. Most of the time they made out nothing was wrong, and my mother put her aches and pains down to old age."

"Is your mother still alive?" asked Gardener.

"No," said Proctor. "She passed away peacefully in a nursing home about ten years ago."

"And she never offered anything at that point as to what it might have been?"

"No," said Proctor, "I only wish she had."

Gardener felt that that line of questioning would not produce any further results, so he turned his attention more to Joe's father. He knew the logistics surrounding the death of Ken Proctor.

"What do *you* know about your father's death?"

"Is this relevant?" asked Ferguson.

"We won't know until he tells us," said Reilly.

"Pretty much the same as you," said Proctor. "It was a hit and run."

"That's all you know?" asked Reilly. "He was killed in a hit and run in the Nineties, around the time of these contracts being signed, and that's all you know? You don't know who he signed the contract with, why he signed it, or whether his death was anything to do with it: or who killed him?"

"Isn't it your job to find that out?" asked Ferguson. "It's bad enough that my client lost his father in such mysterious circumstances without you raking it all up again. But perhaps if the police had found out who was responsible, we might have saved some time."

Gardener pushed on. "Did he have any enemies that you can think of?"

"None that *I* know about, but he was a farmer. Believe it or not, farmers make enemies for all sorts of reasons."

"But you can't think of any?" asked Gardener. "Did he have many friends socially?"

"Yes, but none that would kill him for anything."

Reilly suddenly lit the blue touch paper.

"Were you involved?"

"That's out of order, Mr Reilly," said Ferguson.

"Just asking," said Reilly. "Farm involved, everything passing to Joe, you never know what folk will do for a bit of power and money."

Gardener appreciated why his partner had said it. He wanted a reaction. Proctor's almost purple faced expression told Gardener what he needed to know – that it was unlikely Joe was involved.

"It has no relevance to what's happening today," claimed Ferguson.

"We don't know that," said Gardener.

Proctor did confess to having a disagreement with his father. He told them all about the argument over farm machinery, and the fact that his father refused to spend any money on stuff, preferring instead to bodge it up: another suggestion that Ken Proctor was desperate for money. The reason for signing the ninety-nine-year leases must definitely have played a part in what was happening today, if only Gardener could figure out the reason.

"Maybe that's why he was killed in a hit and run?" suggested Gardener. "He may have been involved in something that *does* relate back to what's going on here."

"Pure speculation," said Ferguson. "Still your job to prove it, but we're here talking about bodies being found on my client's premises, not what his father got up to, or to speculate as to why he was killed."

"Maybe," replied Gardener, "but if his father wasn't responsible, that means someone else is, and the only person in the frame at the moment *is* your client."

"Then, as I said, you still need to prove it."

"That's what we're trying to do, so where is the fourth body, Joe?" asked Reilly.

Gardener nearly dropped through the floor, whilst both Joe Proctor and Alec Ferguson nearly went through the roof; never a dull moment with the Irishman.

"Don't answer that, Joe," said Ferguson. "It's up to them to find it, and then try to prove your guilt. These two are just fishing, and this one here" – Ferguson pointed to Reilly – "is trying to rattle you. They have nothing on you."

"Apart from the bodies being found on his land," said Gardener, "not to mention a chemical connection."

"All of which could be a set-up," offered Ferguson, "but, as I keep saying, you need to come in here with some real proof. Now, is there anything else, or can we go?"

"Okay," said Gardener, "so let's talk about who might be responsible: have *you* upset anyone recently, Mr Proctor?"

"Not that I can think of."

"Family life okay?" asked Reilly.

"No different to anyone else."

"What does that mean?"

"It means, that in general, we get on fine but like all families we have the odd disagreement."

"How do you get on with your son?" asked Gardener.

"We get on okay."

"Do you have any differences with him like your father had with you?"

"Not enough to kill for."

"You must know your son pretty well," said Gardener. "How likely is it that he may have found out something about his grandfather that you didn't know, that he might have an axe to grind about what happened all those years ago?"

"Ask him," said Proctor. "Neither of us have anything to hide, so feel free to speak to him after me. I'm not doing your dirty work for you."

Gardener didn't quite expect that, so he turned his attention to something else. According to the contracts Gardener had, the derelict house on Joe Proctor's land was leased by a company called Atlas Transport on Thorpe Arch Trading Estate owned by a lawyer by the name of Mark Trot, and the lock-up was leased by a company called MCC Holdings owned by an accountant called Richard Monarch.

Gardener tapped Reilly's foot under the table, which meant they needed to rattle out a succession of rapid-fire questions, some of which may have been covered, others that would be new, in an effort to unseat Proctor to see if he made a mistake or contradicted something he had already said. He started by returning to the buildings.

"Have you ever had any contact with anyone connected to the buildings?"

"No. I've told you, I've never met them personally."

"Do you know anyone called Wendy Hubbard?"

"No, never heard of her," replied Proctor, shaking his head.

Gardener opened the manila folder. He extracted the photos of heads they had and slipped them across the table.

"Do you recognize either of these people?"

After some consideration, Proctor said he didn't.

"Do you know if your father knew them: can you remember if he ever mentioned those names in the contracts?"

"How do I know if he knew them? And he certainly never mentioned them as far as I can remember."

"Did your father never tell you about the deal?" asked Reilly.

"Don't you think I'd have mentioned it if he had? I'm in enough trouble without adding any more."

"So when did you actually find out?" asked Gardener.

Proctor didn't answer immediately, he was obviously thinking about the answer.

"When I took over the farm, not that long after his death."

"Did you try to contact these people then?"

"As a matter of fact, I did," replied Proctor. "Well, my wife did. She takes care of the legal and financial stuff."

"And?"

"As far as I recall, she never found out who any of them actually were, or where they were from, and she never met any of them. I know it's strange, but like I've said, the money kept coming in."

"Who has keys for the locks to the buildings?" asked Gardener.

"I suppose we do, but I thought it was only the leaseholders that had them."

"Bit naive, isn't it?" said Reilly. "You own the land but someone else leases the buildings. You'd think only they had the keys, did you not question why you had them?"

"Not until the other day when you told me there were a new one on the lock-up. So it wouldn't have mattered anyway, would it?"

"And you have no idea who put it there?" asked Gardener.

"No, I didn't know it was there till you told me."

"It wasn't your son?"

"He says not, you were there when he came into the room, he thought it was me."

"When was the last time you were at the lock-up?" asked Gardener.

"Before Tuesday, I can't really remember, it might be as much as a month ago, but I remember talking to Harry Corbett one morning. I were going into Morley and he were going into the field."

"Has anyone else been seen going to and from the field to your knowledge?"

"Only Harry Corbett, and the man you're claiming were from the water board."

"Who pays the electricity and the rates etc?"

"We do, it all comes under the farm, but you've seen the places, it's little more than a standing charge."

"Have you ever noticed anyone visiting the buildings?"

"No, 'cause I'm never there."

"Have you ever used them for anything yourself?"

"No."

"Has your son ever used them for anything?"

Proctor shook his head. "Not to my knowledge."

"Your man with the horses, Corbett," said Reilly, "does he have anything to do with any of those buildings?"

"Again, not to my knowledge."

"You need to ask him, Inspector," said Ferguson.

Gardener continued. "Last time we spoke to you, you said he paid cash but you didn't really know much about him. How did you find each other?"

"He found me," said Proctor, "came up to the house one day and inquired about the place. Said he needed to house a couple of new horses until they had been seen by a vet and treated, and before they could go to his own stables."

"So it's only a temporary arrangement?"

"Seems like it. But that's on the other side of the field, nowhere near the lock-up."

"And you don't know where he lives?"

"No."

"Don't you find that strange?" asked Reilly.

"Not really. Do I need to know? It's temporary, he's paying cash, and he isn't doing any wrong."

"That you know of. You see, none of this is looking good for you, is it, Joe, old son?" said Reilly. "Here you are with a farm, a load of buildings that you know nothing about, but you take money for them, then you do a bit of dodgy dealing with one of your fields for cash. All of this leaves me wondering what else you're up to."

"Like I said, Inspector," added Ferguson, "you need to find evidence for what you're suggesting. My client may be taking a bit of money he's not declaring, but so far, you've presented no evidence of his guilt involving murder. You're going to have to do more than this if you want to keep my client."

Gardener figured Ferguson was right. There were other problems with Proctor that he needed to consider. He genuinely didn't think the farmer was a killer, but that didn't mean he wasn't working with the person responsible. Once again, Gardener could not find a connection between Proctor and the people he had so far identified, other than the buildings they had been found in. Nor could he find any connection to Proctor and the missing girls.

There was also no evidence, as yet, that the methanothorox used on the victims belonged to Proctor, mainly because they were cold cases. There was no CCTV from the old house with the latest victim.

Gardener threw a complete curve ball question in. "Do you play chess, Mr Proctor?"

"What in God's name?" said Ferguson, glancing at the ceiling.

The question appeared to take Proctor by surprise.

"Chess? I've never played in my life. Where do you think I get the time?"

A search of Proctor's place did not reveal a chessboard. Gardener also knew that Proctor had alibis for all the murders, and the farm bank details did tie up to the people who supposedly owned the buildings. The account was also very healthy in general.

"So you don't have a score to settle with anyone?" asked Gardener.

"You're not finishing what was started years ago?" added Reilly.

Proctor spread his arms and his expression was genuinely sincere.

"Why would I? I'm not going to incriminate myself, am I? If my father had done all of this and I'd known, why would I have left the bodies where they were in the first place? All of this is a bit bloody elaborate, where would I find the time with a farm to run?"

He had a point. And Gardener had nothing else he could throw at him. After everything they had covered, Gardener felt there wasn't enough. If Proctor genuinely didn't know anything about the leases on the properties, it meant that Gardener was going to have to investigate Ken Proctor more closely. He would need access to the police archives again; to find out exactly what had happened to Joe's father on the night he died, how deeply it was investigated, and what conclusion they came to.

But in all honesty, how long could he keep Joe? Probably not very long at all, because his lawyer would make sure of it.

He was going to have to let Proctor go.

Chapter Thirty-two

As per usual – mainly because Gardener and Reilly had otherwise been tied up – the incident room meeting was held in the late evening. Following Proctor's release, Gardener had had a visit from another witness claiming recognition of the head of the second victim whose photo had been released to the newspapers. He would be able to share that with the team, as well as the findings of victim number three from Fitz that had been delivered only five minutes previously.

After entering the room and placing folders on the desk in front of him, Gardener first asked the team to share with him what they had discovered. The rag-and-bone man, the water board official, and his 4x4 had yielded little to nothing: some people had seen the vehicle and the man, but most had paid scant attention.

A follow up on vans in the station car park revealed that most of the owners were there on official business. The rest were work vans whose drivers were able to prove their reason for being there. One belonged to a local builder who was carrying out renovations on some flats nearby. He was waiting for a delivery of goods by train and happily passed a few minutes with the detectives.

Gardener shared his thoughts with the team that whoever was responsible had to reside locally, allowing them to blend in very well; something he would return to later in the meeting.

Further checks on Debra Gosforth revealed that she had not gone to Ireland, or if she had, it hadn't been to

Rosscarbery to live with family. There were other avenues to check, but it didn't seem likely that the story Elizabeth Holmes had been told was true. Debra Gosforth was a misper.

There was a glimmer of hope for Lisa Small. Paul Benson and Patrick Edwards believed they had located her aunt Marion in a care home in Guiseley. Despite suffering from dementia, she did have good days and they were going to try their luck the following day; the likelihood, however, was that Lisa Small would also be classed a misper.

Rawson and Sharp confirmed their thoughts on the rhyme; *Sing a Song of Sixpence* didn't appear to have anything to do with the crime scene: it simply fitted with the fact that Monarch was an accountant.

During the day, Gates and Longstaff had had a chance to study chess pieces to see if it led them anywhere.

The one found with Hubbard was the queen. Monarch's chess piece was the knight.

These pieces represent the protective knights, shaped like a horse because it is symbolic of what knights rode during battle. They were thought to be protectors of the royal family, the first line of defence in case the enemy broke through the castle walls. Gates and Longstaff drew very little from the information they had found.

Thornton and Anderson mentioned that Monarch and Trot's Street Lane premises was a non-starter. There was no one there who remembered them and the building was now a travel agent.

That left only *The Guardian* newspaper. Following a phone call, Longstaff had emailed the editor with what she wanted but as yet, she'd had no reply. No one held out any hope with that one.

"*We* have a bit of positive news," said Anderson.

"Go on," said Reilly.

"We called on Elizabeth Holmes again," continued Thornton. "She recognized the picture of our clergyman as being that of Jeremy Cleeves."

"No doubt about it," said Anderson.

"Actually," said Gardener, "we might find there is some doubt. I believe Elizabeth Holmes might have been given a false name."

Thornton's face dropped. "Why?"

"After interviewing Joe Proctor and before coming in here," said Gardener, "we had another witness come forward with the identity of our clergyman. A Mrs Stella Watson who *lives* in Morley."

"If our witness is right," said Reilly, "he isn't just a clergyman."

"Marvellous," said Anderson, wiping his face with his hands.

Gardener took up the story. "Apparently his name is Charles Pitman and he was none other than the Bishop of Leeds."

"Bishop?" exclaimed Rawson.

"Yes," confirmed Gardener, "according to Watson, she knew him for many years because of the involvement they both had with the church. She was a church warden."

"What did she say about him?" asked Sharp.

Gardener checked his notes. "According to her he was always pleasant, well spoken, mild-mannered. The usual thing you would expect from a man of his calibre."

"But that said," continued Reilly, "she always felt there was something odd about him. Nothing she could put her finger on, but she just didn't like the way he looked at her."

"Leered was the word she used," said Gardener.

"There was nothing concrete," said Reilly, "but she heard rumours that he'd abused his position; stories of him touching up young girls."

"But," said Gardener, "she stressed that's all they were, rumours. There was nothing official, nothing concrete."

"Wouldn't surprise me," said Rawson. "It wouldn't be the first time."

"Even so, Dave," replied Gardener, "I doubt there'd be much we could prove on that score."

"Did she describe this Jeremy Cleeves, or Charles Pitman in any detail?" asked Sharp.

"He was a large man, most of which had turned to fat," said Gardener. "He was balding with wisps of white hair, green eyes, a fat nose and fat lips with nicotine-stained teeth." Gardener glanced at the whiteboard, to the picture. "That last bit seems about right. She reckoned he was almost always seen in formal dress, which tied in with his occupation."

"Otherwise, ill-fitting suits," said Reilly.

"Seems he disappeared sometime in 1990 when he was seventy years of age and semi-retired."

"But here's the big one," said Reilly, a comment that grabbed their attention.

"What big one?" asked Gates.

"Apart from being the Bishop of Leeds he was pretty much a bigwig here in Morley," said Gardener. "According to Stella Watson, he spent a lot of time in Morley at The Convent of All Hallows in the Wood. This building is still situated on the corner of Troy Road and Commercial Street."

"Might be the breakthrough we're looking for," said Briggs, sitting in the corner of the room with a mug of tea.

"I'm now wondering," said Gardener, "if this is the connection to everything that happened forty years ago. I'd like someone on that tomorrow, please. Put his name into the system and see what comes out. If we're really lucky, we might find all the others that we have names for."

"We'll take that," said Anderson. "This bloke's been leading us a merry dance so I'd like to get to the bottom of it."

Gardener nodded and made a note on one of the whiteboards, of which, there were now several. The team scribbled notes before Gardener turned his attention to the folder he'd received from Fitz.

After reading through various papers, he told the team the basics.

"Fitz has managed to match up body number three with other body parts. The torso belongs to a man with an enlarged liver, prostate problems, and high blood pressure. The head we know is Wendy Hubbard's; apart from being female it also has cancerous cells. The arms are male and have evidence of osteoporosis. The legs are male and show signs of HIV."

Gardener placed photos on the whiteboards and turned to face Gates and Longstaff.

"The chess piece is the castle, also known as the rook. Do you have anything in your notes about that?"

Longstaff checked, before adding, "Not much. This piece is positioned on the corners of each player's side. As the name 'castle' suggests, this is the protective barrier, or the walls that protect the higher-ranking pieces. This is why they are placed on the sides to symbolize protection over royalty, in the same way as a castle or a tower protects those on the inside."

"That it?" asked Reilly.

"Afraid so," said Gates.

"Not much to go on," said Gardener.

Unwilling to waste any further discussion time, because he realized it would go nowhere, he placed the two laminated documents they had found at scene three into the overhead projector and switched it on.

Veronica Walsh

DOB: 09/09/70

Description: Veronica was by far the most beautiful of all the girls and could have had a modelling career. She had fine, long blonde hair, blue eyes and a voluptuous figure, with a smooth complexion, thick lips, aquiline nose and white teeth. Her voice was as smooth as silk.

Background: Veronica had always been told that she had been taken into the care of the convent staff when she had been found in a basket on the doorstep one stormy night. The Mother Superior said she had tried in vain to find Veronica's parents, but no one ever came forward.

Date Missing: 09/03/85

"There we have it," said Gardener. "Veronica Walsh appears to be the third nun to have gone missing. She was found in a basket on the doorstep of the convent. There might be something there when we start looking into convents.

"I know this sounds bad," continued Gardener, "but I don't want any of you spending much time on the missing girls. So far, we've drawn a blank. I don't think the information the killer is leaving us is meant to help. He or she is simply telling us, they know more than we do."

"I agree," said Briggs, "this investigation needs to focus on what's happening today and what we can do about stopping whoever is responsible."

Gardener nodded again, glancing at his watch. "I'll come back to that. Time is moving on and we have one or two things more to discuss."

He pointed to the cryptic message:

A man of the law made his bed – but no one's sorry he's dead!

"The killer is obviously referring to Mark Trot, the lawyer," said Gardener. "It's probably the killer's candid opinion that no one's sorry he's dead."

"Probably shared by a lot of other people," added Briggs.

Gardener read it out again, before asking. "Does anyone recognize the rhyme?"

"It's from *Little Mother Goose*," said Anderson. "Another I've read to the grandchildren."

"Not before bed, I hope," said Thornton. "Christ, some of these nursery rhymes are a bit like horror films."

Gates laughed. "I know, you wouldn't catch me reading them to my kids."

"I think the most important thing on the page is this." Gardener pointed to the symbol.

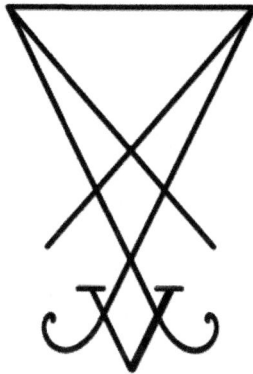

"What the hell is that?" asked Briggs.

"I have absolutely no idea," replied Gardener. "Never seen it before." He opened it to the room. "It's obviously a symbol of some sort; anyone?"

From the vacant expressions no one did.

"The only thing I recognize," said Reilly, "is the letter 'V' at the bottom, but that could mean anything."

"It could be pointing us to a name," said Rawson.

"But it's no one we've come across so far," said Sharp.

"Unless we've been given some duff information," offered Gardener. "Elizabeth Holmes knew our clergyman as Jeremy Cleeves, but another witness claims his name was Charles Pitman. Hopefully, when we put that into the police computers we'll have a hit, and maybe it will lead us to the others and what really happened forty years ago."

"Surely if it was anything that bad," said Briggs, "we would know, someone would remember."

Gardener nodded, "It *was* a long time ago."

"So were some of the suspects in Operation Yewtree, but a lot's emerged over those cases."

"Fair point," said Gardener. Hoping to move on he said, "Okay, Sarah and Julie are probably the best we have at surfing the net. Can you dig into this, please? Put the symbol into Google, see if it comes up with anything. What is it? What does it mean?

"And finally," continued Gardener, "the personal message." He turned back to the screen.

> *No more help now, Detective, you're on your own again. But don't hang around, or you'll miss the train.*

Gardener turned back to face the team.

"The one word that stands out for me is 'train'. Does it pull us back to the station?"

"But we haven't found anything at the station, sir," said Patrick Edwards.

"So we look again," said Gardener, "but that's a job for Sean and myself. We're going round to the station tomorrow. We're not going to ask any questions, we're just going to observe. There might be something we've missed, something obvious, that's shouting out at us."

Gardener wrote it on the whiteboard, before turning, intending to finish the meeting with news of Joe Proctor, and hand out any actions connected to what they had discovered. He filled them in about the interview in the cell, concentrating on the leases.

"Having investigated those, it appeared that none of the companies physically exist, but someone somewhere knows something about them, and he or she is playing games to a level that I do not appreciate.

"I want the banks connected to those leases – and the shop where we found the first victim – turning upside down. Why are the companies listed registered to dead people? Who is behind it? Get as much information as you can, and if the banks refuse to cooperate, see DCI Briggs for the necessary paperwork.

"Continuing with what we found in the barn, I still want as much information about the chemicals as possible."

"Do you still think Joe Proctor is involved, Stewart?" asked Briggs.

"If I'm being honest, I don't think he's our killer, but I believe that whatever happened to his old man is somehow tied into all of this, so I want Ken Proctor's death investigating further. Is there anyone connected to Ken that is still alive? If there is, see if we can find and speak to them, see what they remember. Someone connected to Proctor senior may be responsible for the murders in the past, may even be responsible for his murder, and what we're coming across today.

"The other thing about the discovery of the third body is," said Gardener, "I believe that whoever is responsible has to be a local person. He or she could not do everything if they didn't live close by. They obviously blend in because people know them. It's probably someone very ordinary in everyday life, someone who has a normal job, who does normal things."

"And someone who everyone trusts," added Reilly.

Gardener nodded his agreement. "So something to concentrate on there for two of you – perhaps Colin and Dave. Ken Proctor, he might be the key to all of this."

"Where is Joe Proctor now?" asked Briggs.

"I had to let him go," said Gardener, "but he's under caution, he knows we are watching him. I've asked him to surrender his passport and to report to the station every day.

"Let's also have someone round at the ex-convent on Troy Road, see what we can find out. On a final note, I want to make a comment on what I think is relevant and important, and something DCI Briggs has mentioned. We cannot save any of the victims we are finding, or the missing girls. There is nothing we can do for them. It was forty years ago.

"*We* need to concentrate on who is leaving the bodies now, and what the ultimate aim is – because they will not stop at four from the past. I honestly believe they will have something else in mind.

"My guess is they will be going for someone current, someone who is actually still alive and connected to the case. God only knows who that will be, but we have to find whoever it is, and stop them."

Chapter Thirty-three

Emily entered the shop early on Friday morning and found Patterson already there. All the meat was cut, the trays were laid out. The ovens were on, and he was sitting with a mug in his hand, simply staring into space. She suspected he wasn't even aware of her presence.

Emily coughed, more loudly than she should have done.

Patterson jumped, nearly spilling his tea. "What the hell are you playing at?"

"I could ask you the same question. How long have you been here?"

"Feels like all night."

"Oh dear, that bad, is it?" She glanced at his cup and nodded. "Fresh one?"

"If you're making."

She chose to say nothing further. Whilst the kettle boiled and the tea brewed, Emily checked the meat in the ovens with a temperature probe. She opened the fresh bags of breadcakes ready to slice and butter. She made the tea and placed one in front of Patterson, and in all that time he hadn't moved a muscle. He hadn't even put the radio on.

"What the hell is wrong with you? You've been like this for days."

He shrugged, took a sip of tea. "Nowt to worry about."

"For me, maybe," replied Emily. "I suspect it's a different story for you."

Patterson changed the subject. "How did it go with Greengrass the other night?"

"Who?" asked Emily.

"You know, that scruffy fucker who persuaded you to go out on a date with him. Did he manage to get the spuds out of his ears?"

"If you mean Harry, very well."

"Give over. I bet *you* paid. He doesn't look like he's got two half-pennies to rub together."

"Shows what little you know."

"Seen his place, have you?" questioned Patterson.

"No, but I know where it is."

"Where, Oil Drum Lane?"

"Scotchman, if you must know."

"Scotchman Lane?" repeated Patterson. "I live on Scotchman, there's no shanty-town houses on that lane, I can tell you."

"He lives way past you, my lad."

That shut Patterson up, for a few seconds at least. "Where?"

"The white house, after the golf club."

"Fuck off," replied Patterson. "What is he, the gardener?"

Emily had long since been used to his language. "In a manner of speaking."

"Thought as much."

"You've got no idea, Patterson."

Emily went on to explain what a wonderful evening they had had: the arrival in a horse and cart, what Corbett had been up to in his life, what a gentleman he was; perhaps too much of one. Emily mentioned how disappointed she was to have been taken home but not by him.

"Why?" asked Patterson, "where did he go?"

"I've no idea, and the footman never said. Anyway," said Emily, "never mind changing the subject. We were talking about you, not me. I've worked here far too many years, Patterson, to know when stuff's right and when it isn't. And at the moment it definitely isn't. So you'd better get on and tell me. Is it the business?"

"Business is fine," replied Patterson. "You should know that."

"I do, but things can go wrong. If it's not business, is it the kids?"

"No, they're both doing well."

"Paula?"

"No, she oils the hinges of her mouth on a regular basis so there's no problem there."

Emily leaned forward. "Whatever it is, love, you can tell me. I might have worked here since it opened and you might be a right sassy bugger when you want but I've become quite fond of you, and I know summat's not right. What is it?"

Patterson hesitated. He glanced at the ceiling and she noticed for the first time that his eyes were damp, which worried her all the more.

"What is it, love?" she asked. "It's obviously something serious."

"Oh, God." Patterson put the cup down, ran his fingers through his hair and down his face.

"Come on," said Emily, "out with it. I want to help you."

"I can't believe it's come to this."

"What has?"

"It's a mess."

"What is?" asked Emily. God only knew what was going on, what was affecting him so bad. She'd never seen him in such a state. "Have you done something?"

"Like what?" he asked, sharp eyed.

"You tell me, love, I'm not a mind reader. If it's not the business or the kids, or Paula, it has to be you. So what have you done? Whatever it is, it can't be that bad, and between us I'm sure we can fix it."

"I doubt it."

Emily sighed. "Are you having an affair?"

Patterson seemed appalled. "No, I'm bloody well not. I'd be happy if it were that simple."

Emily's stomach lurched. An affair was bad enough but whatever he was up to sounded worse. She took a gamble.

"Is there something wrong with *you*?"

He stared at the ceiling and then down at his feet, wringing his hands together, breathing heavily.

"Surely it can't be all that bad. You're worrying me now."

He still didn't spill the beans.

"Come on. What's wrong?"

Finally, he stared at her, aware that she was giving him no option. "It's embarrassing."

"What's embarrassing?"

Patterson finally plucked up the courage to tell her that he had found a lump.

"A lump, where?"

"On the back of the shed wall, where do you think?"

"That's the Patterson I know and love, sassy as ever. Where is the lump?"

He glanced down. "You know."

She followed his eyes, cottoning on. "A lump, is that all?"

"All? It's e-fucking-nough, isn't it?"

"How big is it?"

"Well I didn't get the tape measure out."

"You know what I mean – big or small?"

"Well, quite small, I suppose."

"Does Paula know?"

"No."

"Don't you think you should tell her? I bet she's worried about your behaviour. She deserves to know. You need to tell her. Have you seen a doctor?"

He shook his head.

"Why not?"

"I've told you, it's embarrassing. What if I make an appointment and it's a woman?"

Emily raised her eyebrows. "For God's sake, you're all the same, you lot. It'll be nowt she hasn't seen before."

Emily stood up and took the cups to the sink and then returned to her chair.

"Right, get on the phone and get an appointment made. Doesn't matter when it is, I'll cover the shop. I'll tell you something for nothing, Patterson, better to be embarrassed than dead."

She softened her approach.

"If it's any consolation it happened to me. Found one on my breast. I were worried, just like you are. I needn't have been. It was just fatty tissue – nowt to be bothered by. Go and get it sorted, and cheer up."

For some reason he started laughing, and he couldn't stop. She suspected that it was the first time he'd spoken about it, and it was sheer relief. He must have been worried sick. She thought for one second that he was going to confess to the strange murders going on in Morley.

Her expression darkened as she suddenly thought about her date. Why had he left early? Did she really know enough about him?

Patterson must have sensed it.

"Are you okay, now?"

Emily decided to return the favour. She told Patterson some more about Harry; the fact that he'd left early and had become very secretive.

"I don't know why I'm telling you all this. He were a perfect gentleman, treated me like a princess. What's it got to do with me if he left early, it was probably business?"

"But?" asked Patterson.

"What do you mean, but?"

"You're worried about something."

Emily felt awful. She was putting two and two together and making fifty. She told Patterson about him renting the field at Proctors, and he seemed to know quite a bit about the murders, and he left early, and then another body had been found.

"Doesn't mean anything," said Patterson.

"You're right, it doesn't. Could be something, could be nothing, but what do I really know about him? What if he's harbouring a bit of a dark secret?"

"Well if that's how you're feeling, tell the police."

"The police?"

"You can't be too careful, Emily, love, and you're a good judge of character."

"What will I tell them? We had a date and he left early and I think he went to kill someone?"

Patterson stood up. "Maybe he did, maybe he didn't. But what if you're next?"

Emily suddenly went cold, as if someone had walked over her grave.

Patterson turned to leave the back room but faced her before going through the doorway. "And if you see him, ask him if he plays chess."

Chapter Thirty-four

Dave Rawson brought the car to a halt on Commercial Street opposite a building housing LJ Priestley, the funeral director. Both officers jumped out but it was Sharp who opened the conversation.

"Jesus Christ, it's a bit nippy this morning."

"Hardly surprising, it's nearly November," said Rawson, glancing at the old derelict building, nestled at the corner of Troy Road and Commercial Street. "Guess this is what we came to see."

Sharp stared on. He did not find the place at all inviting. A few empty buildings and some cottages stood on Troy Road. Further up Commercial Street on their left were a number of stone-built cottages that formed St. Mary's Square, which backed on to the churchyard.

"Seen better days if you ask me," said Rawson.

"Such a pity" said Sharp. "Looks to me like it might have been a lovely old building."

"Shall we check it out?" asked Rawson.

"We can have a quick look," said Sharp, "but I suspect we're wasting our time. It must have been like this for years."

Rawson nodded. "You're probably right."

A quick search of the perimeter and the grounds revealed the remains of an empty shell of what would have been something special in its day. Little was left of the roof or the stained-glass windows. Most of the brickwork was crumbling but the four walls of the building, and the spire, still stood firm. A large wooden door barred entry.

As they came back around the front, Rawson stopped and stared around.

"What's up?" asked Sharp.

"Did you hear something?"

"Like what?"

"I'm not sure," replied Rawson. "I thought I heard a voice."

Sharp shrugged. "I doubt it. The wind's pretty loud and piercing and there's plenty of crows around the place. It was probably one of them."

"You're probably right," said Rawson, but the expression on his face said otherwise.

As they approached the front door, Rawson said, "Should we try and have a look inside?"

"Don't think it would be a good idea, Dave," replied Sharp. "It looks like a health and safety nightmare. If we go in there and anything happens, the boss will have our guts for garters."

"You're right," said Rawson. "If we're going to send anyone inside it might as well be the Irishman."

The pair of them laughed. "I'll leave you to suggest that one."

Sharp glanced around. The grounds were overgrown, grass nearly as tall as they were. The trees were erect but would have benefited from trimming. A number of headstones had dropped at angles, and it was easy to see that no one cared enough for the building to even try to make it presentable.

"I wonder who owns it?" asked Rawson.

"Nobody by the look of the place," said Sharp, feeling the pinch again. A quick glance upwards saw mushrooming grey clouds that threatened rain. A cold wind nearly cut through him. "I don't think there's much to be gained here. What we need to find out is some sort of potted history, who owns it now and whether or not there are any plans for it."

"Good idea, but first let's have a coffee in town somewhere. This fucking wind isn't doing much for me."

As they left the grounds and wandered back to the car, two women walked by. The older one pulled a two-wheeled shopping trolley behind her; the younger one, possibly a neighbour or her daughter, was carrying a bag.

"Morning," shouted the younger one, in a Northeast accent.

Sharp noticed she was slim and blonde, wore a padded jacket over a knee-length skirt and boots up to her knees. She also wore thin wire-rimmed spectacles.

"Are you with the builder?"

"Such a shame, this place," said the older one. "It's about time someone did something with it."

"So long as they don't turn it into a home for young offenders."

"Ooh no," said the older one, "I don't want any of them living here. We'll all be killed in our beds."

"I wouldn't go that far, Mam," said the blonde.

Sharp stopped the conversation mid-flow. "Did you mention a builder?"

"Yes, builder," replied the blonde, "that's right."

Sharp and Rawson displayed warrant cards and introduced themselves, dragging names from the women: Charlotte and Florrie. They both lived a few yards up on St. Mary's Square.

"Can you tell us anything about the builder?" asked Rawson.

"Not really," said Charlotte, "I never spoke to him, or anything."

"When was he here?"

"A couple of days back."

"Where did you see him?"

"In the grounds, looking round."

Charlotte pointed to where Sharp and Rawson had been, near the front door.

"How did you know he was a builder?" asked Sharp.

"My friend told me. I haven't lived here long and I need one myself, see. Have you ever tried getting a builder to come and look at a job? It's bloody disgraceful. They quote you an arm and a leg and then tell you they can't come for six months."

"The builder," Sharp reminded her, "what else was he up to?"

"What do you mean?"

"Did he go inside, or just stay outside?"

"I don't think he went inside," said Charlotte. "He was over there at the front door, and then he disappeared around the other side for a minute or so. Then he came back and went across there to his van." She pointed to the funeral director.

"What did he look like?" asked Sharp.

"Big bloke," said Charlotte. She glanced at Rawson. "About his size but not as much hair. Come to think of it he never had any hair that I could see."

"Did you notice much about the van?" asked Rawson.

"Not really. It was a big white one with a door on the side."

"Any logo on it?" Sharp asked.

"No. It was plain white."

"Didn't see the registration, did you?" asked Rawson.

"No, sorry. I was with my friend, Tracey Collins, she lives up on St. Mary's Square as well, number three. We were rushing to see the funeral director, her father's just recently died."

"Sorry to hear that," said Sharp.

"Maybe we should go and see Priestley," said Rawson, "see if he can shed any light."

"I doubt it," said Florrie. "That's his old building. They moved to Queen Street a while back, but he might be able to tell you something about the old church. He's been in Morley since God were a lad."

"Christ," said Rawson, pointing to the church, "he must have placed a fair few in there, then."

"I'll say."

Sharp let the women go and immediately jumped on the phone to Gardener to report what they'd found.

Chapter Thirty-five

Gardener and Reilly had arrived at the railway station early. Gardener had with him a list of vehicle registrations that had previously been taken, and most of those matched the list that had been cleared. Reilly took the numbers of those that were new.

The station was open, which was why he felt the wind cutting into him. The road down led to a dead end, with a car park on the left. He noticed a number of portacabins behind a wooden gate bearing the name 'AmcoGiffen'. Gardener wondered about those. He mentioned as much to Reilly.

"You're thinking our man is a railway worker?"

"Might be an answer for why and how he's managed to evade us so well."

"Then maybe we should have a few operational support officers down here to check out them there portacabins."

"Just what I was thinking, but this being Network Rail, we'll need to do things by the book."

"A warrant, you mean?"

"There's no way we'll get into that compound without one."

Gardener couldn't see anyone, and the gate was locked, so he made a mental note to call back later.

Casting an eye over the station itself, it was basically a platform with a shelter. Research had informed him that it formed part of the Huddersfield Line.

"There's not much here," said Reilly.

Gardener had to agree. "To be honest, Sean, I didn't think there would be. I'm sure the team have done an excellent job canvassing the area, but even trained eyes can miss things."

Reilly pointed to a group of buildings on Station Road, leading to the station approach.

"Let's have a poke around that lot, see if anything gives."

As they set off, Gardener noticed a number of detached and semi-detached houses built on an incline to their right, overlooking the track. At the end of the road, in front of them, stood a large apartment block called Barwick Court. Gardener figured they were private because the car park was gated and entry was by pin number only.

"Did we cover this place?" Reilly asked.

"I'm sure we did, Sean, and I don't recall anything standing out. Whoever this person is, they're clever enough to have covered all of their tracks."

"I doubt they've covered them all," replied Reilly. "They'll have overlooked something."

"It'll take some finding," said Gardener. Pointing to his right, he said, "let's have a walk up there. Nothing I've seen here merits further investigation."

The road was pretty desolate, except for a white house in the distance on the left. It was, however, the building on the right that held his attention.

"This looks interesting," said Reilly.

"Just what I was thinking," said Gardener. "What was it the last clue said? 'No more help now, Detective, you're on your own again. But don't hang around, or you'll miss the train.'"

"We're not hanging around, we only found body number three a couple of days back. And the clue about the missing the train was probably *too* obvious to be the station."

Gardener nodded and returned his attention to the dwelling. Situated on Station Road, the old, three-storey building was brick built, including the arched windows, each of which supported ceramic plant holders in the style of hanging baskets. The upper storey window frames were rotten and most of the glass was smashed. The wooden front door was latched with a new hasp and lock, which immediately brought to mind the lock-up on Proctor's land.

Whilst Gardener was busy with the front of the building, Reilly toddled off around the back.

To his left, Gardener saw a small wooden fence built around a six-foot square patch of grass. To the right were two shutter doors: one roller, the other concertina. He noticed brackets where the CCTV cameras had been removed. The building didn't appear to have seen any action for quite some time, but then neither did any of the other buildings where they had found victims.

On the opposite side of the road he noticed a tall, Yorkshire-stone wall with a bank of trees, the land rising upwards, leading to more buildings on Albert Road. Gardener had no idea what they were. Turning back, by far the most prominent feature on the building of interest was a 'For Sale' sign on an exterior wall, belonging to Crossley's on Queen Street.

Reilly returned. "Everything around the back's pretty much closed up but there is a window open."

Gardener pointed upwards.

"Well look what we have here," said Reilly, "are we back full circle?"

"Give Crossley's a call, Sean, ask them about this place, and see if someone can meet us immediately, even if it is Crossley himself."

Gardener glanced at the white house in the distance. It wasn't that far away, so he was pretty sure that whoever lived there might have seen some kind of action, or perhaps know something about the building's owner.

"How soon?" asked Gardener, as Reilly disconnected.

"Not at all."

"Sorry?"

Reilly pointed to the sign. "They didn't put that there. The sign is theirs but they have no idea where it came from because this building is not on their books."

Gardener's spine tingled. He immediately headed for the white house, with Reilly in tow.

When they arrived, Gardener discovered that the owners were called Simpson. Both husband and wife were at work, but Gemma the daughter was home. She was tall and skinny and blonde with blue eyes, and the make up and dress sense of a model.

She mentioned an odd incident. She had spotted a man unloading a van at two o'clock in the morning. She'd been in her bedroom listening to music on her headphones. It was only when she returned from the bathroom that she actually saw anything. Because of the angle all she could see was the side of a white van. It had no logos on it, but she did notice a side door. She definitely could not see the registration. She knew absolutely nothing about the owner but said her parents would be back around teatime if they wanted to send someone to talk to them.

"I know the angle isn't very good," said Gardener, "but did you get enough of a look at the man to give us a description?"

"I suppose so," replied Gemma. "He was quite tall, well-built, and from what I could see, he had a shaved head. I think he was wearing a leather jacket and jeans. But given it was two o'clock in the morning that's the best I can do."

"That's great, Gemma, love," said Reilly. "We're lucky you saw him at all."

"I can tell you he was walking backwards and forwards into the building, carrying boxes in."

Gardener thanked her for her time, gave her a card and asked if she would call him if she remembered anything else. He headed back toward the building. Only as he did so, did he see the name Station House stencilled into the concrete lintel running the width of the place.

Gardener stopped. "That's good enough for me, Sean."

"Good enough for what, though? We go in there now, we have to break in. That will be illegal, and if we find anything it will be inadmissible in court."

"Maybe," said Gardener, "but if we *do* find anything, we already have enough on the killer to drag him before a court when we catch him. So, let's enter and leave via the open window you noticed around the back."

"Let me enter, you mean," smiled Reilly.

They agreed that Gardener would continue checking out the front, whilst his partner slipped around the back.

"Before you do that, Sean, will you go back to the station and get the car? We have some scene suits in the boot. If we're going to do this, let's do it properly and not give anyone any further excuses to have a go at us."

Reilly agreed. The whole operation took about fifteen minutes. The Irishman finally slipped around the back and, five minutes later, the front door opened and he waved Gardener in. The place was a working building and perhaps belonged to a carpenter or a builder of some description. Already, Gardener had the feeling it had been worth their time.

Suddenly, his mobile chimed. Gardener answered and had a short conversation. Reilly asked who it was when the call was finished.

"Colin. He's over at the church with Dave Rawson, he thinks they may have found something." He told Reilly the details.

"Might tie in to what we have here."

"Let's have a look, shall we?"

For a building that didn't appear to have been used from the outside, the interior told a different story. Surprisingly, it was quite warm given the weather. It was rather cavernous and the whole of the ground floor was full of wood of every description, colour, size and length, and stored in a number of metal frames scattered all over, but despite that, Gardener felt there was something methodical about the design.

Along one wall, a pallet of bricks had been placed, and a number of loose ones were piled up next to it. Charts covered the walls with calculations. At the far end, Gardener noticed a band saw, and a variety of power tools on more shelves, including a circular saw, at least ten different hand saws, chisels, knives, screwdrivers and practically everything else a tradesman would need.

Builders' tools were also present: trowels, levels, chisels, hammers, and a concrete mixer.

To the left of those, he saw a door that led into another room. Gardener also registered a humming sound but couldn't quite locate it.

He strolled forward and opened the wooden door. Inside was someone's personal quarters. The size of a normal living room, it housed a bed, a couple of chairs, a TV, a fridge and some cooking utensils, amongst other basic items one would need to live.

"Boss, over here," shouted Reilly.

Gardener's scene suit rustled as he strode over to his partner, and his spine tingled when he noticed what Reilly was staring at: an old-fashioned hand cart with a roof on. It was made completely of wood, even the wheels. Two handles extended approximately four feet from one end. The whole construction was very sturdy and the wood had been heavily treated with stain and lacquer.

"I think we should call this in, Sean. Let's get everyone down here and turn the place over."

"We're not," said Gardener. "Technically, we broke into Proctor's barn and that paid dividends, and it wasn't questioned." He quickly made the call and then placed his mobile in his pocket.

"Have you any idea what the hell that humming is all about?"

"No," said Reilly, "but I figure it's coming from the back of the place."

The pair of them threaded their way around a number of cardboard boxes that Gemma Simpson had mentioned, before finally heading through an archway into another section of the building that had the roller-shutter door Gardener had seen from outside.

He realized he was now staring at possibly two industrial freezer units, but only one of them had a white envelope on the door, with a large question mark printed on it.

Gardener stepped forward and opened the door.

"Jesus Christ!" said Reilly.

Chapter Thirty-six

It was almost six in the evening before Gardener, Reilly and Briggs slipped into the incident room. It had been one hell of a day, and it was very likely, far from over.

Earlier, inside Station House, the industrial freezer with the envelope on the front door contained another body, number four as far as the police were concerned. Of that there was no doubt. It was naked, hanging on a meat hook, conveniently inserted into the neck. The rough heavy stitching connecting everything was immediately evident and had to have been good because the head had not become detached. Although the body had a thin, almost transparent coating of white frost, the dark colours of heavy bruising and nasty abrasions were still visible.

As there was absolutely no rush to do anything with the body, Gardener and Reilly had stepped outside and waited for everyone to arrive: his own team, the PolSA team, the SOCOs and the Home Office pathologist. Once the body had been removed and taken for inspection, Gardener issued actions; his own team were to continue with the actions he'd set them the previous night in the incident room, and the operational support officers would do the legwork within the immediate area.

Now, in the incident room, his team had assembled. All of them had hot drinks, not only because it was late, but it was bloody cold outside, and that was probably where they had spent most of their day.

"Okay, thank you for coming," said Gardener.

Reilly stood to one side, with his arms folded, leaning against one wall. Briggs had taken a seat at the back.

"There's no doubt the body in the freezer is the fourth one we've been expecting, but I have a funny feeling that there will be a further surprise in store from this killer. However, before you guys tell me what you have, I'll share the contents of the envelope with you. He slipped the first piece of paper into the overhead projector and switched it on.

Isabella Moorcroft

DOB: 01/04/67

Description: Isabella had jet black shoulder-length hair, with blue eyes, and a slim figure.

Background: Isabella had always been told that she had been taken into the care of the convent staff after her parents had died in a car crash on the outskirts of Harrogate returning home from her christening. Family and friends had been shocked and many had offered to care for the infant but a will had been found

indicating that the parents had wanted a life in the
diocese should anything happen to them. Robert
believed the documents were in fact fabricated because
according to rumour, Isabella was in fact the love
child of the Mother Superior, Wendy Hubbard, and
the Bishop, Charles Pitman.

Date Missing: 01/04/85

"I can't see the point of spending much time with this piece of information. We know we have four bodies that make up four victims, and four missing girls. Once again, the killer is revelling in his or her extensive knowledge about the situation: very little of which we'll be able to prove."

"But it does mention two people who are currently on our radar," said Briggs.

"True," said Gardener, "but it's still a forty-year-old mystery with little we can do about it."

"At least we have it for the records," said Bob Anderson.

"Which is why I wanted to mention it," said Gardener.

"What was the chess piece?" asked Gates.

"The only one it could be," said Gardener. "The Bishop."

A collection of sighs rose around the room.

"That figures," said Longstaff, who went on to give them a little bit of info. "He stands close to the king and queen because it represents the church, which many royal courts held near and dear to their hearts. It's also considered as the third most powerful piece on the chess board because back in the day, religion could influence many people, even without the help of the royal family."

"Well *he* certainly seems to have influenced a lot of people," said Gardener, "particularly when you think about Elizabeth Holmes. He's obviously managed to fool more people in order to be able to entice young girls away from possible guardians.

"So what else was this man – or to be more precise – were these four people up to?" asked Gardener. "It seems logical to assume they were directly involved in the disappearance of all these girls, with their fabricated stories, but what really happened forty years ago?"

"Somebody obviously knows," said Briggs, "but what I don't get is, why wait all this time to bring it to light?"

Gardener replaced the paper in the overhead projector.

"Maybe the killer's final cryptic clue will give us something to go on."

53.74792268, 1.30146689, 139.35027338a, 156.91746992d, 35y, 295.96856177h, ot.

"What in God's name is that?" asked Bob Anderson.

"Could be anything," said Colin Sharp.

"Whatever it is," said Reilly, "it won't be random. Our killer has been methodical all the way through the investigation."

"It's gonna take some deciphering," said Gates.

"Funny you should say that, Sarah," said Gardener.

"Me and my big mouth," she replied.

"I think I might have to look for a new partner," quipped Longstaff.

"I doubt it would have mattered anyway, girls," said Reilly. "The boss man was always going to give that one to you two."

"I've already emailed it," said Gardener, smiling. "As Sean says, whoever is responsible for what we're finding has been methodical throughout. Every one of their clues has pointed us to a new piece in the puzzle, and there's no reason to think this one won't. Whatever you can do and as soon as you can do it, girls, would be great."

"Question is," said Briggs, "what are we going to find when we get there?"

"Another body?" said Paul Benson.

Gardener slipped another piece of paper into the projector, which revealed the possible final rhyme – or at least he hoped it would be.

> *One more! There is no wall, but he's still heading for a great fall!*

"That's the easiest one of the lot," said Anderson. "Humpty Dumpty."

"In the past, the rhymes have told us something about one of the bodies on the slab," said Gardener. "This one is telling us there is definitely someone else."

"Who?" asked Briggs. "Who will we find and what condition will they be in? And what part will he or she have played in all of this?"

"Whoever the killer holds responsible," said Colin Sharp. "I think what we've found so far are minions, but there has to be someone at the top of the tree; someone who controlled it?"

"Now we have all four names, we might find out," said Gardener. "Whatever was going on has to have been part of an investigation somewhere, so maybe there will be something in our own records."

Patrick Edwards spoke up. "We have something on that, sir."

As he said that, Steve Fenton, head of the SOCOs walked in with hopefully some more information.

"Okay, Patrick, let's come back to that." Gardener turned to Fenton. "What do you have for us, Steve?"

"Not a lot, I'm afraid," said Fenton. "We've been working flat out on Station House." Fenton opened a manila file. "We do have four sets of prints. Sadly, three are not on our files. So, either they haven't committed any crimes, or they haven't been caught."

"I take it then that one set *is* on file?" asked Gardener.

"Yes," replied Fenton, "a petty thief by the name of Martin Fowler, from Bramley."

Gardener didn't know him. "Why would a petty thief have his prints in that place?"

"It's always possible it's been empty for some time and Fowler knew about it," said Fenton.

"Maybe he's been sleeping there," said Reilly.

"Do we have an address for him?" asked Gardener.

"We have a last known address," said Fenton.

"Okay," said Gardener. "It's unlikely he's responsible for what we've been finding – a bit out of his league, I would think. But we'll bring him in for questioning anyway. It won't do any harm. You never know, he might lead us to a bigger fish."

Pleased with something positive, Gardener noted the action on the whiteboard before moving on. Glancing at his notes, he asked if Gates and Longstaff had discovered anything regarding the symbol the killer had left as a cryptic message from scene three.

"Oh my God," said Gates, "are you going to love this."

Gardener's heart sank. "I doubt that very much."

Everyone pulled their chairs forward. Whatever these two were going to say sounded good.

"That symbol is known as The Sigil of Lucifer," said Longstaff.

"Pardon?" asked Gardener. He'd heard of Lucifer – hadn't everyone? But the last thing he'd expected was for it to come up in his investigation.

"The Sigil of Lucifer," said Gates, "was first documented in the sixteenth century – 1517 to be precise – in the Grimorium Verum also known as the Grimoire of Truth. Apparently it was written as a practical guide to invoking and working with Lucifer, or Beelzebub or Astaroth, or however many other names he has."

"Where the Christ is this leading us?" asked Briggs.

Longstaff took over. "By performing the appropriate ritual, the sigil acts as a gateway to invoke and bestow the power and presence of Lucifer."

Gardener ran his hands down his face. "So are we now getting into in the dark arts?"

"Sounds like it," said Rawson.

"Which could make it a whole different ball game," said Sharp.

"Over time," continued Gates, as if she was really loving it, "the graphical elements of the sigil have been identified with certain characteristics. The overall sigil appears as a chalice, which represents creation, the fertile darkness awaiting and ready for untold possibilities. Although the sigil is an instrument used to invoke Lucifer, that demon is considered to be the bearer of light and wisdom into the darkness."

"The letters in the symbol mean something as well," said Longstaff. "The 'X' over the sigil indicates the power and realm of the physical plane; its passion and sensuality that drives all entities. The inverted triangle represents water, often referred to as the original 'Elixir of Ecstasy' without which physical life could not exist. The 'V' at the bottom of the sigil represents the duality of all things; dark and light, male and female and the power of convergence of the two into one manifesting balance, creation and existence."

That pretty much silenced the room before Gates finally added, "The Sigil of Lucifer is also known as the Seal of Satan."

"I'm sure that's what we all wanted to hear," said Gardener.

"So what is the killer trying to tell us now?" asked Thornton.

"That maybe these four were satanists," said Gardener, "on top of everything else."

"Might be one answer for why the nuns disappeared," said Briggs.

"Nothing would surprise me," said Rawson. "There is documented evidence of this stuff going on all the time, especially where the church is involved."

"If that was the case," said Anderson, "wouldn't you think we'd have found something about that by now?"

"I doubt it," said Edwards. "We've only just managed to put together who these people are."

"He has a point," said Gardener. "But now we do know, let's stop guessing and add that to the list of actions. As Sean mentioned earlier, every clue the killer has given us has pointed to something."

"But why?" asked Briggs. "Why is he telling us all of this… unless he wants to get caught?"

"He's showing us what we didn't do forty years ago," said Gardener.

Briggs conceded with a nod and the raising of his arms.

Gardener wrote the action down on the whiteboard, seriously concerned about how far they had come, how little they had discovered, and how much more they might have to unearth before they had an answer.

He turned to Sharp and Rawson and asked them for an update of their day. They summarized the abandoned convent and then mentioned the conversation with the two women they'd met on the way out.

"And they had no idea who the builder was?" asked Gardener.

"No," replied Sharp, "but the younger one, Charlotte, mentioned a friend who lived nearby called Tracey Collins; said *she* might know him."

"Have we spoken to her?"

"Not yet," said Rawson. "We tried a couple of times today but she was out. We put a message through her door and spoke to the neighbour opposite who said she didn't know Collins very well, but she would speak to her when she appeared."

"Okay," said Gardener, making a note. "I suppose we should be thankful for small mercies. I'll leave a message with switchboard to try calling her tonight. Anything else?"

"We went over to see Priestley, the undertaker," said Sharp. "He was quite knowledgeable about the building itself."

"Apparently," said Rawson, "the All Hallows in the Wood church was built in 1878, at a cost of £7,000. It became the site of the convent in the 1980s. One of its historical features was The Pancake Bell in the tower, which originated at Kirkstall Abbey and became part of an annual Shrove Tuesday tradition. The bell was taken from the tower and hand rung on the steps of the church for one hour between 11:00 and 12:00am. Hot pancakes were then served inside."

"But it doesn't end well," said Sharp. "It closed permanently in 2008. Shortly afterwards it was revealed that the site had been bought by an entrepreneur who wanted to turn it into a hotel complex. However, in 2010 the old church was set on fire and what you're left with now is the burnt-out shell and tower."

"None of that really helped us," said Rawson, "but as we were leaving he came out with an absolute gem."

"Apparently, forty years ago," said Sharp, "over a four-month period, it was said that four nuns disappeared from The Convent of All Hallows in the Wood. The convent was a home for girls who had lost their parents at a young age and had nowhere else to go."

Gardener grabbed all four pages of the names and extra information about the girls from the killer's notes, reading them out loud.

"It has to be these girls. So what happened to them? Where the hell did they go?"

"He didn't know," said Sharp. "All he did know was that they were never found."

"It must have made the newspapers," said Gardener, "something this big."

"So why haven't we come across it?" asked Briggs.

"Because we weren't looking for it," said Reilly. "We had no idea *what* we were looking for."

"It didn't make the papers," said Sharp.

"Didn't?" questioned Reilly. "Something as big as four nuns disappearing in close succession and all from the same place, and it didn't make the papers?"

"It was all local suspicion," said Rawson, "Chinese whispers, the rumour mill. No one was ever able to actually prove anything."

"That can't be right," said Gardener. "Surely the diocese can't have controlled it all to such a degree. This Priestley must remember something else about it all."

"Not really," said Sharp. "You see, we were talking to Priestley junior. At that time, Priestley senior was running the business."

"Where is *he*?"

"Nursing home," said Rawson.

"Not another one," said Reilly. "Is *he* okay?"

"No," said Sharp. "Dementia, but Priestley junior is going to see him. He's brilliant with stuff in the past, just can't remember anything recent."

That gave Gardener some hope, but it was cotton thin.

"So," said Reilly, "we've got supernatural symbols and four dead people, two of which were involved with the convent. If we manage to uncover this lot, there's no telling where it will end up."

"We have a mother superior and a bishop," said Briggs. "They're the connection to the convent. I wouldn't mind betting that when we do find out something more, the other two – the lawyer and the accountant – will also have been involved with the diocese somehow."

"We need an all-out attack on archives," said Gardener. "Something as big must have made our records, somehow."

"Problem is, Stewart," said Briggs, "whatever we do find out, someone has a head start on us."

"But we have something else that might help," said Rawson, "an even bigger scandal to rock Morley, sometime in the Nineties."

"Yes," said Sharp. "We mentioned the names of our four victims and he definitely remembers those names."

Chapter Thirty-seven

"Disappeared?" said Gardener. "Without a trace?"

Sharp nodded. "As good as, nobody ever found them."

"Until now," replied Gardener. "We know that, because we have them."

"Surely there must be something in our archives about that," said Briggs.

"There is," said Bob Anderson.

"We came across some information when we were looking for stuff on this Pitman character," said Thornton.

"We heard a bit of a whisper that sent us into the archives," said Anderson. "We read up about Pitman when he was the former Bishop of Leeds. It seems that he spent a lot of time at the convent in Morley, and there is something in the police records about an assault."

"By him?" asked Gardener. "Or on him?"

"On him," said Thornton.

"What happened?" asked Briggs.

"Nothing, according to what we've unearthed," said Thornton. "It was the Mother Superior, the Hubbard woman, who made the phone call when she saw the state he was in one night. He'd been out on pastoral duty and he was late coming back. His nose was bleeding and his eye was starting to blacken."

"So why did nothing happen?" asked Gardener.

"Because when the police attended, he claimed he'd fallen down the stairs because he was drunk. He said it was nothing and that they were wasting their time. There were no charges to press."

"That doesn't sound right to me," said Reilly. "With everything that had gone on – despite it only being rumour and kept underground – it sounds to me like *someone* found out."

"And took the law into their own hands," said Briggs.

"We have the notes with us," said Anderson. "The bottom line is, the Bishop kept his mouth shut so no one could prove anything, especially if they couldn't find who was responsible. At that point no evidence had been brought to the table as to the reason for the attack. If it did happen, it was random, happened after dark, and there were no witnesses."

"But then those two main players disappeared," said Gardener. "So how long after the assault claim before they were removed?"

Thornton rifled through his papers. "About five years."

"So it could have been random," said Briggs.

"Or it could have been our Mr patience," said Reilly. "When did all this happen?"

"I think it was some time in the early Nineties," said Anderson, also checking notes.

Gates coughed and attracted Gardener's attention. "Actually, that ties up with something we've found."

"Go on," said Gardener.

"You asked us to go all out on the banks," said Longstaff. "And here's what we managed to piece together."

"We made a check on properties where we've so far found bodies," said Gates. "After Pitman, Hubbard, Monarch and Trot disappeared, bank accounts were set up with different banks in Morley in their names. Fifty thousand was put into each."

"Fifty thousand?" questioned Gardener. "That's a tidy sum of money now, never mind back in the Nineties. I wonder where all that came from?"

"Could it have been something to do with Pitman and Hubbard?" asked Briggs. "Let's face it, given their positions in life, they wouldn't be short of a bob or two."

"And we had a dodgy lawyer and an accountant," said Gardener.

"And if our killer had done his homework – and it sounds like he has – he would know about the money," said Reilly.

"If the killer took each of these people," said Gardener, "they could have had them some time before they were finished off."

"In order to get all the information out of them," said Sharp.

"Not to mention the money," added Rawson.

"Two of the accounts are tied to the ninety-nine-year leases," said Gates.

"The other to the shop on Brunswick Street, but that was set up as recently as last year. From what we could see there had been no activity on that account until then."

"Last year?" questioned Gardener, shaking his head. "Someone has some real patience."

"Not to mention intelligence," said Paul Benson, "given the nature of the clues they've been leaving."

"And they were set up in the names of the victims we've been finding?" asked Reilly.

"Three of them, yes."

"And you two have no means of being able to trace any further back than that?" asked Gardener.

"Not yet," said Longstaff.

Gardener believed them. Gates and Longstaff were as good as anyone he'd seen in the world of IT. If they hadn't completely cracked it yet, he doubted it could be cracked.

"Any mention of the name Proctor in all of this, aside from owning the leased properties?" asked Gardener.

"Not that we've come across," said Gates.

"Which still leaves the question, where and how *does* Ken Proctor fit in to all of this?"

"He's a farmer," said Briggs. "Didn't Fitz say we might be looking for a farmer or a butcher?"

"Initially," replied Gardener, "but you still have to ask why? Why would a farmer or a butcher get involved in all of this? It's a lot to lose if it all came out, and a long time to try and keep it a secret."

"But Joe Proctor mentioned the farm being in trouble some years ago," said Reilly.

Gardener nodded, "which is probably why the leases were set up."

"Can't be," said Briggs. "We've seen what those leases are paying. It's not lucrative enough."

"Maybe not," said Gardener, "but a lump sum to kick-start it would be."

"Maybe our killer had something on Ken Proctor, as well as the clergy," said Reilly, "something big enough to coerce him into getting involved."

"That's another conversation with Joe Proctor," said Gardener, "but after the last one he might be less cooperative."

"And the likelihood is, he might not know," said Briggs.

Gardener glanced at Gates. "Sarah, Julie, see how far back the banks go with their records. Maybe we can see if a lump sum was put into the farm account it might give us a starting point."

"Still wouldn't mean he was guilty of anything," said Briggs. "It would depend on whether we could trace back where it came from."

"True," said Gardener, "but it *would* give us something else on which to quiz Joe Proctor."

"Got it," shouted Bob Anderson, startling everyone. "I've got it."

He waved a sheet of paper in the air.

"What have you got?" asked Gardener, smiling.

"We did a bit more digging on that assault case. A detective sergeant investigating that so-called vicious attack on Pitman also went missing some months later."

"The sergeant went missing?" shouted Gardener. "Are you serious?"

"Missing, as in for a few days?" said Reilly. "Or missing as in this lot?"

Anderson nodded. "The latter; he was never found either. The attack on Pitman remained unsolved, as did the subsequent police investigation into the missing sergeant. The case was closed."

"Jesus," said Reilly. "I'm not sure I'm believing what I'm hearing here. How can so many people all connected to the same place go missing, and there not be more on it?"

"If we find anyone else has gone missing," said Rawson, "I want off this case… before I disappear."

"I doubt we'll be that lucky," said Reilly.

"Who was the DS?" asked Gardener.

"A newly promoted police sergeant called Robert Blanchard," said Thornton, "with his DC, Eddie Perrin."

Patrick Edwards quickly put his hand up.

"Yes, Patrick," said Gardener, as if they were all in the classroom.

"That's what me and Paul Benson have been looking into. You asked us to keep trawling through the records of *The Guardian* newspaper, as that was where a previous clue was pointing us."

"Sorry, Patrick," said Gardener. "This must have been what you were going to tell us earlier. What did you find?"

"We came across an article revealing the missing policeman, sergeant Robert Blanchard," said Benson. "Same era, same case."

"Hey, wait a minute," said Gates. "That's also the name of the person who apparently owns Station House in Morley."

"Blanchard?" asked Briggs.

"When did he buy that?" asked Gardener.

"According to what we found out, early 1990."

Gardener glanced at Bob Anderson. "Yet he's supposed to have disappeared?"

"According to our report, yes."

"When?"

Anderson scanned his notes. "1985."

"Interesting," said Reilly. "Could he be our man?"

"Be a bit old, wouldn't he?" questioned Briggs. "If it is him, he'd be in his eighties."

"I take your point, sir," said Gardener, "but it wouldn't be impossible."

"Especially if he's determined," offered Reilly.

"Do you think he would fit the descriptions we've been getting?" asked Rawson. "You know, well built. All the witnesses claim he's well built. When you're eighty-five, you're usually on the small, thin side, a bit doddery."

"Generally speaking," said Gardener. "As I said, though, not impossible."

"Okay," said Briggs, "we won't rule it out. It was only an observation."

Gardener nodded, wrote it down on the whiteboard and then returned to what he was going to say. "So, according to Bob, Blanchard investigated the possible assault on Pitman."

"Only, according to Pitman, it wasn't an assault," said Reilly.

"The nuns disappeared before '85, Blanchard apparently disappeared *in* '85, the clergy and, we'll assume, the accountant and the lawyer went missing in the Nineties, and a whole series of bogus accounts are opened up around the same time in the names of the people connected to the convent. The question now is, *did* Blanchard really disappear?"

"Could Robert Blanchard be our man?" asked Reilly. "Did he investigate an assault and come out with a whole lot more?"

"Did he get too close to everything?" asked Sharp.

"Was he made to disappear?" asked Rawson. "If he got the lowdown on these missing nuns, maybe he wanted to blow the whole case open but the diocese had too much to protect and acted accordingly."

"That does sound a bit far-fetched," said Gardener. "It's one thing to take on a bunch of nuns that were little more than schoolgirls, but a police sergeant is a different matter altogether."

"Potentially, you're taking on the entire police force," said Briggs.

Gardener nodded. "The only other conclusion you can come to is that maybe Blanchard did find out what was going on, found out that the diocese were too big to take on but chose to remain invisible and become a vigilante."

"Which is equally as far-fetched," said Reilly.

"On the face of it, yes," said Gardener, "but nothing would surprise me with this case." He suddenly turned to Steve Fenton. "Steve, every policeman's fingerprints are on file for elimination purposes. Can you check to see if any of the prints we have for Station House belong to Robert Blanchard?"

Fenton nodded and left the room. The buzz of anticipation was quite immeasurable.

Gardener asked Benson if anyone else was mentioned in the report he'd found in *The Guardian*.

"There must have been other people on the case."

It was Patrick Edwards who answered. "Eddie Perrin, Blanchard's right-hand man."

"Has he gone missing?"

"It didn't say," said Benson.

"So maybe he hasn't," said Gardener. "Who was in charge of the case?"

"A bloke called Edward Winstanley."

"Winstanley," repeated Reilly. "I've heard that name recently."

"Where?" Gardener asked.

Reilly left the room without answering.

"Poor lad," said Rawson. "It's all too much for him."

"Maybe he's decided to get out before you, Dave," said Gardener.

Reilly returned with a newspaper. He placed it down on the table in front of Gardener.

"That's what I was reading a few days back, you remember? The article is about a retired police superintendent, aged eighty-five, who has gone missing."

Gardener read the report and glanced upwards.

"I'd like every available one of us on this now. Check our archives for everything you can find connected to this group of people.

"This case is no longer about missing girls, it's about whoever is taking revenge today, and whoever that is almost certainly has Winstanley. We need to find him to prevent his death. Whoever killed the members of the diocese got some kind of twisted justice for the nuns, but he hasn't finished. So is it Robert Blanchard?" Gardener asked.

Steve Fenton came back in the room. "Negative. We have not found Blanchard's prints in Station House."

Benson's mobile suddenly chimed. He excused himself and took the call in one corner of the room. When he returned to the centre, he said, "I know where we can find Eddie Perrin."

Chapter Thirty-eight

Emily had taken the bull by the horns following another conversation with Patterson, which meant she now had

Saturday morning free. She was standing outside the large white house on Scotchman Lane. The gates were open. Parked inside on the drive, a large silver-grey Bentley caught her eye. Glancing upwards, a deep blue sky shone with few clouds, but the temperature was low and biting; threats of a thunderstorm after lunch were rumoured.

Emily rang the doorbell and the chime sounded somewhere in the distance. Her stomach performed summersaults, her throat was constricted.

She had not heard anything from Corbett since their date. Not that it was all that long ago, and he was free to come and go as he pleased. On the night of the date, he seemed smitten. Why hadn't he called? She feared however, that she knew the answer to that one.

The door opened and his expression was far from welcoming but he still invited her in. He was dressed in a pair of grey slacks, with a white woolly jumper.

To her immediate left was a cloakroom. The hall was long, with regency wallpaper of red and cream stripes, and a twisting banister rail leading upwards. The carpet was so thick she thought she had shrunk. There were paintings on the wall that probably cost more than her house. Everything smelled of fresh linen.

"You'd better come through," he said; no greeting. He turned and led the way into a kitchen at the back of the house, which ran the entire width, full of cupboards and domestic appliances and dried flowers on the walls, and ornaments that had a feminine touch.

She smelled coffee. He poured her one without asking, placing it at the table, opposite his.

"How have you been?" she asked, not knowing what else to say, quite clearly out of her comfort zone.

"I can't complain." He gestured for her to sit.

They both did.

To her left, she noticed a small alcove; inside, a gaming table with a chessboard on top, and two chairs. Whoever played was in the middle of a game.

"Oh, I didn't know you played chess." She thought back to Patterson's comment, wondering why he'd made it.

"There's a lot you don't know about me, my dear."

She took a sip of coffee. The blend was very mild and velvety, perhaps the best she'd tasted.

"Who do you play against?"

"Myself," he replied.

"How can you play a game of chess by yourself? Surely you know all the moves; can't be very interesting."

"On the contrary; gives you the chance to become two different people. Get inside someone else's mind. People are very interesting, don't you find?"

Emily wondered what was coming. He was upset, guarded; nowhere near as open as the night of their date.

"I tend to take them as I find them."

"I'm not so sure that you do, Emily, dear."

"What do you mean?"

"Come on, let's not play games. Why have you come here this morning? Was it to try and salve your conscience?"

She took another sip of coffee but it didn't go down so well.

"I'm not sure what you mean."

Corbett finished his coffee and stood up. "Come, let me show you something."

Emily didn't like the sound of that. Had he asked her the night of the date she'd have gone anywhere with him. She had been in seventh heaven, relaxed, and eager to see and hear anything he had to say.

Now, it was a different story. His manner was cold, his eyes dark and impenetrable, and she was already at a disadvantage because she was in his territory.

"Trust me, my dear. I have no desire to hurt you. I never have had," said Corbett. As he turned and made his way into the hall, he muttered the words, "I wish I could say the same for you."

She followed him through the front door and out on to the drive. He was standing by the open passenger door of the Bentley, gesturing with his arm that she should hop inside.

Against her better judgement, she did. It was daylight. The chances of him doing anything were slim. And despite her conversations about Corbett with Patterson, she did not feel deep down that he *would* do anything.

The whole journey was taken in silence, lasting little more than ten minutes, as he negotiated traffic through the centre of Morley, finishing up on Brunswick Street, outside a care home called Morley Manor. Because of Covid restrictions he could not take her inside but led her to the large bay window of a ground floor room.

Sitting in a plush red velvet, high wingback chair was an old lady with silver hair and glasses, currently dozing. One of the blue uniformed nurses entered the room to check on her and gave Corbett a wave. He waved back.

"The lady in the chair is my ninety-five-year-old mother. They take excellent care of her here. She has everything she wants. When I left you the other night I came here to say goodnight to her before she went to bed, as I do every night."

Emily didn't simply feel bad; she wanted the ground to open up and swallow her, and to close again so that she could never crawl back out.

"Harry," she said.

He raised his hand. "Please, my dear, don't make it any worse."

"But I need to explain."

"No, you don't. I have a very small circle of friends. It wasn't very hard to work out who told the police that I could be the man they were looking for in connection with the recent murders in the town."

"I didn't…"

Once again, he raised his hand. "Please, my dear, don't embarrass either of us, yourself mainly."

As he walked back to the car he said, "I trust you can find your way home. And just for the record, I am not their man."

Chapter Thirty-nine

Gardener and Reilly pulled into the car park of The Glass House, a rural pub, two miles south of Skipton on the A629. Reilly parked the car, killed the engine and jumped out before Gardener. The pair of them dashed across the car park and entered the front door, out of the rain.

The pub was built on three tiers, with wooden beams and a rustic theme running throughout. The floor was parquet, the walls Yorkshire stone. Most of the scenes and prints adorning the walls were of the town from a bygone era.

The top tier catered mainly to the serious foodies. The middle tier served bar snacks and drinks, and the lower tier was for those who wanted only to drink, with a number of private wooden booths around the perimeter, allowing customers the chance to be alone if they wished. Pan Pipes music at a gentle volume attracted the clientele that the pub actually wanted.

The landlord was small but rotund and of indeterminate age, with wiry jet black hair, which ran down his face and formed a beard and moustache. His eyes were as black as his facial hair and his expression said he would rather be anywhere but work on a Saturday evening.

"I'll have a pint of the black stuff," said Reilly, meaning Guinness, "and a still orange for my colleague."

"He's driving, is he?"

"You could say that." Steering straight to the point, Reilly said, "We're looking for a man by the name of Eddie Perrin. We've been told he drinks in here."

"Might do," replied the landlord. "Who's asking?"

"We are," said Reilly, waving his warrant card in the landlord's direction.

With both drinks served, the landlord pointed to the corner. Gardener glanced over. Sitting alone in one of the booths was a man whose head was as large and as round as a football. His hair was sparse and silver in colour. His eyes resembled olives in the snow. He was dressed in a grey overcoat and trousers with brown loafers on his feet; on the bench seat next to him was a brown trilby. Perrin was finishing the dregs of his pint. He didn't appear to have missed many meals over the last few years.

"Can you pull another of what he's having?" asked Gardener.

"No problem," said the landlord.

Gardener collected his orange and nodded to Reilly before walking over to join his prey. When he reached the table he asked, "Eddie Perrin?"

"Who's asking?"

"Is that the standard question around these parts?"

The man glanced up. "It is if you're a tax inspector. And if you are, he left half an hour ago."

"Do I look like a tax inspector?" Gardener asked, checking his clothes as Reilly joined them, placing Perrin's pint in front of him.

"Not now," replied Perrin, "they're not exactly known for their generosity." He picked up his drink and took a sip. "Well, now the pleasantries are out of the way you'd better sit down and let's get down to business. We know it's not tax, so you must be the boys in blue."

"You've not lost your touch, Eddie, old son."

"I can sniff out a copper a mile away."

"You should be able to," said Gardener, "given how many years you served as one."

Perrin nodded, took another sip, and then said, "Either someone's said too much or you've been doing your homework, and I know which one *I* think it'll be. I'm guessing you're not here to buy me pints, or to pass the time of day, so it must be information you're wanting. At least you're going the right way about it, a couple of these and I'm anybody's. Three and I'm everybody's."

Perrin laughed at his own joke; a hearty, infectious laugh that lit up his face like a lightbulb, and had his body rocking.

Both officers sat down. Reilly took a sip of his drink, pursing his lips. "That's pretty good, so it is."

"Aye," said Perrin, taking a mouthful of his pint. "It must be. Judging by your accent, I reckon you'll have tried a few of them back home. He keeps a good pint, our Gerry."

"I wish I could agree," said Gardener, orange in hand.

"So, what do you two do? I'm gathering you're not local."

"No," said Gardener. "MIT, Leeds Central."

"Oh, the serious squad. I were only ever in Morley, never made it as high as Millgarth, as it were called in those days."

"How long *were* you on the force, Mr Perrin?" asked Gardener.

"A good thirty years."

"Do you miss it?" asked Reilly.

"Some days," replied Perrin. "I'm not sure I could cope with the kind of crime you lot investigate now. In my day it were mainly burglaries, muggings, traffic crime, a few deaths, and a bit of armed robbery with violence." Perrin laughed. "I sound like I'm auditioning for summat. But nowadays there's all sorts of technical stuff going down: computers, phones, hacking scandals… I don't know how the hell you cope with it all. How do you chase somebody you can't even see? Criminals can do all manner of things without leaving footprints."

"Oh they still leave footprints," retorted Gardener, "but they're digital."

"My point exactly. How do you catch summat you can't see?"

"You get used to it," said Reilly.

"Suppose you must." Perrin took another mouthful of his drink. The music changed; it was a bit more uptempo but still Pan Pipes.

"So when did you retire?" Gardener asked.

"The start of the millennium. I'd had enough by then, and I could see what were coming."

"How do you pass the time now, then, Eddie, old son?"

"You're looking at it."

Gardener glanced around. "Here?"

"Not all the time. I have a nephew who runs his own business. I do a bit of driving, like, delivering stuff around the country, twice a week. Pays me cash in hand: helps wi' groceries and the odd pint in here. And while I'm doing all that it keeps me out of mischief and keeps the bills down at home. Anyway, lads, this is getting us nowhere," said Perrin. "If we're gonna participate in valuable drinking time, then let's at least have some decent questions. You're here because you want information, which you must think I have, so what is it?"

Reilly came straight out with it. "What happened to Robert Blanchard?"

"Jesus," said Perrin. "Dress it up a bit, why don't you?"

"You asked us," said Reilly, laughing.

Perrin laughed as well. "He's alright, your mate, isn't he? I reckon he's got a right sense of humour."

"He's okay in small doses," replied Gardener.

"Like penicillin." Perrin laughed again and nearly rocked himself out of the booth, before becoming a little more serious. "Robert Blanchard, now there's a name I haven't heard in some time. What's dragged that cold case up?"

"Not quite as cold as you'd think," replied Gardener, realising that Perrin was no mug, and if he wanted information it would have to be on a quid pro quo basis. Gardener would have to answer Perrin's questions if he wanted answers to his own.

"How do you mean, like?" Perrin stopped drinking and his eyes narrowed before they started twitching. He laid his pint to rest on the table, as if it suddenly tasted bad.

"We're not strictly investigating Blanchard, or what happened to him," said Gardener, "but he's cropped up in a current investigation."

"That wouldn't be these bodies you're finding all over Morley, would it?"

"Still up to date, Eddie?" said Reilly.

"It pays to be in the know, son. But as it happens, yes, I am. I've read the papers and watched the news, and I must say I don't envy what you're trying to unravel, but it must be quite interesting if Robert Blanchard's name has come up. He's been gone nigh on forty years and I've thought of nowt else for nearly as long. So if it *was* my attention you wanted, you've got it all now."

"What was he like?" asked Gardener.

"He were a big bloke, physically, you didn't argue with him. At the same time, he had a heart of gold, daft as a brush if he liked you: very conscientious, hard working. He were a dedicated family man. If he had the bit between his teeth he wouldn't be put off the scent. He didn't just *know* the difference between right and wrong, he lived and breathed it, and the justice that followed, no matter what the sentence, and I reckon that's what did it for him."

"We've been reading the records, Mr Perrin," said Gardener. "We know that he went missing. Left home for work one morning and never returned."

Perrin's eyes glazed over, as if he was reliving the moment.

"What nugget was he chasing, Eddie?" asked Reilly. "What was going on that appears to have cost him his life?"

"I'll be honest, son," sighed Perrin, "I don't rightly know. I've had plenty of years to try and work it out, and I've still not come up with a satisfactory answer. All the main figures seemed to disappear in the early Nineties, and although I had my suspicions I had nothing concrete to act upon."

"What *have* you come up with, Mr Perrin?" Gardener asked. "Have you any idea what Robert Blanchard uncovered?"

"Possibly," Perrin stood up. "If you don't mind I'm gonna answer the call of nature and then I'll order another drink. I've bottled this up for long enough, but it's nice to see someone else taking an interest, someone who isn't tied up with bureaucratic red tape, with people blocking the way every time you ask a question. I think I'm gonna enjoy finding out what you have to say, and with a bit of luck, I might be able to fill in some gaps."

When Perrin returned he asked Gardener and Reilly if they wanted another drink. Only Reilly accepted. Once they were all seated, Perrin had with him two packets of crisps, two bags of dry roasted peanuts, and a sachet of pork scratchings.

"I'm partial to the odd snack."

"So I see," replied Reilly.

"Help yourself," said Perrin.

Gardener laughed, wondering if Perrin would regret that, as Reilly dipped into the dry roasted peanuts.

"So," said Perrin, after opening the crisps in the novel way of squeezing the middle and popping the top. Only the top didn't pop, but the bottom instead.

"Shit, it's never done that before," he said, watching the crisps fall out of the packet. Once he gathered them round in a mound and threw a couple in his mouth and took a drink he said, "So, you want to know what Robert Blanchard was up to."

Gardener nodded.

"Well if I'm to be honest here," said Perrin, "I don't rightly know for certain. I remember the night we were called to the convent, to investigate an alleged attack on the Bishop, Charles Pitman. We questioned him for about an hour, but he said there *was* no attack, over and over again."

"That's what we've been told," said Reilly. "The story we heard was he walked into a door."

"That's not what we were told," said Perrin. "Pitman – despite being a bishop – had indulged in one drink too many, and he'd tumbled down the convent steps. The Mother Superior were with him and she dragged him inside and into the vestry to help clean him up. As far as the diocese were concerned, no one from the convent made the call, so they had no idea who had informed the police, but whoever it was they had it wrong."

"Is that the feeling *you* got?" Gardener asked.

"Not really," said Perrin. "But what could we do? You can't force someone to tell you the truth, especially if they had summat as big as they did to hide. We were on our way out when we spotted a young nun. I still remember it now, the look in her eyes. She were dead worried, looked desperate to tell us something. But *they* were hovering around and she wasn't willing to speak. When we got outside, we stayed and listened for a few minutes. We definitely heard raised voices, as if someone were putting the girl through her paces. And I can bloody well guess who."

"The Mother Superior?" asked Gardener.

"Aye," said Perrin. "Old Mother Hubbard. But Robert didn't forget it, so he waited a bit; went back a week later. He actually managed to talk to that young nun. Her name were Isabella Moorcroft, and they met three more times after that, pretty much in secret before Robert had what he thought were enough information about *missing* nuns to start the ball rolling."

"How much did he confide in you?" asked Gardener. "Can you remember the names of the girls who went missing, and what happened to them?"

"According to Isabella Moorcroft, Debra Gosforth endured years of sexual, physical and psychological abuse by the diocese during her childhood and teenage years. Isabella also believed that Debra were forced to participate in Satanic rituals."

"Satanic," repeated Gardener. "Did they have any actual evidence of this, or was it on some nun's say so?"

"It took a lot for that girl to open up," said Perrin, "but she described being placed in a coffin crawling wi' cockroaches, being forced to eat a human eyeball and penetrated wi' a snake to consecrate her orifices to Satan. They were known as The Black Angels, you know."

"Who were?" asked Gardener.

"Them four: Pitman, and Hubbard from the diocese. Trot was a lawyer, and Monarch was an accountant, both of them represented the diocese. Debra Gosforth claimed that one of them had previously killed children, mutilated dogs, *and* performed an abortion on *her* as part of their devil worship."

Perrin finished his pint before continuing. "The next time they came for Debra to do whatever it was they were doing, she never returned. Isabella were told that Debra Gosforth had been taken to another convent in Ireland. No further details were supplied."

"Any idea where all this happened?" asked Reilly.

"Not officially, but I reckon it had to have happened at the convent in Morley."

"Did you have a poke around, see anything to back up the story?"

"No," said Perrin. "We weren't allowed to on the first visit. When we left, we hung around outside for a few minutes, talking about what we'd heard, throwing around ideas when suddenly, Lord Almighty Pitman appeared from nowhere and asked what was going on. We made something up, which I forget now but he weren't stupid. Madam Hubbard then appeared and they closed ranks on us. Got all high and mighty and said that if we wanted meetings, speak to people, or to have a look around we would have to go through the proper channels."

"What about the other girls?"

"It were similar for Lisa Small, but she also told Isabella that a man referred to as the *devil* assaulted her while she lay on a slab surrounded by candles. She said before the attack, she and other girls were taken from their rooms at night to a nearby field where The Black Angels danced naked in a circle around a tree. She were later taken to the back of a candlelit chapel and dragged downstairs. She had no idea where the chapel was.

"According to Lisa, everyone sat round a square slab, and she were given some sweets and told that someone were coming to see her specially, and he were known as the devil. She also claimed she were assaulted then taken back outside and left in an open grave all night.

"She were lifted out the following morning, and put in a blood bath as part of a terrifying ritual. When Isabella asked what Lisa meant about the blood bath, she were told it was blood, but she wasn't sure exactly what it was, or where the blood had been taken from.

"On another occasion she were also forced to perform a sex act on a woman at an orphanage but she didn't know who the woman was or where the orphanage was."

"Jesus Christ," said Reilly. "Are you sure about all this?"

"I'm only telling you what I were told. Lisa also said she were tied to her bed and beaten and warned not to speak about her ordeal. And she claimed she were regularly gagged and had her hair cut off. Isabella vouched for the fact that she were almost bald the last time she had seen her. They never had another chance to speak because Lisa disappeared one night. Isabella were told that Lisa had been taken to another convent in Northern Ireland. Once again, no further details were supplied."

"And the third girl?" questioned Gardener.

"Veronica Walsh alleged that she were made to perform sexual acts by men brought into the convent and that the nuns would deliver her to a priest, who would then rape her.

"That witch, Hubbard, ruled the institution through continuous terror, inflicting shocking abuse and cruelty on the children in her care. Some of the children were known only by a number, not a name. Veronica, she were known as '69'. She were once so badly beaten that her leg needed twenty stitches. On another occasion a kettle of boiling water were poured over her thigh.

"Further allegations were directed against The Black Angels. The sexual abuse, which was commonly associated with physical violence, ranged across inspection of genitalia, kissing, fondling of genitalia, masturbation of a witness by an abuser and the other way around, oral intercourse, rape and gang rape. It were horrendous. When confronted with evidence of sexual abuse, the typical response of the religious authorities was to transfer the offender to another location, where they were free to abuse again. Only in these cases it were the girls that were moved out. In Veronica's case, she had apparently been taken to another convent in North Wales."

"Did you and Robert check any of this out?" asked Reilly.

"We tried but as far as I remember, we didn't get anywhere. I'm not actually sure when and how the girls went missing, but Isabella Moorcroft really believed that the girls had been offered up as human sacrifices."

"Are you serious?" asked Reilly.

"I'm as serious as I can be but I have no proof of anything I'm telling you. But I can tell by the expressions on your faces that you *believe* what I'm saying, and I'll bet it fits in with things you've found out."

"We haven't really found out much," said Gardener. "Torturing people is one thing, but human sacrifice is something else altogether. What exactly would they be hoping to achieve?"

"Let's have another quick toilet break and some more drinks."

Perrin made his way to the toilet whilst Reilly went to the bar. By the time Perrin returned, more drinks and bar snacks were on the table.

"Now you're talking my language," said Perrin.

"And his," said Gardener, glancing at Reilly.

Perrin took a sip and immediately started where he left off.

"I've read a bit about it. You see, human sacrifice requires the exchange of a life – willingly or not – in return for supernatural assistance, or for a greater cause. I have no proof, but nothing would surprise me where them lot were concerned, and it wouldn't be the first time the church had been involved in stuff like that.

"Whether we like it or not, human sacrifice has been with us for more than five thousand years and, in the form of altruistic suicide, is one of the many characteristics that distinguish us from other animals."

Gardener was keen to change the subject because all Perrin was giving them was hearsay. He needed more.

"Let's get back to Robert Blanchard, you really have no idea where he went?"

"To be honest, no. Everyone said it were summat to do with the church because of everything that were going on, but no one knew for certain. If you want my opinion, I believe they played a part in it. I think he got too close to the truth, and those that made the nuns disappear did the same to him.

"I even wondered if the police were in on it at one point. I remember he were told by the superintendent that it was highly unlikely that any of Isabella's claims were true.

"The official story from the diocese was that the girls had been dispersed to other convents around the UK. Robert wasn't so sure, so he spent his own time investigating it privately. He studied the situation, documented everything in a journal so that he had his facts right, and returned to speak with Pitman and Hubbard to check all of those facts, before reporting one more time to his superior officer. But having spoken to the diocese, Robert suddenly failed to report for duty one night, and he were never seen again. There were even an investigation to trace his final movements but we drew a blank."

"Did you ever see the journal?"

"No."

"Any idea what happened to it?"

"No. Probably went missing wi' him."

Gardener figured that some of it was in their possession now. "What did the police do about it?"

"What could they do? The diocese closed ranks, they looked after their own. You have to remember just how bloody powerful the church is. You only have to look at what happens today, still; priests assaulting altar boys and abusing youngsters. Have you ever seen any of them go to prison? Not on your life, they don't. The diocese provided paperwork; it gave the supposed location of the missing girls but it couldn't be fully checked out."

"And then Blanchard disappeared?" asked Reilly.

Perrin nodded. "The official police story seemed like a load of cobblers to me. I reckoned the police knew nothing either. Or they investigated but they didn't get anywhere."

"How many times did you go with him?" asked Gardener.

"Twice. Once for the original investigation. The second time were when we went to see Isabella. After that, Robert went on his own."

"So you only ever met Isabella?"

"Aye, and from what I could see she were a nice lass, not the sort to go making up fancy stories."

"Any idea what happened to her?"

"No. The trail went cold with her. That's when the whole thing came to a blinding halt and the police launched an investigation into my partner's disappearance. Paperwork were provided for Isabella to confirm that she was transferred to a convent in Southern Ireland, somewhere on the West Coast, but we could never prove it."

"Did you check it out?"

"Aye, but whoever we spoke to said it was true and that we were not allowed to speak to her personally."

"If you know all this," said Reilly, "why didn't you say something at the time?"

"What? And end up like Robert?" replied Perrin. "No thanks. Anyway, bloke you wanna be talking to is Winstanley. He were the Super at the time all this kicked off. He were investigating it all: Robert and the nuns going missing, and the attack on that bishop bloke. Only, you can't, can you?"

"Have you ever considered that your friend might *not* have disappeared?" asked Reilly.

"Do you know summat I don't?" asked Perrin, through narrow eyes.

"We don't know anything, Mr Perrin," said Gardener, "but an alternative suggestion has been made."

"Which is?"

"You know him better than we do," said Reilly. "An alternative scenario would be that he chose to disappear so he could continue working through the mess without drawing attention to himself."

Perrin smiled, as if he liked the suggestion. "Well if anyone were capable, it would be him."

After a strained silence, Perrin said. "There is someone else who might be able to help you."

"Who?" asked Gardener.

"His wife, Betty. She's still alive, but she's not in a good way these days. Still lives in the same house on Troy Hill in Morley."

Chapter Forty

Gardener and Reilly stepped into a cosy little parlour. The room was tastefully decorated with a Welsh dresser and a small table and chairs. An open fire was spitting and crackling, next to that was a high wingback chair and a coffee table, on top of which was an envelope and a book. Background noise was provided by an old-fashioned radio on a shelf behind the chair.

What did pique Gardener's attention was the chessboard in an alcove. That could prove interesting.

"God, that's a welcome sight," said Reilly, creeping closer to the flames, rubbing his hands together.

Gardener wiped himself down a little. The weather outside had grown torrential: winds and very heavy rain battered the small town.

Betty leant forward on her cane, reaching towards a log on the hearth.

Reilly stopped her. "Don't you worry yourself, love, I'll do that. Park yourself in that chair."

"I can't do that," replied Betty, "you're my guests, and you need a cup of tea."

"As I said, you park yourself, dear lady. I'll take care of the tea."

"Are you sure? I'm not having a good day today."

As she explained her problem, Gardener helped her into the seat.

"Don't you worry, Mrs Blanchard, we'll take care of everything. Do you have any help?"

"I have my son."

"What about carers, or meals on wheels?"

"No, love," said Betty, "no need for them. I've cooked and baked all my life. No need to start falling back on things now, just 'cause I'm getting on." She turned to Reilly. "In that cupboard on the wall to the right of the sink you'll find some chocolate cake. Help yourself."

Reilly's eyes lit up.

"You might regret saying that, Mrs Blanchard," said Gardener.

"I like to see a healthy appetite."

The conversation continued as small talk until Reilly returned with everything they needed.

Once Gardener had finished his cake, he explained the reason for the visit, and the fact that they had met with Eddie Perrin earlier in the day and, if possible, they may need her help to clear up one or two things.

"I've not seen him for a while, how is he?"

"He seems okay," said Gardener, "but he indicated that you might be able to fill in some blanks. I wonder if we could get a little bit of background, please, Mrs Blanchard. How long have you lived here?"

"All my married life," she replied. "Me and my husband, Robert, bought it when we were first married."

"You've not lived anywhere else?"

"Not since we married, love."

"And your son was born here?"

"Our Andy? Aye." She smiled. "The big lummox. Yes, he grew up here. He's a builder now, keeps himself fit."

"Does he have his own business?" asked Reilly.

"I believe so. To be honest, I've no idea what he does but he's not short of a bob or two, and he looks after me," she replied. "He's a grafter, I'll give him that. He were devastated when Robert disappeared; they shared so much together. He'll not agree with me but it were his dad disappearing that were the making of him."

"How so?" Reilly asked.

"I forced him to pick himself up, dust himself down, put one foot in front of the other and start living his life again. He had a good job with a local builder called Fred Jibb, who had given Andy a great start when it came to employment, was willing to teach him everything he could about the building trade. Fred had most of the local contracts for the council and the police force.

"And then I gave Andy another piece of advice. I'd been saving money, for quite some time and I was able to give him enough to buy an old tumbledown cottage at the edge of Tor Wood just outside the town. No one else would touch it because everyone believed it was completely beyond repair.

"He renovated the place himself. Mid-December it was, and most people wouldn't have bothered with the place until the New Year. But Andy isn't most people. He was up on scaffold on Christmas Eve, in the driving snow, putting on new roof tiles.

"His mates all laughed at him on the way to the pub, telling him that's where *he* should be. By the time March came round, Andy had finished the renovation and a young couple expecting their first child moved into a spotless, up to date, and safe as anything new house.

"That was his first house, and the wisest move he had ever made. Do you know, he saw those same mates ten years later, on their way to the pub again; he was taking me to a rather posh restaurant in his new car. Funny really, they weren't laughing at him then."

"Sounds like he has a wise head on his shoulders," said Gardener. Although he found it interesting, he needed to move on.

"He has. He's not just a builder, he surprised me once when he told me about an IT course he were doing, when he reckoned computers were going to be the next big thing. You wouldn't think a builder would be into computers, would you. I know I'm not; I can barely work the telly."

Reilly stood and moved over to the chessboard.

"Who's the chess player?"

"That's our Andy as well. Bloody good he is. His dad taught him."

A chill ran down Gardener's spine: computers, chess, builder; all fitted in with the man they were searching for.

"Does he play against himself now?" Reilly asked.

"No, not that I know of. That game hasn't been touched for forty years. Robert made the last move on his way out of the door that fateful morning."

Reilly glanced at Betty. "And no one's made a move since?"

"No. Our Andy's waiting for his father to come home. He thinks it would be an unfair advantage if he made the move without his father seeing it."

"Interesting," said Reilly, taking his seat.

"Can I ask you, Mrs Blanchard," said Gardener, "have you ever heard from Robert since his disappearance?"

"No," said Betty. "Although they could trace his whereabouts to the last place he had been and roughly at what time, when he had left that building he was never seen again, nor did we ever hear from him. His bank accounts and building society savings were never touched. He simply disappeared and no one could tell us where."

"Mrs Blanchard," said Gardener, "I would like to discuss a little of what Robert found on the final investigation, if I may."

"Of course you can, love. My memory's not as good as it was but I'll try my best."

Gardener covered the things that Perrin had told them, and Betty backed up the fact that Robert also believed the nuns had been sacrificed. No one could ever prove that; nor could they prove the nuns had gone where the diocese had said. The church elders simply confirmed it but wouldn't let anyone from the outside world interfere with the nuns.

Gardener found that ironic, since most of the people on the inside seemed to be interfering with them.

"Eddie Perrin said that Robert had kept a journal of everything he had discovered, but Perrin never saw it. Did you?"

"I did, love. I helped him prepare it."

"Do you still have it?" Gardener asked.

"No, love. I have no idea where it is. I've not seen it since the day he left."

"Where was it when you last saw it?"

"In an upstairs cupboard in my bedroom, but it's not there now."

Gardener asked Reilly to pop to the car and bring back the photocopies of the pages they had. Within minutes, Gardener was showing Betty those pages.

"Do you recognize the handwriting?"

Betty's eyes misted over. "Aye, love, I do. That's Robert's. Is this all you have, four pages? There was so much more to it."

"I'm afraid so," said Gardener.

"Where did *you* find them?"

"I shouldn't really tell you, Mrs Blanchard, but I don't think it will make much difference now. We found them at the crime scenes."

"It's a crying shame what happened to those girls, officer. I hope to God you get some justice for them, and for my Robert. No one should be allowed to get away with that."

"Justice for Robert makes *me* think that you don't believe he just walked out and disappeared of his own accord," said Gardener.

"Why would he? He had a good job, well paid, nice home, family, and he were a good detective," replied Betty. "No, love, he didn't walk out, whatever happened to him was made to happen, and likely as not, it was them lot at the convent who were responsible. But that's just my opinion – not fact."

Betty put her arms on the arms of the chair and pushed upwards. "Would you excuse me whilst I nip to the toilet?"

As she stood up, so did Reilly, grabbing and passing her walking stick. She shuffled out of the room, and Reilly returned his attention to the chessboard.

Gardener noticed how intensely his partner was staring at the board.

"What's up?"

Reilly glanced back. "Some of the pieces are missing."

"Pardon?" said Gardener, on his feet. "Which ones?"

"There are five black pieces missing," said Reilly. "King, queen, rook, knight and bishop."

Gardener grew cold inside. "Are you sure?"

Reilly glanced around. "There are pieces on the board, and pieces at the side. Those at the side have been taken during the game, but they don't match up to what's on the board."

Gardener glanced around. There was nowhere else they could be. There were no cupboards and no spare shelves. The Welsh dresser was full of ornaments and plates. Fully aware that he shouldn't really be snooping, he leaned over and opened up the drawers, which were full of knick-knacks – tablecloths, place mats, extra cutlery, coasters and many other kitchen utensils – but no chess pieces.

He turned to face Reilly. "So if they're not at the side of the board, where are they?"

"I'd say we had them."

"There's no way Betty Blanchard is responsible for any of this, so maybe Robert really *didn't* disappear."

"But how the hell would he get in and out of this house without his wife knowing?"

"He'd still have the keys," said Gardener. "They've lived here all their married life. But I have to be honest, I don't really buy it."

"What other explanation is there?" asked Reilly.

"That it's Andy and not Robert," said a voice behind them. Betty Blanchard was standing near her chair. In one hand she had the stick, in the other a couple of black and white photographs. She struggled and finally dropped herself into the chair. "I brought these for you."

Gardener and Reilly sat down and Gardener took the photos.

"That's Robert, on the right," said Betty. "Andy on the left."

Gardener was amazed. "They're like two peas in a pod." He passed them over to Reilly.

"In every way," said Betty. "They look the same, they talk the same, have the same mannerisms. Andy's just a carbon copy of his dad."

"Mrs Blanchard," said Gardener, "you must have heard some of our conversation about the possibility of Robert never having disappeared."

"A little, but I don't believe for one second that he went missing of his own accord, or that he's still alive and seeking out justice for what happened to those poor girls. I think the person seeking justice is our Andy."

"Why would he?" Reilly asked.

"He was always hell bent on revenge for the disappearance of his father. He was convinced it had something to do with the diocese, and he felt that the police failed us. He's never given up on his dad, but he always said that one day he would see to it that justice would be served… one way or another."

It made sense to Gardener, certainly more sense than a serving police officer going missing and coming back years later to avenge the crime.

"Where does your son live, Mrs Blanchard?"

"That's just it, officer, I've really no idea. He owns that many properties. The first place you should start is the flat above Patterson's butcher shop on Queen Street. He's mentioned that place a few times."

Gardener immediately pulled out his phone and called Colin Sharp and asked him to follow up that piece of information, and to pay a visit to a cottage at Tor Wood once Betty had told him which one. He gave Sharp further details and said he wanted a background check running on Andy Blanchard, any bank accounts, and any property.

"Why have you never said anything?" Gardener asked Betty, once he'd disconnected his call.

"He's my son."

"So why tell us now?" asked Reilly.

Betty Blanchard sighed and sat back in the chair. She glanced at the table, and the envelope that bore the NHS logo.

"Because time isn't on my side, officer, and when I go to meet my maker, it's important to me that I have a clear conscience. Call it the last rites if you will. In other words, I think it will be the last right thing I do."

Chapter Forty-one

Andy Blanchard brought his van to a stop outside his mother's house and switched off the engine. The weather was horrendous; torrential rain and heavy winds had battered the town for what seemed like ever, causing localized flooding. Water blasted the windscreen like a hail of bullets.

He glanced at the dashboard: 8:00pm. He was quite surprised that his mother's house was in darkness. He knew she went to bed early but not at eight; too many soaps to watch.

His mind wandered to other things. The constant bad weather had certainly impeded his plans for Winstanley. Moving him was a nightmare, but worth it. He hoped the bastard had not yet had a heart attack, therefore robbing Andy of any pleasure yet to come.

He sat back in his seat, smiling to himself. Nearly forty years ago his father went missing. Andy never believed any of what was said at the time and he didn't now. But he *had* decided back then that something had to be done, and it was unlikely the police were going to do it. He understood their hands were tied. But his weren't.

Patience was a virtue, something he had picked up over the years, and it had paid off. The plan was finally coming to fruition. It had started with Old Mother Hubbard, and tonight it would end with Winstanley, the police superintendent who had done nothing despite knowing plenty. He would pay for sitting idly by, making up excuses.

Andy jumped out of the van and caught a face full of rain. The door swung wide and it took all he had to close it again, so powerful was the wind.

"Fucking weather," he shouted, as he locked the door.

He quickly opened the gate and ran down the path to the back door. The security light lit up and he let himself in.

The kitchen was also in darkness and the first thing he noticed was how cold the house was. His mother had never kept a cold house, certainly not in later years when she was struggling with her condition.

"Mam?" he shouted.

There was no reply. He didn't like that either. He could hear the radio in the parlour. She *could* be listening, but why in the dark? And why not answer him? Unless she'd nodded off.

He switched on a light, glanced around the kitchen, noticed pots in the sink. Another no-no. Betty always washed and dried her dishes after her meals no matter what. She would not go to bed and leave pots in the sink.

Andy's heart raced. He scurried through the kitchen into the parlour, switching on another light. He found his mother sitting in the fireside chair. The flames of the fire had long since died. They were not the only ones. Betty's skin had a blue tinge. In her right hand she clutched a letter.

"Mam?" shouted Andy, bending down.

Her skin was cold to touch. She wasn't breathing.

"No," said Andy. "Come on, Mam, not now. We're so close to the end."

Instinctively, he grabbed the letter headed NHS. Betty had recently had two scans on her lungs. The results of the second insisted that she make an appointment with her doctor so they could discuss the results. That wasn't good. They never said as much, but the tone of the letter and his mother's recent ill health meant it was likely to be bad news.

Too late now. Andy wondered if she *had* spoken to her doctor.

A tear meandered down his face. He felt so heavy and yet, hollow, as if he was treading water. Andy stood up, walked back into the kitchen, taking the door that led upstairs. When he returned he had a thick woolly blanket, which he placed around Betty.

"It's alright, Mam. I'll finish this now. By the time tonight is out, every one of those bastards will have paid."

He knelt down beside her and held her hand.

"I know he's not coming back, Mam, and maybe I've let you down. I suspect you knew all along what I was doing, but don't think badly of me. Don't you worry, I'll finish what Dad started."

He placed her hand underneath the blanket, tucking her in completely.

"You rest in peace, Mam."

Chapter Forty-two

The incident room was a hive of activity when Gardener and Reilly finally returned to the station. Gardener was cold because of the torrential weather, so he appreciated the warmth of the building.

Reilly went straight to the coffee machine. As Gardener glanced around, he noticed Benson and Edwards at the whiteboard. Anderson and Thornton were on the phone. Rawson and Sharp were studying documents; he couldn't even see Gates or Longstaff. Phones were ringing, chatter was incessant, and everyone appeared to be deep into something.

Reilly passed Gardener a freshly made cup of tea.

"And before you ask it's not from the machine."

Anderson and Thornton finished their calls, joining the others around the whiteboard. Gardener and Reilly updated them on the meeting with Eddie Perrin, and then with Betty Blanchard.

"I felt sorry for her," said Gardener. "She clearly knew what was going on but felt powerless to do anything."

"Or she figured blood was thicker than water," added Reilly.

"Do you think she's known all along?" asked Sharp.

"Probably not all along," said Gardener, "but there must have come a point when she started adding things up."

"God, she must have been tortured," said Anderson.

"Not wanting to believe the obvious," added Thornton.

"Sounds that way," said Gardener.

He turned and faced the whiteboard as Briggs entered the room.

"Okay, I realise it's Saturday and very few people want to play ball on a weekend, but we have a job to do, and if we're going to save Edward Winstanley's life, it doesn't matter what day of the week we choose."

"There's always the possibility he's missing for another reason, Stewart," said Briggs, "that our man doesn't have him."

"I don't think there's much chance of that, sir," replied Gardener.

Gardener glanced at his watch. "I know it's late but we need every scrap of information you guys have collected, no matter how little or insignificant, before we go tonight. It could be the difference between life and death for someone."

"We visited the butcher on Queen Street," said Benson. "Patterson claimed that he had not seen Blanchard for some time – about a week."

"He used to live in the flat above the shop until then," said Edwards, "but he rented it out to another couple."

"I assume then that he *owns* the flat above the shop," said Gardener.

"He owns the shop as well," said Benson.

"Christ," said Reilly. "He has been busy."

"Patterson said he hasn't seen him since then but he knows that Andy Blanchard has lots of other properties so he could be anywhere," said Benson.

"Did you find out where those properties are?" asked Gardener.

"Only a couple of them," said Edwards, "but he wasn't at those either."

"Nor was he at the cottage in Tor Wood," said Anderson.

"We paid a visit to that place and the young couple reckoned they'd been renting it for a couple of years," said Thornton, "from Blanchard. They said he's a brilliant landlord; doesn't overcharge, fixes things on time and doesn't show up very often unless summoned."

"When he shows up right away," said Anderson, "or within the same day."

"Looks like we have a manhunt on our hands," said Reilly.

"Have we been able to run a list of *all* the properties he owns?" Gardener asked.

Bob Anderson consulted his notes. "We're still on with it but we have a few here to go on."

"Okay, let's jump on it first thing tomorrow morning, see what we can find."

"He has to be in one of them," said Reilly.

"Depends how many he has," said Briggs. "We might be days finding out where they all are, especially if they're not in his name."

"And I have a feeling we don't have days," said Gardener. He turned to Sharp. "Anything on bank accounts?"

"In the time that we've had, not a lot," said Sharp.

"It is Saturday... night," added Rawson.

"But we did manage a little nugget, thanks to the wonders of modern technology," said Sharp. "As we already know, accounts were opened in the Nineties under the names of Pitman, Hubbard, Monarch and Trot."

Rawson took over. "Two were opened in the traditional manner, and two were opened online. It's the traditional method that's let him down."

"He opened them using the names Mark Trot and Richard Monarch," said Sharp. "One with Lloyds in Leeds and the other with HSBC in Shipley."

"Both banks required photo ID," said Rawson, "which *he* supplied, and *they* still have on file. They emailed it over. His big mistake was using the same photo with false paperwork for both."

"The photos are old," said Sharp, holding the black and white photo that Betty had supplied, "but you can tell it's him. He hasn't changed much."

"Have you found anything in the records that connects Ken Proctor?" asked Gardener.

"Not so far."

Gardener was a touch frustrated. "What part did *he* play in this?"

"Maybe he didn't," replied Sharp.

"He had to have played a part somewhere because of the leases. But at least we finally have something," said Gardener. "There is something I don't understand. Our man has made very few mistakes, why would he make such an amateur move with this?"

"Early days, wasn't it, Stewart," said Briggs. "The longer he went on, the more careful he will have become."

"Maybe in the early days," said Anderson, "he was in a rush."

"Or too confident," added Thornton.

"What about transactions?" asked Gardener. "Are they usually online or in person, and have there been many?"

"Nothing in the early days. More recently, online," said Sharp, "switch card at first, but contactless now. He was obviously thinking things out more. Paying with cards and using computers kept him away from the banks."

The door to the room suddenly flew back and hit the wall when an excited Gates and Longstaff rushed in.

"Pleased you could join us, so we are," said Reilly.

"You'll change your tune when you hear what we have to say," said Gates.

"Go on," said Gardener.

"We've cracked the final cryptic clue from scene four," said Longstaff.

"What have you got?" asked Briggs.

"That long, strange puzzle is in fact a Google Earth coordinate," said Gates, "and we know exactly where it is."

Chapter Forty-three

Four squad cars pulled up on Commercial Street, all of them parking in the car park of the former funeral directors, opposite the former Convent of All Hallows in the Wood. Gardener and Reilly, along with Anderson and Thornton were in one. Sharp, Rawson, Benson and Edwards in another. Gates and Longstaff in the third.

Gardener jumped out and peered at the building through the blistering rain, trying to hold on to his jacket and hat. The wind whistled through the trees and he could barely hear himself think. He peered at his watch. It was after ten at night, the place should have been in darkness, but beams of light were shining through the roof. The building – if the stories were to be believed – had seen enough grim goings on in its life, but God only knew what they were going to find when they walked in tonight. Gardener issued tasks quickly.

"Listen closely everyone. I appreciate all your hard work and it looks as if the girls were right in reading the final clue. I want you all to spread out: Bob, Frank, Patrick and Paul, take the rear of the building, please, and keep your eyes open. Colin, Dave, you come with me and Sean, we'll take the front door."

"What about us?" Gates asked.

"Can you guys stay here in the car park? I've no reason to suspect our man is working with anyone but if he is, forewarned is to be forearmed. See anything you don't like, call me."

"See anything, in this weather?" said Gates. "You must be joking."

Eight officers sloped across the road and into the grounds, holding on to their clothing. Four of them took the path around the building leading to the rear. The others headed for the front with the senior officer.

For Gardener, the eeriest feeling of all was the fact that it was so silent. There were lights inside the building, but no sound, so he had no idea what the hell he was walking into.

Standing at the front door, he noticed it was open two or three inches, and the shape of the building allowed him some respite from the weather. Before going in he turned, speaking to Rawson and Sharp.

"Give us a minute or so. Just wait here to see if anyone else turns up from anywhere."

"And then come in?" asked Sharp.

"You might as well," said Reilly. "I think we're gonna need you."

"Fucking joking, aren't you," said Rawson to Reilly. "You don't need anybody. If we go in there, it won't be to save you from him."

Reilly smiled. "Very funny."

Gardener pushed open the door and immediately thought he'd walked into Dante's Inferno.

Everything had come full circle. Forty years ago, the former convent was the scene of the original crimes. Now, it was witnessing yet further death and destruction.

The man Gardener took to be Edward Winstanley was fastened onto a giant crucifix. But it was in fact more than that. Knowing what Gardener knew about Andy Blanchard, he suspected the additions were his handiwork.

Winstanley's arms, legs, and head, were connected to ropes, each of them running through a series of pulleys, which appeared to turn at will, taking the retired police inspector one step nearer to a grisly end. The wheels all turned a little at the same time, the ropes tightened. Winstanley gasped and grimaced. Rain leaked in from the holes where the tiles should have been and despite the wind outside, Gardener could hear the constant dripping of water.

"Jesus Christ," said Rawson, as he slipped in behind the senior officers.

The wheels turned again, and Gardener figured they needed to do something quickly, because the old man would not survive much more.

The big question was where Blanchard might be hiding. To the right of the crucifix, Gardener saw a cage the size of a shipping container, but it was empty. He turned to Rawson and Sharp.

"You two take the left side of the building, we'll go to the right."

As soon as all four men made their first move, a voice shouted, "Stay right where you are, you lot."

Gardener glanced upwards but he couldn't see anyone. All of them stood still, obviously unaware of what possible danger they might be in.

Andy Blanchard suddenly appeared from behind the cage: big, shaven-headed. Gardener guessed his weight at around eighteen or nineteen stone. Very little of that was fat. He wore a T-shirt under a leather jacket, and jeans, with trainers.

"I've waited forty years for this moment, don't think you lot are going to muscle in here and spoil it for me."

"You won't get away with it," said Reilly.

"Funny you should say that," replied Blanchard. "I know four people that nearly did forty years ago. And this piece of filth" – he pointed to Winstanley – "didn't do a thing."

"I know how you must feel, Mr Blanchard–" started Gardener.

"I very much doubt that," said Blanchard.

A sudden clap of thunder burst overhead, drowning out anything else that Blanchard said. A sheet of lightning lit up the night sky and the crucifix, the scene reminiscent of a Hammer horror film.

The wheels turned again, the ropes tightened and Winstanley let out a yelp.

"For Christ's sake man," shouted Reilly, "this is not the answer."

"How would you lot know?" shouted Blanchard. "You never had any answers for my dad."

Suddenly, the four officers outside the building all appeared inside, behind Gardener and Reilly. Gates and Longstaff also wedged themselves in.

"I thought I told you to stay in the car park."

"What, and miss all the fun?" said Gates, staring up. "What the hell's happened to him?"

"He did," said Reilly, pointing to Blanchard.

"It's what's going to happen if we don't do something soon," said Gardener.

More thunder, more lightening and more rain all drowned out his words. Gardener noticed Blanchard suddenly glance up, and then down at the ground. Something had caught his attention.

A large plasma screen to the right of Winstanley came to life. Gardener had not noticed it before, and he didn't stop to question where the power was coming from, or how safe it would be. On the screen he saw a chessboard. The pieces were all set up and ready for a game.

Blanchard glanced at the ground again, turning his head left to right. Something was obviously bothering him.

"Right, listen up, because I'm only going to say this once," he shouted. "One of you needs to go over to that TV and play a game of chess against the computer."

"For what?" Gardener asked.

"His life," shouted Blanchard, pointing at Winstanley.

"Don't be ridiculous," said Reilly. "The game's up, Blanchard. We've caught you. Don't make things any worse for yourself."

"I'm finished anyway," shouted Blanchard. "I don't care what happens to me. At least I'll have the satisfaction of knowing every one of these bastards has suffered for what they did to those poor girls, me and my family. Now get one of your fucking officers over to that TV and start playing the game."

Gardener took a few steps forward. "Look…"

"No buts," shouted Blanchard. "Here's the rule; there are no rules. One of you needs to play against the computer, and you need to beat it if you want to save his life."

The wheels turned again, pulling the old man's limbs tighter than Gardener would have thought possible without them coming apart.

Winstanley screamed, and said something, but no one understood it.

"And there is a time limit. If you don't beat it within ten minutes, him up there" – Blanchard pointed at Winstanley again – "will become part of the landscape."

"I'm on it," said Longstaff, rushing forward.

"Julie," shouted Gardener, but it was pointless, she was halfway to the destination.

Gates also ran forward. As Gardener was about to speak, another peel of thunder rattled and vibrated the building, and a sheet of lightning lit up overhead, Gardener saw a gap in the ground open up, and the cage behind Blanchard suddenly dropped on one side.

"Jesus Christ," said Reilly, "we might be in the middle of a landslide."

Blanchard suddenly took off very swiftly and disappeared through a door at the back of the building.

Gardener turned to the team.

"One of you phone for an ambulance. The rest of you, see if it is possible to free Winstanley. Sean, let's you and I go and see if we can talk some sense into this madman."

Chapter Forty-four

Once through the door, Gardener realized they were not in another room of the church, but in fact, outside, in a graveyard, with the rain coming at them from all angles.

"Brilliant," shouted Reilly. "How the hell do we find him in this place?"

As he said that, another peel of thunder, followed by a flash of lightning lit up the grounds and they saw Blanchard in the distance, dodging around the gravestones.

"Come on," said Gardener, "we need to catch him somehow."

The pair of them set off but it was very difficult to work out a clear path, there was so little light. Gardener tripped and Reilly waited to see what had happened.

"I'm okay, Sean, just carry on."

As Gardener reached his feet he was tired, wet and very likely dirty but now was not the time. He peered into the graveyard, able to make out two figures. Another sheet of lightning helped enormously, especially when he heard a scream and saw one of them lose his footing.

But it wasn't Reilly.

Gardener then heard his partner shouting, and a small light appeared in the distance, which must have been his phone.

As he made his way across the cemetery, he could hear Andy Blanchard bawling and screaming, in fact, almost squealing.

He caught up with them and found Reilly on the edge of what appeared to be an open grave – but it was much deeper, much wider. The earth around it continued to pour in, as did more water. Gardener was suddenly shocked when a headstone fell forward, into the gap, landing on Andy Blanchard, who was stuck at the bottom, his leg now trapped by the stone.

Most shocking of all was that he could see bones: legs, arms, a skull. Despite everything that had happened, he couldn't help but ask if Blanchard was okay.

"Do I look okay?" he shouted back. "Get me out of here!"

"I can't reach him," said Reilly, standing up.

"We need a rope," said Gardener. "Did you see anything in the building?"

"No," said Reilly, "but I wasn't really looking."

Reilly actually set off before Gardener could say anything else.

The senior officer turned his attention back to Blanchard.

"Don't panic, we'll get you out."

More thunder, more lightning, another sudden gust of wind, and a faster hail of rain all added to Gardener's discomfort.

"For God's sake, get me out," shouted Blanchard. "I can't stand being enclosed."

"Mr Blanchard," shouted Gardener, "you need to stop panicking. We'll do everything we can."

Blanchard was desperately trying to remove the headstone, when another one fell in, on the same leg. He screamed and his eyes shot upwards.

"Get me out of this fucking place!" He started to babble. "I once saw a bloke fall in a cement mixer. He were a right fucking mess, got cut to ribbons, his fucking head fell out. And that Billy bastard Doyle forced me into it afterwards to clean it out because he thought it would be funny."

Gardener didn't know who or what the hell he was on about but at least he was talking. He dropped to the ground and leaned in closer, asking a question.

"Why now, Mr Blanchard?"

"Why now, what?"

"Why have you waited till now to do all of this?"

"Why not now? Is there ever a good time? I saw what them bastards did to my mother after my dad went. She were never the same again. Someone had to get even, get justice for what they did, and you lot didn't do anything. That's why Winstanley's in there, paying for what he didn't do; put that lot away. Me mother needed justice and closure, and maybe now was the right time, before anything happened to her. But it has happened, and I'm too late, she never saw it, did she? Them bastards got away with it again."

"What do you mean she never saw it?" asked Gardener.

"She's dead, isn't she? Died before I could finish this."

Chapter Forty-five

The nightmare *inside* the convent was equal to the one outside.

Longstaff played the chess game on the computer, aided by Gates, but they were going nowhere fast. The game must have been set on the hardest level and they had lost half of their pieces already.

"This is mental," said Longstaff, "I can't play against this, it's impossible."

Gates glanced at Winstanley, who was hanging, motionless. She hoped he'd only passed out. Four of the team circled the bottom of the crucifix, searching for something.

Two were trying to climb the framework in order to reach Winstanley, but even that appeared to be more difficult than they had thought.

The wheels suddenly turned again but the retired police officer made no sound.

"Oh, Christ," said Longstaff. She'd lost another two pieces, and had only about six left, none of which were the queen.

"This isn't working," said Gates.

She noticed Reilly suddenly rush into the building, crossing the ground at warp speed. He ran into the container-sized cage, and back out again very quickly, carrying a rope.

"There's only one thing for it," said Longstaff.

"What?"

"Pull the plug on the computer."

"What good will that do?" asked Gates.

"It'll stop the game, buy us some time… maybe."

Although Longstaff wasn't convinced she still followed the electrical supply, which ended up inside what might have been a vestry. When she found it, she pulled it out and ran back into the main building.

"Any good?" she asked Gates.

The turn of the wheels gave her the answer.

Chapter Forty-six

Gardener was still on the ground when he heard clomping footsteps to his right as Reilly returned.

Before his partner could say anything, Gardener also heard the sound of a siren, and saw flashing blue lights in the direction of the road outside the church.

"How are they doing inside?" asked Gardener.

"Not very well, by the look of things."

Reilly tied the rope to a gravestone.

"Are you listening to me, copper?" shouted Blanchard, still struggling to remove the headstones from his leg.

It was going to be difficult due to the angle he was laid at. The softened ground underneath him meant he had no leverage.

"I'm sorry, Mr Blanchard," said Gardener, "please go on."

"You wanted to know about Ken Proctor," said Blanchard, obviously tiring because his sentences were breaking up. "He did the dirty work. Cut the bodies up and sewed them all to each other in a different order."

"How did you get him to do that?" asked Gardener.

Reilly had finished tying the rope to the stone. He pulled on it a few times.

"Do you think it's wise?" Gardener asked his partner.

"No choice."

"I made him sign a ninety-nine-year lease," shouted Blanchard, "for the use of the lock-up and the old house, which is why he kept quiet."

"Why would he do that?" Gardener asked.

"The farm was losing serious money. Looked like going under. Mounting pressure from other local farms made it look as if Ken was going to have to sell up."

"Must have been more to it than that," shouted Reilly, taking the rope, trying to gain a foothold.

"There was. Ken's wife, Jean, were dying. Or she would have done if she didn't get the operation she needed. The only way they could do it were privately, and that were going to take some serious money. I turned out to be a lifeline to Ken Proctor."

"There must have been more," said Gardener. "The leases wouldn't have been enough to keep him quiet. What else did he do?"

"He kept quiet because he was implicated in the murders," said Blanchard. "Who do you think were cutting up the bodies and rejoining them? He couldn't let that cat out of the bag, could he?"

"Did you kill him?" asked Reilly.

Blanchard laughed. "Loose lips sink ships and all that."

A crack of lightning suddenly blasted the church roof in a direct hit, causing roof tiles and a lot of debris to fall inwards.

Gardener and Reilly both ducked and covered their ears out of instinct.

"What the fuck were that?" shouted Blanchard.

"Sean, we have to wrap this up as quickly as possible and get out of here."

"Then I have no choice."

Reilly lowered one foot down the side of the chasm that Blanchard had fallen into but he could not gain a foothold.

"Sean, for God's sake," shouted Gardener. "Be careful."

Another blast of rain hit Gardener in the face and almost knocked him into the open grave. He lost his footing, falling down on one knee.

Suddenly, a great sucking sound emanated from the open chasm and the wet ground gave way, turning the whole thing into a mudslide.

Another headstone fell forward and into the opening, landing on Blanchard's chest. He let out a great wheezing sound and Gardener was sure he'd cracked a few ribs.

With no further warning, the earth beneath Blanchard gave way. More bones came tumbling out. The headstones slid forward and the whole lot disappeared from view as a great sweeping tidal wave of water coursed into the gap, taking everything in its path.

The headstone with the rope suddenly upended, falling forward into the opening, taking Reilly with it.

As his partner fell past him, Gardener hit the ground, grabbing Reilly's ankle in the process.

The force of Reilly falling into the plot, dragged Gardener forward, and because the ground was wet, he could do little or nothing to stop himself joining his partner.

Reilly shouted something that Gardener could not hear, but he held on to him for dear life.

"Sean, hold on."

"To what?"

Gardener suddenly stopped sliding forward. Something had snagged his ankle. He didn't know what, but he was grateful for now.

The only problem was, he was unable to pull Reilly up on his own.

Gardener suddenly felt himself being pulled backwards.

"Hold on, boss," shouted Dave Rawson. "We'll soon have you both out."

Gardener turned and peered behind him. Dave Rawson held one leg, Colin Sharp the other. Together they managed to drag Gardener clear of the opening, who held on to Reilly's ankle like a trap. He was not prepared to lose his partner.

It took a minute of tugging and pulling before both men were pulled clear. Gardener bent over to catch his breath. Reilly stood by his side.

"Thank you," Reilly said to Rawson.

The big man smiled. "You'd have done the same for me."

The team may have thrown a lot of banter around in the incident room, but Gardener knew how much respect they had for each other.

With the rain still tearing down, Gardener stood up and peered into the opening that had contained Blanchard. There was nothing left: no headstones, no rope, no Blanchard – lots of water. All of them had disappeared deep into the ground.

Gardener turned. "There's nothing we can do here. We'd better get back in there, see what's happening."

As Gardener stepped into the church from the rear, he was pleased to see that the place had been vacated, which must have meant they had managed to free Winstanley.

He found them all outside the front door. The ambulance was leaving, blue lights flashing, sirens blaring. Another one had pulled up behind and was still parked at the side of the road.

"Is he still alive?" Gardener asked Gates.

"I don't know."

"What happened? Did you manage to beat the game?"

"In a manner of speaking," replied Longstaff. "We pulled the plug on the computer, stopped it."

"We were hoping to stop the wheels turning," said Gates.

"Did it work?" asked Reilly.

"Not at first," replied Gates, "but there must have been some connection to the computer because they made one more turn after it was switched off and then stopped altogether."

"The medics freed him from that crucifix," said Longstaff, "but he didn't look good. They couldn't tell us anything."

"Did you finally catch the madman who'd built it?" Gates asked Gardener. "The man responsible for this mess?"

Gardener shook his head. "Afraid not. But he won't give us any more trouble."

Epilogue

Two days later

The rain and the bad weather had finally stopped sometime in the early hours of Sunday morning. Gardener and Reilly had met with Briggs at the station and explained everything. As the old building was still a crime scene, Briggs ordered a team of investigators in to comb the grounds to see if they could retrieve the body of Andy Blanchard.

It was now Monday and Gardener and Reilly were at the rear of the church. A surprising development in the shape of a skeleton had been found, chained to the cellar wall of the disused convent, and Gardener had been called immediately.

The forensic anthropologist met the pair of them at the side of the church.

"Thank you for coming."

She introduced herself as Claire Sutton; approximately thirty years old, slim, with chestnut coloured hair peeking out of the hood of a scene suit. She wore glasses and spoke with a husky, mellow voice.

Gardener nodded. "What can you tell us?"

"It was the torrential weather that brought all of this to light, otherwise we'd have had no idea," said Sutton. "The skeleton chained to the wall was male, tall, probably well-built when he'd been alive."

"Would you like to estimate how long he's been there?"

"It's not easy to say, but a couple of quick tests suggest between thirty and fifty years. What I don't understand is why he was chained to the wall, underneath a convent."

"We could hazard a guess," said Reilly.

"He wasn't by himself."

"You mean you've found our man as well?" asked Gardener.

"Hopefully. He actually ended up right next to the skeleton chained to the wall, with his arms around it. He couldn't have been better positioned if he'd been placed. But there was also another skeleton chained next to the male skeleton."

"Another one?" questioned Gardener.

"Yes," replied Sutton, "a young female, I'd say."

"Jesus," said Reilly, turning and glancing up at the sky, which was surprisingly blue and clear.

"Anyway," said Sutton, "before we can continue, or even get started with our job, would you be kind enough to identify the body, confirm he was the man you wanted to question in connection with the recent murders?"

Gardener nodded. He suited and booted and followed Clair Sutton. It took some time to reach the area because the ground was so uneven and unstable. Finally, they reached the scene and he leaned in close, studying everything. Eventually, he turned back to the anthropologist.

"Yes, that's him."

She thanked him and they made their way to firmer ground. Claire Sutton reached into an inside pocket, dug out an evidence bag and passed it over to Gardener.

"Not sure if this helps with your investigation but it was around the neck of the male skeleton."

Gardener took it, wished Sutton well, and told her he was only a phone call away if she needed anything.

When he reached his partner, he explained everything before they returned to the front of the building where they found Eddie Perrin waiting outside the gates.

"I bet you two had a rough night on Saturday."

"You don't know the half of it," said Gardener.

"News travels fast in these parts, especially if it's bad. They reckoned there were a bit of trouble up here."

Gardener briefly told him what had happened; adding the fact that he'd also discovered Betty Blanchard had passed away. Perrin's expression was pale and downbeat.

"I'm sorry to hear that. What have you got there?" he asked, staring at the bag.

Gardener put on a fresh pair of gloves, opened the bag and withdrew a locket. Though a little stiff, it did part, revealing two photographs, one of Betty Blanchard, and the other of Andy.

"Where were that?" asked Perrin.

"Maybe best you don't know," said Gardener.

"Too late," said Perrin. "I've already seen it, and I know it's Robert's so I wouldn't mind knowing."

"I'm sorry, Mr Perrin," said Gardener, "but from what we've seen, your friend and partner never left the convent."

"What do you mean?"

"Robert Blanchard is still in there. They found a skeleton chained to the wall, underneath the building in what was probably a cellar. The locket was around his neck."

"The bastards," said Perrin, with a very sad expression.

"There was also a female skeleton chained next to him. From what we've been told, we suspect it was Isabella Moorcroft."

Perrin sighed and glanced at the building.

"So Robert didn't come back after forty years to take his revenge, then? I'll stick my neck out and say it must have been Andy."

Gardener nodded. "Andy died only a few feet from where his father was entombed."

If you enjoyed this book, please let others know by leaving a quick review on Amazon. Also, if you spot anything untoward in the paperback, get in touch. We strive for the best quality and appreciate reader feedback.

editor@thebookfolks.com

www.thebookfolks.com

ALSO AVAILABLE

If you enjoyed IMPIOUS, the eighth book, check out the others in the series:

IMPURITY – *Book 1*

Someone is out for revenge. A grotto worker is murdered in the lead up to Christmas. He won't be the first. Can DI Gardener stop the killer, or is he saving his biggest gift till last?

IMPERFECTION – *Book 2*

When theatre-goers are treated to the gruesome spectacle of an actor's lifeless body hanging on the stage, DI Stewart Gardener is called in to investigate. Is the killer still in the audience? A lockdown is set in motion but it is soon apparent that the murderer is able to come and go unnoticed. Identifying and capturing the culprit will mean establishing the motive for their crimes, but perhaps not before more victims meet their fate.

IMPLANT – *Book 3*

A small Yorkshire town is beset by a series of cruel murders. The victims are tortured in bizarre ways. The killer leaves a message with each crime – a playing card from an obscure board game. DI Gardener launches a manhunt but it will only be by figuring out the murderer's motive that they can bring him to justice.

IMPRESSION – *Book 4*

Police are stumped by the case of a missing five-year-old girl until her photograph turns up under the body of a murdered woman. It is the first lead they have and is quickly followed by the discovery of another body connected to the case. Can DI Stewart Gardener find the connection between the individuals before the abducted child becomes another statistic?

IMPOSITION – *Book 5*

When a woman's battered body is reported to police by her husband, it looks like a bungled robbery. But the investigation begins to turn up disturbing links with past crimes. They are dealing with a killer who is expert at concealing his identity. Will they get to him before a vigilante set on revenge?

IMPOSTURE – *Book 6*

When a hit and run claims the lives of two people, DI Gardener begins to realize it was not a random incident. But when he begins to track down the elusive suspects he discovers that a vigilante is getting to them first. Can the detective work out the mystery before more lives are lost?

IMPASSIVE – *Book 7*

A publisher racked with debts is found strung up in a ruined Yorkshire abbey. Has a disgruntled author taken their revenge? DI Stewart Gardener is on the case but maybe a hypnotist has the key to the puzzle. Can the cop muster his team to work some magic and catch a cunning killer?

IMPLICATION – *Book 9*

When a body is found in a burned out car, DI Stewart
Gardener quickly establishes that a murder has been
concealed. But with a missing person case and a spate of
robberies occupying the force, he will struggle to identify
the victim. When the investigations overlap, he'll have to
work out which of the suspects is implicated in which
crime.

IMPUNITY – *Book 10*

After a young woman passes out and dies, the medical
examiner makes a grim discovery. Someone had surgically
removed her kidneys. Detective Stewart Gardener must
find a killer evil enough to think of such a cruel act, let
alone have the gall to carry it out. It looks like revenge is a
motive, but what had the victim, by all accounts a kind and
friendly girl, done to anyone?

IMPALED – *Book 11*

When Gardener is called to investigate a crime, he has no
idea of the terrible scene that awaits him. The corpse of a
man has been found with nails driven into his chest and no
hands. There are no witnesses to the crime, just reports of
a strangely dressed man seen nearby. Gardener feels a
serial killer is at work, and the clock is ticking.

All FREE with Kindle Unlimited and available in paperback.

www.thebookfolks.com

Printed in Great Britain
by Amazon